Praise for Tara

'A fabulous new ta[...]
Colin Bateman

'A highly original new voice.'
Daily Express

Fodder

'The story rattles along like an express train and Tara West is clearly an excellent writer. A deeply cool book . . .
Great stuff.'
Irish Independent

'Energetic and painfully funny . . . A highly entertaining debut.'
Belfast Telegraph

'*Fodder* is simply a must-read debut novel, with its fast-paced plot and dark humour it takes the reader on a constant rollercoaster ride.'
Women's News

'Tara's first novel was an instant hit with critics, universally praised for its daring, its sharp wit, intelligent writing style and highly original theme and approach.'
Damian Smyth, Head of Literature, Arts Council of Northern Ireland

First published in 2013 by
Liberties Press
140 Terenure Road North | Terenure | Dublin 6W
Tel: +353 (1) 405 5703
www.libertiespress.com | info@libertiespress.com

Trade enquiries to Gill & Macmillan Distribution
Hume Avenue | Park West | Dublin 12
T: +353 (1) 500 9534 | F: +353 (1) 500 9595 | E: sales@gillmacmillan.ie

Distributed in the UK by
Turnaround Publisher Services
Unit 3 | Olympia Trading Estate | Coburg Road | London N22 6TZ
T: +44 (0) 20 8829 3000 | E: orders@turnaround-uk.com

Copyright © Tara West, 2013
The author has asserted her moral rights.

ISBN: 978-1-907593-85-7
2 4 6 8 10 9 7 5 3 1

A CIP record for this title is available from the British Library.

Cover design by Anna Morrison
Internal design by Liberties Press

The publishers and author gratefully acknowledge financial assistance from
the Arts Council of Northern Ireland.

Poets Are Eaten as a Delicacy in Japan

Tara West

NORTH

1.

It's not the worst thing, matricide. I thought about it regularly – it used to help me get to sleep at night. But the older I got, the less Mater mattered. Until that Sunday in February, when Georgie rang at eight in the morning to ask if I would come to her house and bring at least five bottles of bleach.

Georgie exorcised her anxiety through the rigorous scrubbing, polishing and stunt-vacuuming of her nooks and crannies. A request for five bottles of bleach was apocalyptic and could mean only one thing. That woman. Gloria. Our mother. I grabbed the first pair of shoes I could find and went to buy bleach before skidding all the way to her house in my frail old Fiat. I winced at the ferocity of my hangover and my ill-judged footwear.

It was snowing as I sat on Georgie's newly decked patio in my flip-flops. She lived in a street of anonymous white semis, in a modest but immaculate house. The garden was manicured even in winter, and walls, windows and doors gleamed polar white. She brought out a tray with newspapers, a white teapot, white mugs and a white plate of pale, soulless biscuits. I took a snow-flecked biscuit and held it between trembling blue fingers. She lifted the bleach from my bag.

'I'm glad you didn't get thin bleach,' she said, stroking a bottle.

'I know you have expensive taste.' My teeth chattered.

'Thick bleach is the best.'

'You spoil this family.'

Georgie was almost two years my senior and with her swaying boobs and prominent jaw, she had an upfront, sassy look. At school, she was the girl who laughed and skulked and smelt of cigarettes and fake tan. She was dubbed 'Two Fucks', because whatever happened, she said she couldn't give two fucks. When she became a mother, that became 'I couldn't give a fiddler's fuck', although how that was an improvement, I wasn't sure. One less fuck, I suppose. And some culture. Her signature style was white jeans and tops that flashed her finer points, and her goose-pimply cleavage and bullet nipples were an eyeful in the snow. She looked exactly like she did in her teens, but she couldn't have been more different.

'So why are we here?' I asked. 'On the patio. In a blizzard.'

'It's not a blizzard.' She shook her foot nervously. 'It's a flurry.'

I tucked my hands into my armpits. 'Georgie. I'm dying here.'

She stirred her tea. 'I don't want Darren to hear us. He's in the kitchen. Don't look.'

I looked at the house, where Georgie's husband Darren moved between dishwasher and cupboards. 'You don't think sitting out here is just a little bit suspicious?'

She smoothed her dark, slow curls and they sprang back into chaos. 'I told him you wanted to try out the new patio furniture.'

'In the snow?'

'It's the kind of thing you'd do.'

I patted the towel that covered the plastic sheet that covered my wooden chair. 'The parasol will be nice when you put it up. Can I see it?'

'It's not snowproof.'

I wrapped my feet together under the chair, my toes throbbing. 'This must be really bad, whatever it is.'

Her sulky eyes flicked to Darren in the kitchen and she rapped the table with her knuckles. 'Hardwood,' she said. 'From sustainable forests.'

'I'll do my poker face.'

'Not until he leaves the room.' She held out her hand like a game show hostess. 'All half price.' She waved under the table to show me the gate legs. 'Practical for storage.' She reached for the newspaper, a quality Sunday, and spread the sections over the table.

'Are they table protectors?' I shook all over. 'Can I have some for my knees?'

She jabbed a finger at the paper. 'No, quick, look, he's gone.'

I looked. A whole page was devoted to a photograph of Gloria. She was draped over a chaise longue in a barely-there Grecian dress, her fleshy ankles tucked together demurely and the nipples of her great, architectural breasts suspiciously stargazy. She eyed the camera, half-coy, half-cow, the sun behind her curls suggesting a halo. I made a mental note of the photographer's name and resolved to kick her Photoshopping ass, if ever I met her. On the opposite page, the article's nauseating headline forced its way into my eye line:

GLORIA REVEALED

Georgie handed me a slim book. 'It's because of this.'

I know a book of poetry when I see one. I quelled my rising gorge. It was the latest from Rory McManus, 'one of the UK and Ireland's greatest living poets,' as he was known. I hated poetry. I loathed poets. It was a book of love poems, graphically describing the man's proclivities and depravities, which he'd only just discovered now that he'd left his wife of thirty-six years for his new muse. It was a hit with lovers and poetry lovers alike, lauded as 'explicit, raw, energetic – and instructive', no less.

'Read the front,' my sister said. 'And think about it.'

I read. And thought about it. The collection was called *Gloria! Gloria! Gloria!*

'That's your poker face?' Georgie primed the bleach. 'I knew this would happen.'

I held onto my temples and sucked in lungfuls of woodstain fumes. I couldn't feel my feet.

'And it gets worse,' she said.

Leaning out the kitchen window, Darren called, 'You two OK out there?'

Georgie gave a huge squawking laugh that chased starlings from the roof.

She waved and pointed at me and mouthed, 'Hungover! Needs some air!'

She fanned me with the picture of Gloria.

'You like the patio?' Darren called out to me.

I gave him a thumbs-up, retching.

Darren ducked back inside.

'Smile. Wave,' Georgie said, showing her teeth.

I smiled and waved at the lovely Darren. Darren who did dishes, Darren who put up with all Georgie's quirks, the quite-a-catch, long-suffering, hard-working, not the real father of Georgie's child, but any-port-in-a-storm, Darren.

'They're serialising it from next week,' she said.

'Serialising what?'

'Her book.'

'*In Utero*?'

In Utero was Gloria's poetry anthology about motherhood, published when we were fifteen and seventeen, in which she described the sense of freedom she felt when, as a baby, Georgie toddled out of sight. In which she recounted aborting me twice.

'No, her *new* book. It's a memoir.'

I leaned over. I couldn't stop it this time. I aimed at the grass. I missed.

Georgie sluiced bleach over the splattered wood, looking worriedly back at the kitchen. 'If everything comes out, Tommie . . .'

'It just did.' I mopped my chin with the Sports section.

'Don't you pun at me. Puns aren't funny. This isn't funny.'

'I know, I'm sorry.' My ankles twinged at the things Gloria could say about us. 'But she wouldn't,' I said. 'She just wouldn't. She has plenty of other things to talk about. The famous people. The commune. Pete.'

'Dad wasn't famous.'

'Good material, though.'

'You, the mental case. Me, the teenage mother.'

Georgie looked back at the house, her hand on her chest. 'I could lose everything. Darren, Joe, everything.'

Joe's bedroom curtains were closed, but they were like that most of the time. He was fifteen, light like a foal and lived inside Andy Warhol's closet.

Georgie put a whole biscuit in her mouth and chewed frantically. 'And if she finds out where I work now.' Which was as a supervisor in an online sex chatroom. 'My God, if it wasn't about us, I'd love to read it.'

'But she doesn't know anything about us.' I swallowed nervously. 'We haven't seen her in what, fifteen years? She wouldn't do it again, not after last time.'

Georgie swirled cold tea in her mug and drank. 'For the smart one, you can be really stupid sometimes.'

I rallied. 'For being the maternal one, you can be really shit.'

'That's not an argument.'

Silence bristled between us.

'There must be preview copies of the book. That's how books get reviewed, isn't it?' she said. 'You work for a magazine, you could get a copy. Then we could read it before it gets to the shops.'

I jerked with shock and cold. 'I never said I worked for a *respected* magazine.'

'Just phone the publisher.'

'You phone.'

'You phone.'

'I'm afraid of phones.'

She covered her eyes with her hand. 'Why does Gloria always have to ruin everything?' She peeped over her fingers. 'What about court? Could we take her to court?'

I clung to my mug. 'We'd have to see a solicitor. And what if we had to appear in court? That will attract even more attention. And it might not be necessary, because she might not even write about us.'

Georgie's shallow breaths rattled through her chest. 'What are we going to do?'

'We could hire an assassin,' I said. 'You can probably do that online.'

'It's not funny,' she said.

'I know, I can't help it.' Poor taste and inappropriate humour were my way of coping with disaster.

She stood up, chin thrust forward, curls tossed back. 'Well, I'm going to take the tiles off the bathroom wall.' After her unhealthy obsession with cleaning products, fretful bursts of DIY were Georgie's next favourite way of keeping chaos at bay. She had laid flooring in the attic when Joe started school and built something from IKEA each time the in-laws called round.

'This is going to be a nightmare,' she said, taking my mug and setting it on the tray. 'I just know it.' She was breathing noisily.

'Look, don't panic,' I said. 'I'll see if I can get an advance copy. I'll . . . use my . . . er, contacts. Then we'll read it and decide what to do.'

'How quickly do you think you could you get it?'

'Give me a chance, Georgie.'

She lifted the tray. 'Right. OK. Right. Ring me. I'll need to know what's happening. And don't forget, Tommie.'

'I'll ring you, don't worry.'

She took a breath and closed her eyes, exhaling slowly as though counting. 'Right, let's go in.'

'Oh, thank God.' I rose stiffly to my dead, blue feet.

'And act normal. No, not like that. Keep your mouth shut.'

I followed her into the deliciously warm kitchen. The air zinged with antibacterial cleaner, hot new appliances and the citrus zest of Darren's aftershave. I couldn't imagine what my sister kept in her clinically clean cupboards but I knew it couldn't be food. Cooking smells made Georgie faint, and in the past I'd seen her shoo Darren and Joe into the garden to eat a takeaway, squirting at them with Mr Sheen. She'd never been to my place. The dust, the plates, the bottles, the crumbs and oh dear God, the smell of toast – I couldn't put her through it.

Darren cleared away the tray. Tall and weathered, he gleamed like he'd been steeped in chlorine.

'On the tear last night, Tommie?' he asked me, setting our mugs in the dishwasher.

'Just the usual,' I said.

'You be careful.' I'd known him since school but his earnestness still took me by surprise. 'Molton Brown in the bathroom,' he said, 'if you want to have a shower.'

Not a flirty invitation, not even an insult. Georgie typed dirty on the internet every night and Darren's job involved sending cameras down blocked drains to clear logjams. It was their mildly obsessive way of compensating.

'I'm fine, thanks.'

Georgie lifted the Arts section of the paper from the tray and slipped it down by her side. 'Tommie's just going now.'

Darren smiled doubtfully. 'That was a quick visit.'

'I want to get the bathroom started,' Georgie said.

'You want to *what?*' he asked.

'I'm changing the tiles in the bathroom.'

'You liked them three months ago when we got them.'

She folded her arms, cleavage inflating. 'Oh right, so I can't make a mistake now?'

'Don't be like that, Bunny Rabbit.' He put his arms around her and she moved in below his chin, mouthing at me to go away.

I reversed towards the door. 'I'll just go then, busy day ahead. Doing busy things. Busily.'

Outside in their driveway, I set the car's heater to full blast, feet pulsing at the onset of chilblains. Georgie opened the car door and threw the newspaper and McManus's book into my lap. I tried to push them out but she was stronger.

'Just bin them somewhere,' she said, eyes wide.

'Darren's bound to know something's up,' I said.

'That's because it's written all over your face.'

'What is?' I peered at my pale skin and smudged eyes in the mirror.

'Dread, panic,' she said.

'This is how I always look.'

'Just get the book, Tommie,' she hissed.

I crunched into reverse. 'I'll do my best.'

She peered into my car. 'It stinks in here. Do you want some Cif or something?'

'No, but it's a kind offer.'

'Febreze?'

'No, I'm trying to give up.'

'And you reek of drink, by the way.'

'Everyone should have a sister like you.'

'Ring me.'

'I will.'

'Don't forget.'

'I won't.'

'I'll be waiting.'

'I know.'

I pulled away and she disappeared quickly into the house without a wave.

The snow clouds dispersed as I drove back to town and the sun reflected off the wet road, blinding me. I scratched my fingers over my tight scalp. Even if I cured my hangover, I wouldn't shake the nausea. Gloria was back. She wouldn't just rock our boats – she would breach their hulls, sink them and eat them.

I hoped Blob was home. He wouldn't be of any practical help, but he could boost morale as ships went down.

2.

The house I shared with Blob was twenty minutes from Georgie's, or fifty minutes in the snow with bald tyres. Narrow and gardenless, our mid-terrace house was off an unfashionable road in Belfast, where industrial redbrick streets culminated in a Glasgow Rangers Football Supporters Club. The neighbours – orbiting families, door-slamming couples, track-suited old women – thought Blob and I were students, and I was charmed.

There was lumpy lino on the floor and every room had gothic curtains, poles sagging under the strain of them. The previous tenants had left ornaments and we held onto them for entertainment value: Bambi's skull on a plinth, a figurine of Jesus helping a boy play baseball and a shimmering painting of a Native American embracing a handsome cowboy. It was show-stoppingly odd and best of all, cheap. It was perfect for us.

We hadn't gone to bed till 4 AM the night before, having spent it vogueing to Jacques Brel, Led Zeppelin and Kajagoogoo. Sunday was the day Blob called to see May, but he usually only stayed for a dutiful cup of tea. In her eighties, May was the great-aunt who had taught him everything he knew, from acidic putdowns and astonishing spite to tucking me in when I was too drunk to deserve it. He'd lived with her since he was six, when his mother died.

I took painkillers, made tea and toast and settled on one of the small red settees in the extended kitchen. Both settees had theatrical gold fringing, cheap throws and tassled cushions. Opposite the settees were plasticky 1970s' kitchen units, walls that rippled with ageing veneer, and a deep, ornate bookcase, which Chris the landlord had probably picked up from Vincent Price. Chris said

13

the room had two distinct personalities, which was unbeatable value for money.

I slid down the settee, an arm over my sick head. I could have brought the newspaper in from the car for something to read, but what if Gloria was waiting behind more pages? My mother adored the limelight and would relish the attention McManus's book brought her. I hadn't thought about her in years and now, hungover and underslept, she could be anywhere, everywhere, exposing our mistakes to fuel her profile. Georgie was right: this was the stuff of nightmares.

That's why, when Blob rammed the key in the lock and woke me, I was surprised to find I had been dreaming about beach balls. The front door swung back and hit the wall. The mirror and our studenty Klimt print quivered noisily and Blob's voice, trained for the stage and Marlboro-rich, rang through the house.

'I could eat the hole off a scabby dog. Here you, you lazy shite, have you anything-to-Jesus fucking eat? I'm starving.' He marched into the kitchen, brushing the fringed lampshade with his quiff.

Blob had left Northern Ireland when he was eighteen to study drama in London. After graduating, he lived in Tower Hamlets and worked full-time in a deli and part-time as a Morrissey impersonator. He did look a bit like Morrissey, with his quiff and black horn-rimmed glasses – albeit a greying, jowly, obese one who hid his bulk under a grubby raincoat. But even Morrissey had stopped swinging gladioli by the time he was thirty and that's why Blob came home.

'Why are you wearing moon boots?' he said. 'Big purple moon boots.'

'Those are my feet,' I said. 'I'm getting chilblains.'

He hung his coat on the floor and fell into the other settee.

'Everything's a drama with you, Fatty.' He had a nickname for everyone – ironic, insightful or just plain malicious. 'So what's wrong with your sister? Scientists admit there's no cure for limescale?'

I told him about Gloria.

'Oh my God, you're going to be famous!' he screamed, wriggling his porky fingers at me. 'Paparazzi at last! But I'm so fat. I'll need a magazine to hide behind.'

'There are better things to be famous for, Blob. This wasn't the plan.'

We had always agreed we would be famous. As teenagers, we lay on our backs in a sunny cemetery and bonded over our feelings of superiority and our conviction that we would soon be discovered. Reunited, we had slipped into the same roles. The difference now though, was that I didn't quite believe it any more. Blob, however, clung to it like a crutch.

We first met at a youth drama group when I was fourteen and he was fifteen. He was the only actor with any talent and I was one of the few 'writers' who showed up. On the first day he performed a sudden and unbidden tap routine, without music and entirely improvised, and by improvised, I mean he had never learnt tap. He had me at the first step heel. He was already 6' 4" and soldiers would train their guns on him as we minced and giggled our way through Belfast city centre, although his attracting attention probably had more to do with the way he flapped his hands, ran in hysterical circles and screamed like a girl.

He leaned back on the settee and crossed his legs at the ankles, squeaking his brogues. 'But mental is in, Fatty,' he said. 'All the best people are schizo, or dipso, or klepto or something. You could become a spokesperson for nutjobs. Think of it.' His eyes were starry. 'You could open hospital wards, kiss babies . . .'

'I don't particularly want people to know. And I don't want people to know I have anything to do with *her*.' I shuddered.

'Just use her just like she used you. Child of a writer. Child of a poet fucker. It's fast track to the big time, babes.'

'She's not a writer. Neither am I.'

'You were when I met you.'

'I liked ponies when I met you, Blob. That doesn't make me a show jumper.'

He pushed up his glasses. 'This could have been *your* book, you know. Your messed-up background. You could have written about it. And her.'

'I don't want people to know about my messed-up background.'

He hooted. 'Too late. I'd say make the most of it. This is the moment you've been waiting for.' He pushed himself off the settee. 'How's Vinegar Tits taking it?'

'Badly.'

'Boo-hoo.' He approached the bookcase like a supplicant. It contained his ancient stereo, a thirteenth birthday present from May. The silver had worn away to reveal the prosthetic-limb white below, the turntable was coated with petrified crumbs and dead skin, and the speakers looked like little coffins. Blob trailed his fingers across the vinyl spread rampantly across the floor.

'If she hadn't been such a slut, she wouldn't have this problem,' he said.

'This could be the end of Georgie and Darren,' I said. 'It could be the end of Joe.'

'Darren's too good for her and Joe will be fine,' Blob said. 'If you can survive that woman, anyone can.'

After *In Utero* was published, I lived with Blob and May for a time. I don't remember much, other than my guilt at their being so good to me. He hadn't changed in all the time he'd been away since then, apart from the six or seven stone he'd gained, but that was just true to form. I spotted him in a crowded bar and we picked up where we'd left off fourteen years before. I hugged him endlessly and drunkenly, and introduced him again and again to my bewildered workmates. He'd boomed in my ear all night and I beamed like a muppet. A few days later, he rang to say he'd found some good houses if I still wanted to move in with him.

Sudden, but not unusual for me. Before Blob, I moved often, sharing with people who moved abruptly after finding a new friend on Facebook or an old friend in a bar, in a relentless, karmic spiral of abandonment and lurch-leaving. Sharing a house with Blob came surprisingly easy, surprisingly quickly. Shortly after we moved in, I had a brain-popping epiphany in the shower – I felt at home. But I didn't tell Blob that. He would have said I was a danger to myself and sent me to a bunnery for some comfort eating.

He settled a record on the turntable. 'So how did you leave it with the bog beast?'

'I made some unfunny jokes and a promise I can't keep.'

He closed the lid of the turntable and struggled to his feet. 'That'll show her.'

'I said I would use my contacts to get the book.'

'Now that *is* funny.' He dropped onto the settee and lifted the crusts from my plate. The Smiths' 'Please, Please, Please Let Me Get What I Want' rose from the coffin speakers. He folded the crusts into his mouth. 'Make me a cup of tea, Fatty.'

'And I agreed to phone the publisher to get a preview copy.'

He stopped chewing. 'That's ridiculous. Even for you.'

I wasn't good on the phone. Phones turned me into a breathy, simpering girl who sought approval to a detrimental extent. Over the years, I had bought insurance against an asteroid hit, ordered two unwanted sofas and, after calling a wrong number, had almost become grounds for divorce. I regularly negotiated away whatever I wanted, including my own dignity.

Blob chewed, mushy crusts visible. 'I'll phone the publisher for you, babes.'

'Thanks, Blob.'

'If you make me a cup of tea.'

I filled the kettle. 'You know, I think you've lost weight.'

Later, eating Doritos with a full-bodied red, Blob said, 'I have a surprise for you.'

'I don't really like surprises,' I said, sipping from my glass. We were lying on the settees listening to The Velvet Underground, my feet toasting over a warm speaker. The electric fire and lamps were on and when I squinted, it looked homely.

He twisted in his seat to pull something out of his back pocket. 'May gave me this. Look. It must be the last address they have for me. You can be my plus one.'

He handed me an envelope and I pulled out a thin card, an invitation to the CAC Youth Theatre Group Reunion, splashed with stars and stickmen doing the twist.

I threw it back. 'No, thanks.'

'I'm phoning the publisher for you.'

'I made you tea.'

'Your tea is like bong water.'

'Why would I want to see any of those people again?'

'They weren't that bad.'

'I had a terrible time at CAC, Blob.'

'You were shy. And they just thought you were creative, what with your smelly hair and everything. With hindsight, that will look charming.'

'I let them all down.'

'I handled it at the time, babes. I covered for you.'

'You're a trooper, Blob. I still don't want to go.'

'Oh, please go.'

'No.'

'Please.'

'No.

'Please.'

'No.'

'Please.'

'I don't have anything to wear.'

'I'll help you pick something,' he said. 'I'm good at disguising bulk.'

'Don't project your obesity onto me. Why are you so keen to go anyway?'

'I Googled a few of the old gang . . .'

'We were never in a gang. I have never knowingly used the word "gang".'

'Some of them are successful now.'

'As what?'

'Media types, producers, agents: London, New York. And it's who you know in this business.'

'Is that why you never made it?' I said. 'Wait a minute, that didn't come out right. I meant . . .' I scrambled around for diplomacy. 'Success has nothing to do with talent.'

He pushed up his glasses. 'I just haven't found the right role yet.'

The needle bumped back and forth at the end of the record. It was late, we'd been pissed the night before and tomorrow we'd go back to work: me to the magazine, Blob to his third call centre job in as many months. My allusion to reality was careless.

'Oh fuck it, I'll go, alright?' I said. 'If it makes you happy. But I won't enjoy it.'

He got up and flipped the record. 'I wouldn't have it any other way, Fatty.'

3.

The magazine was my dream job, in that I spent my whole day dreaming about being somewhere else. It was based in a once genteel Victorian terrace house near the university and, like most of the houses in the redbrick row, had been converted for business using slingshots, hatchets and explosives. Original fireplaces had been sledgehammered out, tiles had been shucked off to the dump and architraves and ceiling roses suffocated under coats of gloss. We spent eight hours a day sweating and shivering in a building that was ill-equipped whatever the season.

I sat right under the boss, Jude's enhanced nose. She sat on a raised platform, so my face was level with her be-tighted feet. Legs crossed, she would swing one shoe on the knuckle of a big toe because, she said, fidgeting burned calories. This was tolerable on Monday and Tuesday. By Wednesday, the fumes puffed out with every shoe-swing. By Thursday, staff reeled against the musk and by Friday, we were drunk on the haze. As Editor and Publisher, Jude scooped buckets of free beauty products but I think she drank them. She had many talents.

I had no 'contacts' because my job almost exclusively involved slashing and burning my way through press releases that Jude forwarded by email or tossed at my desk, and trimming them to plug gaps between ads. I was the Editorial Department, which meant writing nonsensical style tips I made up on the spot, and penning outrageous purple editorials for advertisers. Buy a quarter page ad and you'd get 75 words. Half page, 150 words. Full page, 300 words. Front cover, 500 words and a blow job from Jude. Jude's role was to schmooze with the advertisers, attend launches, take epic lunches and test-drive performance cars after several Tanquerays and a bottle of L'Air du Temps.

Her assistant, Aoife, suckered a procession of eager young freelancers into writing interviews, fashion, interiors and food pages, then waiting a year or more to be paid. The Arts pages were written by the magazine's only long-term freelancer, an octogenarian called Diane Sand. No matter how often Jude queried or ignored her invoices, Diane continued to squander her wit, spark and longevity on us with determined wartime vim.

Copies of the magazine were distributed to shops, where they sat on the shelves for a few weeks before being returned and piled up in the storeroom. Jude multiplied subscriptions to dentists and doctors surgeries by the number of patients in each, and claimed a massive readership which seemed to convince a lot of advertisers. She even found a cosmetic surgeon to sponsor her new nose. The surgeon got 2,000 words, a pole dance and a threesome, I imagined.

Getting out of bed and making it into work was a huge achievement in itself, and I congratulated myself on a job well done every morning I made it in before eleven. Most of the time Jude and Aoife were out of the office, delayed at a 'breakfast meeting' or a launch or, as we secretly hoped, getting arrested for the debauched partying we heard rumours about and could sometimes smell.

As I walked to work, I noticed the traffic was heavier than normal, even accounting for snow. Cars queued around corners and plumes of exhaust smoke drifted up. Passing the university, I crossed the road alongside shiny students and lecturers sporting Asperger's hair, and I thought about my own abandoned degree – how I had dreaded and avoided the academic farts and fusties, leaving after three months to work as half a reindeer in a Christmas grotto.

Turning a corner, I saw what was causing the tailback. An ambulance and police car were double-parked outside work. My prayers about Jude must have been answered. The front door was propped open and behind the miniature pulpit-style reception was a tiny new temp. She had long, dyed red hair twisted over one shoulder and huge grey-green eyes that blinked blankly at me. Behind her, one door led to the open-plan office and another led upstairs to the boardroom.

'What happened?' I asked.

'Somebody took ill,' she said. 'Very ill. Like, died.'

'Oh my God, who?'

She looked round at the stairs and we listened to the low shuffling and shifting above. 'I don't know,' she said. 'There was a meeting with a client or something. It happened before I got here. Bill? Bill somebody . . . ?'

'Not Bill!'

Bill was the Sales Department. He was nearing retirement but saving his money for the double wedding his twin daughters had requested. He'd had polio as a child and Blob called him 'Sack-a-Slack', because he looked like he was heaving a sack of coal onto his back with every step.

'No, no.' The tiny temp waved her hands. 'Bill tried to tell me what happened but I'm getting mixed up. Seamus . . .'

'My God, not Seamus!'

Seamus was the Production Department. He taught Tae Kwon Do on Tuesdays and salsa on Thursdays, and handled the magazine's constant disasters with amiable grace, which I knew couldn't be healthy.

'No, not Seamus,' said the temp. 'Seamus asked me to phone an ambulance. Patricia . . .'

'Patricia? Dead? No!'

Patricia was the Accounts Department. She had two young sons, she was studying part-time for a business degree and she made dinner before she came to work. Maybe even before she got up, in fact. I knew she was overdoing it.

'No, Patricia's not dead. You must be Tommie. Patricia said you'd be like this.'

The phone rang and the tiny temp held up a hand before answering brightly, 'Good morning, *Bellefast* magazine. One moment please.' She sharpened her focus on me. 'Is there a Hans working here?'

'He left two months ago.'

She went back to the phone. 'I'm sorry, Hans is no longer at this company, can anyone else help?' She paused, then asked me, 'Is there a Petra here?'

'She went travelling.'

'I'm sorry, Petra no longer works here. Can anyone else help?' She looked at me. 'Is there a Claire here?'

'Claire went back to university.'

'I'm sorry, Claire is no longer at this company. Can anyone else help?' Back to me. 'Is there a Stephen here?'

'He took over his dad's farm.'

'I'm sorry, Stephen no longer works here. Can anyone else help?' To me, 'Can *you* speak to them?'

I did the jazz hands dance of silent refusal.

She went back to the phone. 'I'm sorry, we've had a death in the building this morning, things are a bit . . . confused.' She listened to the phone – for quite some time – and said, 'Yes, I was beginning to think that myself.'

It took me years to figure out what the tiny temp had discovered in just a few minutes: anyone with any sense got out. Even death was looking good these days. The workforce was made up of a grim hardcore of lifers who had been here too long for anyone else to want us. And then there was the fringe of people who stayed a few days or weeks and escaped with their CVs intact. Their names still appeared on contact lists, creating the illusion of a bustling, buoyant business.

Patricia leaned into reception and twinkled at the tiny temp as she handed her a cup of tea, then she waved me into the office.

The desks were chaotic with paperwork, creaking yellow computers, old copies of the magazine and dead or dying plants. The office smelt of damp, old smoke and sweaty tights. Bill and Seamus sat on desks with their feet on chairs, cradling tea.

'It's Diane,' Patricia said, pouring me a cup. Her small blue eyes glittered, inviting secrets. 'She passed away.'

'What happened?'

Bill cleared his throat, jowls struggling against a stiff, grey collar. 'My new client, Devine Energy. They're upstairs. They were briefing Diane in the boardroom.'

'Briefing Diane? But I write the advertisers' editorial. Diane does the Arts pages.'

'I sold them a sponsorship of the Arts pages,' he said.

'You sold the Arts pages? Is that what killed her?'

Bill was arch. 'Devine Energy are sponsoring some book or literary festival. I told them Diane was covering it and for a fee she'd write it in a way that promotes Devine Energy.'

'But you can't make the Arts pages promotional,' I said. 'They'd have no integrity.'

'Jude said it was a stroke of genius.' Bill pulled at his tie and undid his top button.

'At first they thought she'd fallen asleep,' Seamus said, pushing a hand through his long hair. His low voice could always break up a squabble. 'Aoife asked me to come up and I checked her pulse and her breathing. I think maybe she did fall asleep. And then she stopped living. It was a while before they noticed. She was cold. You know how Jude can talk.'

We sat in silence.

'I was going to get a good commission on that.'

'*Bill*,' Patricia whispered.

'The girls have put deposits on their dresses.'

'She bailed out rather than sell out,' I marvelled.

'*Tommie*,' Patricia hissed.

We drank our tea. Of the four of us I was the newbie, and I'd been there nine years. Bill had been there since Jude took over the magazine thirteen years before, Patricia had been there eleven years, starting out as temporary receptionist like I did, and Seamus joined just before her. Diane was a long-serving satellite and we were fond of her. I was fond of all of them.

My extension rang. It was Aoife, calling from the boardroom.

'This would be a good time to die of embarrassment, wouldn't it?' I tittered, bewildered by the depths I could sink to. I was pinned against the wall as the paramedics manoeuvred Diane's stretchered body round the tight corners of the staircase. One of them shot me a look.

I knocked on the boardroom door.

'Come in!' Jude's voice chimed.

I slithered in.

The boardroom was where Jude plied clients with coffee and wine and encouraged them to get sticky on doughnuts and sloppy sandwiches. She would stab the soft pink carpet with her stilettos as she stalked around, expounding the might of the magazine, then throw herself onto the pink leather sofa, spent by her efforts.

Framed covers of the magazine hung on the walls, including mock-ups showing fake interviews with major stars. The windows in the roof let in weak daylight, but most of the light came from peachy lamps in the corners. There was a pyramid of doughnuts on the table and the air was saturated with coffee and perfume, with a distinct undercurrent of feet.

Jude beamed a massive rictus at me. She was thin and brittle and her skin was stretched Botox-shiny. She stuck out her bottom lip.

'Poor, poor Diane,' she said. 'Such a lovely woman. Such a talent. Tommie, this is Kevin. Kevin Loane, Marketing Director for Devine Energy.'

A small, undernourished man in a dark suit and buttoned-up shirt rose from his chair, glancing at his watch. His hair fell forward in boyish floppery and his scrawny jaw and neck blazed with a shaving rash. He shook my hand, sniffed like he was shovelling slack, and sat down. 'My sympathies. Your colleague seemed very nice.'

Aoife, the Silver Surfer to Jude's Galactus, met my eye but maintained her distance. She poured coffee into tiny cups, her polyester suit barely containing her.

Jude leaned across the table, deep red lips plumping and pumping with nerves. 'I was just explaining the magazine's high editorial standards to Kevin, and the fact that we have a whole team of talented writers downstairs. Isn't that right, Tommie?'

I opened my mouth. Diane's handbag, notepad and leather-bound address book were still on the table. 'I . . . what, sorry?'

'Tommie's our lead writer, Kevin.'

'Indeed.'

'So Tommie. Tommie, Tommie, Tommie, Tommie. With the greatest respect to Diane, who was a lovely, lovely woman, we have needed someone more "with-it", you know, for quite a while now, so, you know' – Jude flapped her hands from side to side – 'cloud, silver lining, that sort of thing? I've always thought that with your talents' – she gestured loosely as if flummoxed – 'you'd make a fabulous arts correspondent.'

'Well, you know, maybe, I was thinking.' I racked my brains. 'Shouldn't we maybe suspend the Arts pages for a month, you know, out of respect? I really think we should. Diane had a big following.' I had no idea if Diane had a following, but I was too young to die naturally in this meeting myself. A month's delay would at least buy me time to find another job.

'Very thoughtful, Tommie. You're so sensitive. And that's exactly why the Arts pages are perfect for you.' She spun a plastic sleeve containing a press release and notes across the table to me, grinning out her threat. 'As Kevin was explaining before Diane . . . before Diane . . . As Kevin was explaining before, we need to cover a festival on behalf of—'

'May I, Jude?' Kevin shuffled his small body forward. He gave another great, wet sniff and rested his hands on the table. 'It's like this, Tom. Devine Energy is about harnessing the power of thought.'

'I thought you sold wind turbines and solar panels.'

'The power of nature, Tom.'

'Not actually the power of thought then?'

'Ours is the power that appeals to people who think. And who are society's thinkers?'

'Well, with all that pacing, I should think traffic wardens.'

'Writers, Tom. Writers.'

'Not sure I agree.'

'According to our research, 71.2 percent of people are writing, or thinking about writing, or are reading, or reading about writing, or writing about what they're reading, right now. This is set to grow by up to 10.6 percent in the next five years, as evolving communities explore their heritage, examine diversity and express new truths. Devine Energy will be there for them.'

'Heating their garrets,' added Jude, laughing like a little bell with a crack in it.

Kevin sighed earnestly. 'We're supporting them because our research says they support us.' He sat back, working the silence. Someone's guts gurgled. Kevin continued, 'We need you to help us win the hearts and minds of writers, Tom. It will mean a better future. For all of us.' Big, wet sniff.

Aoife's throat clicked. Jude's plum-red fingernails tapped the table, once.

I lifted the press release in the plastic sleeve and looked at the headline:

BELFAST'S FIRST POETRY FESTIVAL ATTRACTS MAJOR SPONSOR

'Right, then! Great, then!' Jude said, putting the lid on her pen with a snap and shuffling her notes. Kevin stood up. Aoife gathered cups.

I stared at the press release and swallowed. Poetry. A whole festival of it. My sweating fingertips slid off the sleeve and the papers fell to the floor.

Kevin put a hand on my shoulder as he picked them up and put them back on the table, his face so close he stole the air between us.

'I'll give you a call, Tom. A few things I want to discuss before the Poetry Festival.' Big wet sniff.

Jude shook his hand at the door and Aoife followed him downstairs, chatting about death as if it were another client to gossip about.

Jude lifted a doughnut and threw herself onto the pink sofa. 'Tell you what, that was fucking close – we nearly lost that fucking account. We only just fucking got it. The trouble I had keeping that guy here. His flight's in an hour.' She spat what she'd chewed into a napkin and took another bite. 'Good result, though. He bought the feature. What the fuck did you think you were doing, Tommie?'

'You put me on the spot.'

'Well, fuck me for trying to run a fucking business here. We have a cash flow problem. We've lost half our advertisers to online competitors, we've got bad debtors, and we only got *him* because he's so keen on the written fucking word.' She spat more doughnut into the napkin. 'Without that asshole's money, no one gets paid. If you don't get this right, we're fucked.'

'But I don't like poets.'

'Jesus. It'll make for good journalism.'

'I've never interviewed anyone in my life.'

'Well, fucking learn, Tommie. Your pals downstairs will be out on the street if you don't pull this off. Look,' she said, nodding towards the table, 'take Diane's address book. You'll need to set up an interview with that guy, the one who plays pocket billiards when he reads his dirty poems, what's his face, Rory McManus. He's topping the bill. Do writers top bills? Who the fuck cares. Diane knew just about everybody. His contact details will be in there. And get that dirty stop-out he's fucking as well, she's big news. I have to go out.'

She dumped the doughnut in a coffee, and stalked out of the room. I floated down to my desk.

'Anyone fancy a drink?' I asked the others.

We waited outside until the pub opened. Inside, it was cold and tangy with disinfectant. I pressed into a dark snug and opened Diane's address book. The soft, perfumed pages were crammed with her civilised writing. Patricia slid into the snug as Bill and Seamus ordered drinks.

'Tommie, what are you having?'

'Get me the biggest gin in the world.' I leafed through to the S's. S for Shaw. Gloria Shaw. She wasn't there. *Thank you, God – God that I don't believe in but keep catching myself out with – thank you, thank you, thank you.* I flicked back to the M's. At the bottom of the page, in tiny writing, Diane had jotted: 'Rory McManus. Contact: Fellowes Agency.'

Back at the F's, I slid my finger down the names. Beside Fellowes Agency, she had written the name and phone number of her contact.

Her contact was my ex-boyfriend. The one whose flat I set on fire.

4.

The snow was almost gone when I left work. I scooted through clouds of breath and fumes, nipping between cars, losing patience with dawdlers. I needed to be home; I needed to think; I needed to hide. Approaching the house, I could hear The Cure's 'The Walk' booming through the walls and I wondered what was coming. That was his soundtrack for repositioning a particular kind of disaster. I'd heard it twice before.

Blob was kneeling in front of the stereo, an album cover in his hand. 'Hey, Fatty!' he boomed, dancing with just his neck. 'Guess what!'

'What?'

'I quit work.'

'What?'

'I quit work!'

'I heard you.' I dumped my coat and bag on the settee. 'I was making a point.'

He turned down the volume and faced me on his knees, jowls wobbling in umbrage. 'I wish you'd warn me when you're going to get hormonal.'

I strode across to the fridge. 'What about the rent? We're already behind.'

He stood with effort and followed me. 'I can't work with philistines.'

'You were selling insurance.' There was a bottle with just a little missing. I uncorked and swigged.

'They didn't let me use the internet,' he said, rinsing glasses under the tap. 'I don't see the point in having a job if I can't use the internet. How am I supposed to look for a different job?'

He held up the glasses and I poured.

'I got bad news today,' I said. 'I got promoted.'

He leaned his backside on the sink. 'You should try not to be so talented.'

I leaned beside him. 'I liked having no ambition. It made me feel like I'd achieved something.'

'But you can't leave now,' he said, putting his arm round my shoulders and squeezing. 'We can't both be out of work at the same time. You can hang on another while. Just till I get sorted out.'

'I don't like you,' I said, drinking deeply.

'But I love you. You're such a fuck-up, no one makes me feel as good about myself as you do.' He tapped my glass with his.

'I have to interview Rory McManus,' I said. 'And my mother. For the Arts pages.'

He downed a glass in one. 'No!'

'And the only way to reach McManus is through Liam McMullan.'

'Is that the one whose fingers you shut in a door?'

'No, that's the one whose flat I set on fire.' I drained my glass.

He topped us up. 'You know, some journalists would kill for an angle like that,' he said. 'Rory McManus, motherfucker. And not everyone can say another one of their interviewees tried to abort them. It's juicy stuff. I wonder how helpful your ex will be. Maybe he's used to being almost murdered, I don't know. I think it will sell.'

'Have you ever thought of voiceover work?' I said. 'You have the face for it.'

He crossed his legs at the ankles and waved his glass. 'Funny you should say that. I have a casting this week and was wondering if you would give me a lift.'

'You and Maurice friends again?'

Blob stopped speaking to his agent when he listed Blob on his website with an acting age of fifty-plus.

'He sent me a text.'

'An apology?'

'Not as such, but very humble directions to the ad agency for the casting session. Could be lucrative, TV role plus voicing radio ads.'

'How were they humble?'

'He used lower case.'

I closed my eyes and held up crossed fingers. 'Did you phone the publisher?'

'Would I let you down? No preview copies available, babes. That newspaper has some kind of pre-publication deal. No one gets to see the book until after the paper prints the extracts. There's a lumbago. People pay a lot of money for that.'

'An embargo?'

'That's the one.'

'We need more drink.'

'The casting's on Thursday. Tell work you're doing research or something.'

I tipped my glass to get the dregs. 'I have to get Gloria's book, Blob.'

'Oh for God's sake, you are so selfish sometimes. What about Mo, would she know how to get it?'

'I never thought of that.'

Mo had been my father's wife, Gloria was his lover and we had all lived together in a crumbling farmhouse with tides of artists, musicians, poets, plate-painters, feminists, gardeners, vegetarians and vagrants – most of whom became academics, chief executives, civil servants and management at the BBC.

I perked up. 'It's worth a try.'

'So you're on for Thursday?'

'Sorry, what about Thursday?'

'Thanks, babes. I knew I could rely on you.'

Later that night, Blob bustled in through the door laden with bags.

'Get up, you lazy shite,' he squawked. 'I bring drink, lots of drink, and trifles from the Orient. The Oriental Garden beside the public toilets, to be precise. And it's more sort of chickeny-prawny stuff than trifle. Put the soundtrack to *The Breakfast Club* on. Let's act out my favourite scenes.'

He dropped the bags on the floor and I threw down my book and rolled off the settee.

'I think I'll call up to see Mo tomorrow,' I said as we listened to Simple Minds and hoovered up rice. 'She might know more about the book. And I owe her a visit, I haven't seen her in months.'

'I'll come too,' he said, scooping and forking. 'Mo liked me.' Sauce dribbled down his chin. 'She always said I had star potential.'

'Mo was very generous.'

He looked at my plate, a swamp of rice and lumps. 'You eating that?'

I handed it over. 'Can I be Judd Nelson tonight?' I asked. 'You're always Judd Nelson.'

'I've got a better idea. How about we pretend to shoot each other?'

'That wasn't in *The Breakfast Club*.'

'No, but I would like to shoot you all the same.'

It turned out I was much better at shooting him and he was much better at being shot. I had a tendency to swoon when he shot me, which Blob said was gay and would never win me a part on *CSI*. He, on the other hand, could die with spectacular flair. I shot him at the bottom of the stairs and he blew backwards clutching his chest, slid down the bottom steps and choked to death on his own blood. I shot him while he lay sleeping on the settee – he tipped onto the floor, woke momentarily and died peacefully with a noise like an injured gazelle. I shot him while he leapt from behind the settee to take a shot at me. He crashed to the floor in slow motion, curled up, calling for his partner and gurgled into oblivion. I was just about to shoot him in the tiny yard behind the house, when someone knocked at the front door.

I was still tee-heeing as I opened the door to find Chris, the landlord. I shook the imaginary gun from my hand and let him in.

'I want whatever you're having,' he chuckled. Chris was a chuckler, permanently and often inappropriately bemused.

'Bonhomie, nasi goreng or vino?' I asked.

'Don't know about that twattery, but I'll have a beer.'

Chris's stretch limo – taxi to hens, tourists and celebs – was parked on the pavement behind my car. He was so well connected, no scummy thief or ugly traffic warden would dare. Small and lean with over-primped facial hair, he assumed his usual doorman stance in front of the bookcase. The fringed lampshade was reflected on his shiny shaved head.

'Eighties hits?' He tilted his head sideways at the turntable. 'I love that stuff. See *Miami Vice*? That was me.' He hitched up his trousers to show bone-white ankles with no socks. 'I'm here for the rent.'

Blob handed him a beer and Chris glugged at it, before sucking air through his teeth. He turned to me. 'See you're going to be famous, then?'

I choked on a stray grain of rice. 'What?'

'Picked your ma up in the limo.'

'How did you know she was my mother?'

'You're the spit of her. And I recognised the name. Shaw, isn't it? And the job – she said she was a writer. I asked, like, you know, I always do, I've got an intercom thingie, I do that. And I recognised the big bazongas, obviously. Only joking.' He rubbed a hand over his shiny head and chuckled.

Horror crept over me. 'What did you tell her?'

'You look like you're going to boke. I told you the Oriental Garden was no good. I was taking her past here on the way to the motorway and I just happened to say I owned a couple of houses round this way and she said one of her kids lived around here and I just twigged. She was telling me she has a book coming out? Memoirs? Will you get like, royalties or whatever? Wonder if she'll put me in it. She has my card.'

I felt the rice rise. My cloud of drunken denial was breaking up. How could she suddenly get this close? After all this time?

'Did you tell her I lived here? In this house?'

'Course I did. Surprised she didn't know. Here, small world, isn't it?'

I didn't make it to the toilet but reached the hand basin just in time. Chris had installed a bathroom ripped out of an avocado spaceship and the colour made me worse. I lost the prawns and rice and everything I'd drunk and had to rinse and poke it all down the plughole with the pointy end of my toothbrush. I opened the window and breathed in the darkness, before sitting on the edge of the bath and chewing my freshly minted toothbrush.

Blob filled the doorway, bottle in one hand, wine glasses between the fingers of his other. 'Well, fuck fuckety-fuck. That's from the Bible. First draft of Corinthians.'

'She knew I lived round here, Blob. How could she know?'

He sat beside me on the bath. 'You're obsessing, Tommie. It's not healthy.' He poured wine, setting the bottle on the floor.

'What else does she know? What does she know about Georgie? How could she know anything about us?'

'We'll get the book and see what she's written. All publicity is good publicity.'

'No, it's not.'

'Oh, help me here, I'm trying to make you feel better.'

'She's going to use us again,' I said, taking my toothbrush out to chew my hair. 'I can see it coming and I can't stop it.'

Blob crossed his legs at the ankles, brogues squeaking. 'Well, I'd say most people aren't interested in reading about tragic little teenagers like you and Fishy Flaps. They want to read about your psycho mother having stunt sex with poetry dick.' He stuffed his wrist into his mouth and retched.

Chris shimmied by and unzipped his fly at the toilet. 'Wonder if I should put another toilet in,' he chuckled, pissing like a horse on steroids.

'Apart from that,' Blob went on, 'if she does write about you and Georgie, it's different from last time. She'll know that. This time you can write about her. Maybe that's what she wants. The worse you make her out to be, the more coverage she'll get. I know how it works. I love trash.'

'So we're damned if we do and damned if we don't,' I said.

'Well, if you must resort to clichés, yes.'

Chris's piss went on and on, steam rising. 'There's another driver who's gutting his ma's old house. He'd give me a bog for a couple of quid, no sweat.'

'It's cold as a witch's diddy in here,' Blob told Chris. 'See if he has a radiator too.'

Chris shook, jigged and zipped. 'Pay the rent and I might even give you a roof over your head.'

'Whether I ignore it or react to it, she still wins,' I said. 'All this time and everything's still on her terms.' I shivered.

'You can make this work for you,' Blob said. 'Just sink to her level.'

'Yeah, and you're going to be famous, don't forget,' Chris chuckled, closing the window.

'I'd rather be famous for something meaningful.'

Blob clinked my glass. 'Just you leave integrity up to me. I follow through where you fail. I have a good feeling about this TV ad.'

'Do you?' I asked. He'd been to more than ten auditions in the last few months and not got any parts.

'You going to be famous as well then?' Chris chuckled.

'Absolutely.'

'Good for you, big man,' chuckled Chris. 'But I still have a wife and family and Dorota from the depot to support. She's due in April and she'll need a car. I know yous are arty types and all that, but the rent is overdue and I wouldn't like us to fall out.'

Blob stood up. 'Did I tell you I have Whitney Houston on a compilation album? Come down and have another beer.'

Chris chuckled. 'I'm an easy touch, aren't I? Problem is, I like yous two, you're harmless. You've got a couple more weeks, but that's it. So what do you think of another toilet? Downstairs, beside the kitchen?' He headed for the stairs tweaking his fly. Blob followed.

I put my glass to my teeth and stared at my flip-flops. The last time Gloria wrote about us, the critics adored her 'challenging honesty'. She was a success at last, but it almost destroyed Georgie and me. For the first time in months, I thought about having a cigarette.

Blob leaned back into the bathroom. 'None of your gothic moping, you. Come on.'

It was later than legal when Chris got a sledgehammer out of his car and started knocking through from the kitchen to the yard. We played 1980s' compilations, Blob danced, Chris hammered, I apologised to the police on two occasions and we slept in the dust as Culture Club played. When Gluteus Maximus arrived, I took him upstairs, glad there were still walls to lean on.

I would have called us friends who fuck except we weren't friends. He was someone I met in a drunken queue one night in McDonald's, and he was a good few years younger than me. We didn't go out, I didn't know what he drank, who his friends were or what he did when he wasn't with me. When I was sober, I disappointed myself but when I was drunk, I couldn't stop myself.

5.

My copy of Bob Dylan's *Bringing It All Back Home* was wedged half-in half-out of the cassette player and had been there since I bought the car for £300 seven years before. Everyone I knew had tried and failed to remove it, but I was sure some day my prince would come. The radio was stuck on medium wave and, forced to choose between live sport chat and everything that was wrong with contemporary music, I turned it off. Crammed into the passenger seat, Blob drooled as he slept, glasses and quiff skew-whiff. He could sleep through anything, even my creative driving.

I had a casually abusive relationship with my car: I neglected it and it, in turn, sought attention by letting me down. Shown any mercy it would roll over and play dead, so I pushed it hard – that was the only thing it understood. The low white sun glared off the wet roads and after a near-miss with a livestock transporter, I admitted defeat and put on the only pair of sunglasses I owned. I'd found them in the glove compartment. They had been designed for a mission to the future and made me look like an extra from the porn version of *Metropolis*.

I headed north, left the motorway, and tore through hawthorned country lanes edged with snow. I'd used Blob's phone to text Jude, explaining that I was out of the office, researching Irish poetry for Kevin Loane's feature. The more I thought about Gloria, the more I needed to see the book. I had to talk to Mo urgently.

The roads narrowed and corners tightened and at a crossroads, we slid into the path of an oncoming tractor. I counter-steered and missed it by inches. The farmer glared. Then, on second thoughts, he waved in a very friendly fashion. I apologised in German and drove away quickly. Men, and sometimes women, waved hello more often than I was comfortable with, a consequence of getting too drunk to remember who and what in a city too small to get away with it. Now that Blob was back, I did it less and less, but sometimes I still needed the kind of escape Gluteus Maximus offered.

My arms and legs knew every turn and gear change as I approached Mo's farm. It was a trip I had made every day on the bus back from school and years later, I still drove up to see her, feeling guilty each time for not visiting more. The last time was summer and she had packed the backseat of my car with strawberries, courgettes, broad beans, a baby oak tree, a cannabis plant and a box of Indian cigarettes.

Swinging into the lane up to the farm, I was thrown into the dense shadow of pines and for a second I was blind. I stamped on the brake but not soon enough. The car ricocheted off a *For Sale* sign, slid sideways on frozen puddles and collided with a piano that had been left next to a removals van in front of the house. The piano trundled backwards and pitched into the ditch, emitting the tortured chord progression of the devil as it went down. Two hundred crows lifted up from the trees and rained shit upon us. I was 'home'.

From the field beside the house, Mo's grandchildren cheered me on. Bemused, Mo watched my calamitous arrival from the steps of the house, a mirrored lamp in each of her hands. The piano movers flocked to the wounded piano and Blob snorted awake. He looked at me, straightening his glasses. 'Who the hell are you and what have you done with Tommie?'

'I just killed a piano.'

'Drive on. Nobody saw.'

Mo rapped the window and I wound it down.

'Hello, Tommie. Hello, Robert.' Her voice was low and raspy from a lifetime of smoking.

'Hello,' we replied in unison.

'I'm not sure if you were able to see through those glasses, sweetheart, but you hit the piano,' she said.

Her son Orbital and daughter Astra appeared at the door of the house. They had been born before ring roads and cars became an issue.

'My piano!' wailed Astra, and flew to the ditch-bound casualty, her Avoca layers flapping like an Irish heroine. I shared a father with Astra and Orbital and we had grown up in the same house but not at the same time – they were thirteen and fifteen years older than me, and had left by the time I was old enough to understand who they were.

These days Orbital owned a vegetarian café in the south of the city and was writing a book about the free food to be found in hedgerows, parks and bins. Astra was something called a 'sapiential consultant', which apparently made her very important somewhere, somehow. The house was Mo's, and even though Georgie and I had lived there, Astra made sure we knew it wasn't ours.

Mo joined Astra while Orbital walked round my car. Blob and I stood beside it, our breath misting and mingling. Blob took off his glasses, stretched and lit a cigarette. Orbital peered at my dented bumper and his mouth lifted at one side in his odd half-smile. He had Mo's big nose and he leaned it towards me, like a dog trying to find out where I'd been.

'What on earth were you two drinking?' he said.

'Drain cleaner. I thought it was meths. Don't look at me like that, you've been there. You know Blob, don't you?' I asked.

Orbital surveyed Blob, nodding his half-smile. 'You're the actor. You have a lot of . . . presence.'

'Thank you,' Blob said.

Orbital wiped his hands down his baggy jumper and started whistling.

Mo approached us, still carrying the lamps. She was sturdy and wore a sheepskin coat and the scuffed high-heeled boots she used even when turning the soil. Her long white hair was held back with a hairband and she had been wearing the same brown eyeliner for almost half a century. Her skin was lined and sallow-grey with smoke. She hugged me, lamps and all.

'Sorry about the piano,' I said. 'I'll pay to get it repaired.'

Astra whisked past and into the house, muttering, 'Flaming idiot.'

'I'm sorry,' I said after her.

'You're still a flaming idiot,' she called back. 'Who wears sunglasses like that anyway?'

I caught Mo scrutinising me.

'What?' I asked.

'Come in,' Mo said, leading the way up the steps. 'We haven't packed the kettle yet.'

We followed Mo inside.

The house was a puzzle of dank narrow passageways and dark organic smells. Years of smoke, lentils and rot drifted through unpredictable spaces and tangential extensions. My guess was eighteenth, nineteenth and twentieth centuries: one minute you were rubbing up against naked granite walls and the next you were sinking into swirling brown carpets that had witnessed Charles marry Diana. Rooms begat rooms and tall gave rise to small, with plenty of places to hide and write pretentious piss to a Canadian boy named Arnaud.

Outbuildings had been used as offices, studios, workshops, bunks, yoga rooms and even a music venue, but through the low window of the patchwork kitchen, I could see weeds growing from the stonework, window casings rotted through and roofs that had collapsed. Next to the half-dismantled polytunnel sat Mo's rusting Ford Transit, Orbital's crusty Saab and Astra's monster 4x4. Beyond them, removals men stacked boxes and furniture into their vans.

Mo set the lamps on the worktop and filled the kettle. We sat at the kitchen table as she dropped teabags into cups and poured boiling water. She took three cigarettes from her pack and offered one to Blob and one to me.

'I've given up,' I said.

She frowned. 'Oh right. No, I mean, good for you.'

She lit her own and Blob's cigarettes and set the pack and lighter down by the ugly handmade ashtray. She coughed, a sticky wet hack, and wheezed with every breath.

'You're selling up, then?' Blob said, looking round at the damp-stained walls. 'Why would anybody want to leave a place like this?'

'I didn't know you were selling,' I said.

Mo blew smoke towards the yellow ceiling. 'Why, does it bother you?'

'No, I'm just surprised. Does it bother you?'

She looked at the cigarette between her fingers. 'Yes.' She took a long time to clear the stickiness from her chest. 'It does. Very much.'

Mo had read scary stories to me when I was small and dried my wellies on the radiator. She gave me my first bra (an Astra cast-off), taught me dirty songs and gave me her old records and books. She let me name the kittens and she was the first person to visit when I was in hospital. She grew and dealt drugs and sold hydroponics equipment online, but she was kind and patient, probably too much of both.

'So, anyway.' Mo brightened. 'Nice to see you both, piano aside.'

'I really am sorry.'

'You go ahead and hit that piano if you want, sweetheart,' she said, patting my hand. She leaned in conspiratorially. 'I'm not dead yet.' She sat back, playing with a tarnished gold chain around her neck. 'Well, Robert, what are you up to these days?'

He slurped his tea. 'I've got a casting for a TV ad. And if I win the role, I'll have done it by talent alone, even if it does pay big bucks. It's a capitalist culture. At least I won't be a lonely whore.'

'Well, I hope you get it. It's about time you got a break.'

Blob shot me a 'told-you-so' look.

Orbital shuffled his clogs into the room carrying trays of baby marijuana plants.

'We've had to wind up the farm.' His voice was oddly reedy. 'We took legal advice. We can't sue Gloria for libel or anything because we're on shaky ground to begin with. It's safer this way.'

Mo folded her arms and puffed smoke upwards. 'Well, it was going to happen anyway.'

Orbital's half-smile was fleeting. 'Mum hasn't been well.'

Mo touched the lamps on the table and looked at Orbital. 'Take these and put them in the van, would you, sweetheart? Robert, give Orb a hand.'

Blob's eyebrows rose above his glasses.

She patted his shoulder, a bird tapping on a mountain. 'Go on, chop wood, carry water. It won't do you any harm.'

Like a child sent to stand in a corner, Blob scuffed and dragged his brogues across the room towards Orbital.

Orbital took in Blob's girth. 'I take it you eat meat, big man?'

'A little,' Blob said as they left the room. 'I'm anorexic. When I look in the mirror I see a fat bastard.'

Their voices moved away and I heard Blob refuse point-blank to carry water.

'You're getting very thin,' Mo said. 'Do you think it's a good idea to live with Robert? I know he's your friend, but I'm not sure he's very good for you.'

'Because he eats everything in the house?'

'No, because the last time you two were friends, you . . . you know . . .'

'That had nothing to do with him. He had no idea. Don't blame him.' Poor Blob. I had done a terrible thing to him once. I didn't mean to. We never talked about it and I hoped that meant it wasn't an issue any more. I wasn't sure. But I hoped.

'I know,' she said. 'But you drink too much when you're with Robert.'

'It's just the right amount if you want to be drunk.'

'All I'm saying is, drink's a depressant.'

'I'm fine. I know the signs. I'm OK. What about you, are you OK?'

She waved her hand to dismiss it. 'Getting old, that's all.'

She leaned back. 'You saw the paper then?'

'Georgie showed me. Have you seen the book? Do you know anyone who's got it? Georgie and I have to see it, Mo.'

She shook her head. 'Don't we all? Everyone's tried. Anyone who was involved here could be in it. But there's an embargo so that people will buy the paper to read it first. It's all very grubby.' She watched her smoke spread along the ceiling. 'She was here a while ago. Not long after your last visit.'

My chest thudded. 'I thought she didn't keep in touch.'

'No, well, she didn't. Then when I opened the door, she hugged me. I thought she wanted to be friends again.' The crease between her eyes deepened. 'I welcomed her. I know people don't believe it, but we were friends, once. Or at least I was. My imagination ran away with me. I thought she wanted to make up with you and Georgie.' She hesitated. 'I'm trying to explain but I sound like I'm making excuses.'

I brought my hair round and chewed it. 'Why, what happened?'

'She wanted to chat about how things were and look at all the old photographs. I couldn't remember where they were but she knew. She got them out of the attic and she wanted to borrow a few. I thought she was just feeling, you know, nostalgic. The box is sitting over there if you want any of them. There are a few of your dad.' She nodded towards a dusty, sagging cardboard box near the door. 'I'm going to burn the rest. Although I think she has the most dangerous ones anyway.'

'Dangerous?'

Mo grinned sourly. 'Oh, you know. The head of the BBC when she was a man; the university dean and his wife and her lover during their naturist phase; the senior civil servant sucking on a bong, his wife's Wicca flirtation. It was the sixties, we were young.' She drew on her cigarette until the filter started to burn, then stubbed it out with her thick brown fingers. She hacked into her rolled-up hand. 'They're nearly all retired now. Writing books that give their side of the story.'

That was one angle that Kevin Loane had missed – books that second-guessed old 'friends'. Probably not his kind of thing.

'The sixties were over by the time Gloria came here,' Mo went on, 'but she's a good self-publicist. She'll use whatever she can.' She played with her chain again. 'I didn't notice she'd taken them. Not at the time.'

'Taken what?' My voice came out a whisper. I cleared my throat.

'The pictures of you and Georgie.'

I lifted the pack of cigarettes. 'What did you tell her?'

'I thought she wanted . . .'

'You told her where I lived.' I opened the pack. The cigarettes looked like sacrificial soldiers. I held their sweetness up to my nose. 'Did you tell her about Georgie?'

'I'm sorry, Tommie. I thought she was—'

I put down the pack and stood up. 'Righty-o then. And that's not a word I use lightly.'

'Tommie . . .'

I made for the front door, knocking over a hydroponics lamp in the hall. It smashed on the tiles but I didn't look back. Swearing, I yanked at the door of my car but the malevolent little bastard wouldn't open. Mo caught up and held onto my arm. Her chest was whistling.

'I thought she was a friend, Tommie. I never thought she would use me like this.'

'But you saw her . . .' You saw her use us and we were kids. But I didn't say it. It wasn't Mo's fault. I was a shit. 'I'll pay for the lamp. And the piano.'

From the house I heard Astra's voice. 'What flaming lunatic smashed one of the lamps? Oh, *that* flaming lunatic. Oh well, that makes everything alright then, doesn't it?'

And then Blob's voice. 'So you're Astra. I like your boots. My friend has a pair like that. He's a female impersonator.'

Dan, the elder of Mo's two grandchildren, ran across the drive. 'Granny, look! There's more! This was in the piano.' He handed her a brown envelope crammed with £20 notes.

The delicate touch on my lips, the first fragrant draw, the scratch as smoke flooded my lungs and came down my nose, the charm of a newly spinning head, the heat on my fingers as I drew to the end and the aftertaste and lick round my teeth. I could smell it in my hair and on my clothes and in the air and I drifted up and away on clouds of delicious poison. Oh, how I'd missed it, how I loved it, how could it be so bad?

I stood on the steps and smoked and smoked. A bee flew up and looked at me and I stared back, wondering why it was about so early in the year. The sun was behind the house and with its pale views and silky light, it was a distractingly beautiful place, particularly if you wanted to bury your head in interpretative dance, experimental music and grass during the bloodiest period in Northern Ireland's history. As Mo and my parents did.

Mo was going to be a doctor and my father was studying for a degree in Divinity. They married when they were still students before dropping out and buying the rundown farmhouse with money from Mo's parents. What had started as a place for friends to gather became a haven for peace-loving, creative types during the Troubles. By the time Gloria arrived in the seventies, it was a self-sufficient commune. When my father started the affair, it was because Mo had already set him free. Mo and my father weren't lovers any more – they were twins by then. Mo's words, not mine.

The removals men were closing the back doors of the vans and I caught a glimpse of all the bits that made up Mo: her huge old wooden bed frame, her stained, threadbare armchair, her bookcase, emptied and soulless. I looked away. Over the course of the day they had discovered almost three thousand pounds inside, under or behind furniture. Mo didn't remember where or when she'd hidden it – the agony and the ecstasy of the long-term stoner.

She joined me as I savoured the last few drags, closing the door of the house behind us.

'Where are you moving to?' I asked.

'I'm staying with my sister in Donegal for a while.' She lit her cigarette.

'What will happen to this place?'

'Housing development. Four gentlemen's residences.' She flicked her eyes at me. 'Astra brokered the deal. I better die soon.'

I laughed. 'You're in great shape.'

She shuffled her scuffed boots. 'I was in hospital after Christmas. I had a hysterectomy. Then pneumonia.'

Fuck. She'd been lugging furniture about all day and now she was standing in the cold, smoking her brains out.

'I know what you're thinking,' she said.

I stared at her. 'Shouldn't we . . . ?'

She gave me a warning look.

I tugged on her sleeve. 'Why didn't you tell me?'

'I didn't want to worry you. You have your own life.'

'That's a bit of an overstatement.'

She inhaled and hacked into her hand, her shoulders convulsing slowly. We stood at the door and smoked without talking. Crows rattled in the trees.

'I'm sorry I told Gloria about you,' she said.

I poked a toe in the dust by the door. 'She knew you'd be kind to her.'

Mo shrugged. 'Orb's café will probably do well out of it. Astra will take it in her stride, she'll turn it to her advantage some way. But you and Georgie . . . I was thinking.' She threw her cigarette into the driveway. 'Maybe it's time you talked to Gloria.'

'Jesus Christ.'

She put her arm round me and laughed. 'It won't be that bad. Just have a conversation. Talk. Just . . .' She squeezed my shoulder. 'I know it's hard, sweetheart, but . . . just be grown up about it.'

She grinned. I sniggered into my shoes.

'You look like her,' Mo said. 'But you aren't like her, if you know what I mean. Except, well . . .' She gave me that look of scrutiny. 'Come inside. I want to show you something.'

❧

The kitchen was lit by a harsh, fly-flecked fluorescent light that creaked and plinked above us. Blob and Orbital were at the table, playing Battleship with Astra's sons, Dan and Jack. Both boys had fair hair and glowing skin. Dan was thin and smart, bordering on sneaky. Two years younger, at six and a half, Jack was smaller and rounder, rakish and good humoured.

For a second their presence confused me. 'Shouldn't you be in school?'

Jack, who was wearing my sunglasses, honked with laughter. 'Auntie Tommie, we *were* at school. We're home now. We can't go to school all day and all night.'

Dan leaned over the table and tried to peek at Blob and Jack's battleships. 'Mummy says Auntie Tommie doesn't get up till lunchtime,' he said.

'I could make us something for tea, Mum,' Orbital said. 'What have you got?'

'Have a look in the cupboards, see what's left.' Mo lifted the sagging box of photographs and set them on the table, her lungs whistling. The box smelt of dirt and damp.

'You not playing any more?' Dan asked Orbital, who'd started opening cupboards.

'What do you need me for?' Orbital said. 'You know where their ships are. Jack, he cheated when you weren't looking.'

'Ohhhhhh!' Jack wailed, slamming his hands down on the table.

'There are no just wars,' Blob said.

'Hey, look,' Mo said to Jack. She handed him a photograph. 'Who's that?'

Dan narrowed his eyes at Blob. 'Are you gay?'

Blob nodded. 'Yes.'

Dan smirked. 'You're *gay.*'

'I'm not talking semantics with an eight-year-old. Now fuck off.'

'Granny, did you hear what he said?'

'Sorry, sweetheart, I wasn't listening.'

Jack looked at the photograph and at me. He took off the sunglasses, peered closely at them and lit up with delight. 'It's Auntie Tommie in the photograph. You're huge there!'

Mo grinned and handed me the photograph. It was Gloria. Or me, if I gained forty pounds. The picture was faded, curling and had a dated red hue. It showed Gloria and my father, Pete, sitting on the steps of the farmhouse in the sun, her arm linked through his, their knees together. He was shirtless, and with his long dark hair, wispy beard and solemn face, he looked like a disciple. With her headscarf, huge African beads, swirling layers, horribly familiar sunglasses and pout, she looked like the front cover of a seventies' *Cosmo*. I threw the picture on the table.

'Who's that man?' Jack asked.

'That's your granddad Pete,' Mo said.

'Where is he now?' Jack said.

Dan rolled his eyes and leaned over the table. 'He's dead, stupid.'

'Yeah, but where *is* he?'

We listened to Astra moving around upstairs. Dan and Jack looked at Mo. Mo busied herself in the box again. 'Ask your mum. She knows about that sort of thing.'

Dan lifted the photograph of Pete and Gloria and studied it.

'How did he die?' Jack asked.

'He died of stupid hair,' Dan said.

'But how did he die?' Jack persevered.

Mo looked at me. Pete died a few months before I was born and I had been angry they lied to me about it. 'It was an accident,' I said. And so I lied too. I couldn't not.

'You can have those glasses if you want,' I told Jack.

'Thanks.' Jack put them back on.

'Ew, they're gay!' Dan squealed.

Jack handed them back.

❀

It was dark when we left the farm, our clothes smelling of mushrooms, omelette and smoke. Orbital had loaded up the backseat with a box of old vinyl he had lifted out of the skip and Mo gave me some gooseberry jam, a tray of tinned peaches, an envelope with photographs of my father and a little stick in a pot, which she said was a baby ash tree.

She settled her hand on the roof as we got into the car. 'You two be careful,' she said.

'You too.'

'And don't worry about the piano, sweetheart. Or the lamp. I'll sort it out. I've got all that cash now.'

'No, it was my fault.'

'Not at all. Silly place to leave a piano. Thanks for coming. We haven't much left to do here.' She rapped the roof of the car and I pulled away towards the lane. In the mirror, I could see a light in every window as Mo, Orbital, Dan and Jack waved from the steps.

Pulling out onto the dark country road, I drove towards a ghost in flowing layers and had to brake sharply, a scream caught in my throat. Albums and tins rammed us in the back. Blob oofed and swore.

Astra stood in front of the car, her hand on the bonnet.

I wound down the window, my heart flailing, as she walked round the side of the car. 'Jesus, Astra, I could have killed you.' I clutched my chest. 'You could have killed me.'

Her well-cut hair and long, layered clothes lifted and whipped. Her face was strong like Mo's, but had none of Mo's warmth. 'Why were you here?' she said.

'I ran out of gooseberry jam.'

'I hope you don't think you'll be getting anything from the sale of this house. And I've spoken to her about her will. She doesn't owe you anything.' She pulled her layers tighter. Pious and merciless, she was a medieval pope in the making. She couldn't contemplate any motives but her own and everyone else was guilty.

'OK, well . . . bye, then.' I wound up the window and we pulled away. 'My timing is fantastic,' I said.

'She's just jealous, babes,' Blob said.

'You're right. Who wouldn't want a nothing job and an aimless, childless, loveless life like mine?'

'You brainless bint. Mo prefers you.'

We headed back the way we came, my skewed headlights making driving much more thrilling than was strictly necessary. I wished there was music.

As we filtered onto the motorway, I said to Blob, 'Don't be unkind to Dan. He's just a little kid.'

But Blob was asleep.

6.

I was dreaming about shelves and the car-smoke-radio alarm when Blob, in T-shirt and voluminous boxers, hand over his eyes, marched in and stretched his phone out. I struggled through layers to take it. The phone's screen was white. It was alive. I leaned on an elbow and said hello.

'Where the fuck are you?'

I slapped my hand to my head. I had a nicotine hangover. 'Wuh?'

'Are you coming in today, or what?' Jude's voice cleaved me.

'I was . . . well . . . I wasn't . . . well.'

'Where the fuck were you yesterday?'

'Poetry . . . research thing.'

'All day? Kevin Loane has been trying to reach you. Phone him as soon as you get in here. Are you in bed?'

'No.'

'You sound like you're in bed.'

'How did you get this number?'

'You texted me from it, Tommie. Stop fucking about and get in here.' She paused. Then she was gone.

I lay down and pulled the covers up. The phone buzzed in my hand. It was a text. From Jude. *Get fckng up.*

Blob was beached across the armchair in my room, hand still over his eyes. The pale blue walls were supposed to help with insomnia. And they did, just not at the right time. My clothes – black undies, black outies – were dropped and draped across the furniture and the narrow spaces in between. Divorced shoes, boots, heels and flip-flops were scattered across the industrial carpet tiling. Piles of books spilled in corners and baskets overflowed with cheap

52

accessories. The ageing clock radio beside my bed said 10.12 AM. The gothic purple curtains said forever midnight.

I opened my eyes at 10.47 AM.

Flinging myself out of bed, I caught my foot in an abandoned bra and flew face-first towards the wardrobe. Even as I flew, the words 'booby trap' came to mind. I hit the door with the side of my face and crunched to the floor.

'Jesus!' Blob was kneeling beside me, trying to pull my hands away. 'Let me see, let me see.'

I swore and cried in pain and shock. Then I cried and laughed because Blob's todger was hanging out of his shorts as he fussed around. And then I just cried because I was being looked after by someone whose dick was hanging out of his shorts and this was my life. I mopped my tears with my guilty bra.

'I think that's going to be a black eye,' Blob said, examining my face.

I crawled over to the mirror. My cheekbone and eyebrow throbbed. The skin was raised and a perfect crescent was already developing under my eye.

'It won't be that bad,' I said, surprised at how much my voice shook.

'Yeah, well,' he said uncertainly. 'Come down and I'll make you a cup of tea.'

'I have to go to work.'

'Oh, have a fucking cup of tea.'

I sent Jude a text from Blob's phone saying I'd had an accident but I'd be there ASAP. She didn't respond, which was worse than getting a reply.

Before he'd left the night before, Chris had covered the Chris-shaped hole in the kitchen wall with hardboard and told us in Landlordese that work would begin as soon as possible and there might be some disruption. Blob made tea and poured me a bowl of peaches as the wind moved his quiff and flipped the fringes of the lampshade.

We sat on the edge of the settees as the room rattled around us like a bus shelter. I warmed my hands on a cup of sugary tea and smoked one of Blob's cigarettes, blowing smoke through the hole in the wall. Blob ate the peaches. I felt around in my bag for make-up.

'I have stage make-up,' Blob said.

'OK, but be quick.'

He took the stairs three at a time and thundered down with the bag that Ernest Worthing was found in. He played Talking Heads as he worked, dabbing, lining, smoothing, smearing, powdering and gripping me if I flinched.

He stepped back. 'There. You're done.'

In front of the mirror, I turned my head from side to side. 'I'd make a good Othello,' I said, using a finger wrapped in a sleeve to tone it down.

He writhed on the spot, as his phone buzzed in his pocket. Pulling it out, he looked at the screen and held it to me. 'It's that woman again. Your boss.'

'You answer it.'

Behind Blob, someone knocked at the front door. Blob opened it to find a chuckling Chris.

'My friends!' he chuckled, walking in and slapping Blob on the back.

Blob handed him the phone. 'Speak to this woman.'

Chris chuckled. 'Certainly.' He answered the phone. 'Hello . . . Hello, my love . . . Here, no need to be like that . . . Well, who the hell are *you*? Here, wait a minute, I know you! I taxied you . . . Here, did you ever find your clothes? Oh, don't you worry, wild horses wouldn't drag that out of me . . . Somebody got arrested . . . I know . . . I know . . . Mmm . . . Alright then, no worries . . . Me too. All the best, now. Bye.'

He handed the phone back to Blob, shaking his head and chuckling. 'Small world, small world.' He looked at me. 'Is that a black eye? That's not good. What's going on?' He narrowed his eyes at Blob.

'What are you looking at me for?' Blob said. 'She tripped over her own bra.'

'I wasn't wearing it at the time,' I added.

'Right, well,' Chris said, his chuckle diluted with suspicion. 'I came round to say we're starting work today and I had a brainwave. You, big man, can labour for me and that'll go towards your rent.'

Blob held up a finger. 'Just one second.' He took my elbow and ushered me to the sink. He whispered, 'That's slave labour, isn't it?'

'I don't think we have a choice,' I whispered back.

'The call centre might take me back.'

'One day won't hurt. You might even enjoy it. Physical labour releases endorphins and a feeling of spiritual satisfaction. I read about it. It's the big thing.'

'It's "in" then?'

I shrugged. 'Probably. And it will extend your range.'

He turned back to Chris, his chins held high. 'In the name of spiritual and professional advancement, alright then.'

'Whatever, mate,' Chris said. 'Come out and meet the lads. I have to head on. The town is hosting the second Hirsute Women's Conference this week and I'm the official ride.'

I grabbed my coat and bag and followed them outside. Chris introduced Blob to two wiry, unimpressed Poles who stood smoking beside a flatbed lorry. The back was loaded with pickaxes, shovels, wheelbarrows and tools. Behind that, another lorry unloaded a skip.

'Just do whatever the lads tell you,' Chris briefed Blob, as he walked backwards to the limo. 'They don't speak English but you're not building a rocket, big man.'

I gave Blob an encouraging smile, fished my sunglasses out of the car and set off for work.

I smelled the Wednesday tights before I saw her. She said nothing and I didn't look up. The air was tinged with burnt dust from the electric heater and the radio squeaked quietly on the floor. Bill and Patricia worked with their heads down. Jude threw a pile of press releases at me and put her heels up on her desk. She was wearing pink leather trousers, which meant she must be wearing pop socks. I shuddered. Suddenly she stood up, leaned over and peered at me closely.

'Take the sunglasses off.'

I peeled them off.

'What happened to your face?'

'Accident.'

'You're a dark horse, Tommie. I could start to like you. Article idea: take this down. The truth about abused women, a willing victim writes.'

'What?'

'Sadomasochism. Take it down, you.'

I took up my notebook and pencil, scribbled the word 'knob' and drew a bubbly pair of tits. Then I made them into a bubbly rabbit and dotted a non-existent 'i'. 'Got it.'

Jude spun a block of Post-it notes at me. 'Kevin wants a meeting this afternoon. Here's his number. How are you getting on with your pervy poet?'

'Just about to phone his people.'

She wriggled a finger in her ear and rolled the haul between finger and thumb. 'Phone Kevin first. Chop-fucking-chop.'

I lifted the receiver and tapped in the number, eyes closed tight. It was going to happen, I couldn't stop it – the switch that flicked inside my head when I spoke to people I didn't know on the phone.

'Hello, Kevin Loane's office.'

Cue my breathy, simpering response: 'Ooh, hello, is that Kevin?' I gushed.

'No, this is his assistant, Tracy.'

'Oops, sorry, crikey, that's a bad cold,' I giggled.

'Sorry?' said the assistant.

'Try echinacea.' Perky-perky-perky!

'Beg pardon?'

'Echinacea.'

'Spell that please.'

'E-C-H-I-N-A-C-E-A.'

'And you're calling regarding?'

'Devine Energy's sponsorship of the Belfast Poetry Festival and the coverage in *Bellefast* magazine,' I tittered.

She clicked off and I let my hair fall between me and Jude. The phone clicked again and I heard Kevin's voice, edgy.

'I was really expecting Tommie to call me back,' he said with a big, wet sniff. 'You're the third writer I've been assigned. What kind of name is that anyway?'

I paused for a second before assuming a bright voice with a trace of somewhere very far away. 'Right. Yes, no, I'm Tommie's PA. My parents are from Switzerland. It's a very popular name there.'

Foot clouds wafted up as Jude rocked in her seat.

'Tommie must be a very busy woman,' Kevin went on. 'I wish I was important enough to warrant a personal phone call from her.'

'She sends her apologies but asks if you are free for a meeting this afternoon?' I said, dabbing at sudden sweat.

'Obviously. I suggested it.' I could hear him thinking. 'Will you be there?'

'No, sorry.'

'Shame. You sound talented.'

'Thank you.' I could feel my make-up sliding off.

Kevin continued, 'Tell her to be at my office for two-thirty.'

'I'll enter it in Tommie's diary this very moment,' I said.

He hung up.

'What the fuck was that about?' Jude said, sockets hollowed.

'He thought I was someone called Echinacea. I didn't want to make him feel stupid.'

'Well, as long as he pays, I don't fucking care.' She stood up, swinging her gargantuan pink patent bag over her shoulder. 'Patricia, phone the printer and tell him we're only paying for half of last month's run. There was a problem. Tell Seamus to think of some-thing.' She pulled her pop socks up through her trousers. 'And Bill, I have to put your target up by thirty percent this month.'

'What?' He spun round in his chair as Jude stalked towards the door. 'There's only two days left!'

She stopped in the doorway and threatened us with a grin. 'We make a good team,' she said. Aoife floated out behind her like a familiar.

Hearing her car pull away, Bill put his feet on the desk and dialled the racing results line. Patricia pulled a chair over beside me, the lining of her cheap black suit fissling. She crossed her petite legs and leaned in.

'What really happened?' She twinkled sympathetically.

'I tripped over some clothes.'

She raised an over-plucked eyebrow. 'Come on.'

'Seriously.'

'Did you put ice on it?'

'Never thought of that.'

'Well, at least let me try to cover it for you.'

'It's fine. Blob already had a go.' I took my mirror out of my bag and grimaced. The black crescent under my eye was clear and cartoon-perfect and the smudged make-up made me look like a Barbie that had been left outside all winter. I let my hair fall over my face.

'Let me have a go,' Patricia said. 'I have wipes.'

Patricia's touch was soft and light as a bird. As she removed Blob's panstick, we could hear giggles coming from reception.

Patricia grinned. 'Seamus and Lisa are getting on well.'

'Who's Lisa?'

'The receptionist.'

'The tiny one?'

Patricia nodded, dabbing concealer around my eye. 'He's always out there talking to her.'

'Bless,' I said.

'Don't be like that.' She took out her powder.

Chastised, I listened to their muffled chat and giggles.

'No, you're right,' I said. 'It's good. It's like Cathy and Hareton.'

Patricia got out her lip pencil and gloss. 'Friends of yours?'

'Nnn . . .'

'Don't move.' She drew round the outline of my mouth.

'Ooo . . .'

'Just a sec.' She painted on thick pink gloss. 'You want to look good for our Kevin.' She winked. 'Now do this.' She popped her lips to settle the gloss.

I popped.

'Wait,' she said. 'Your cheeks.' Patricia rummaged around in her sequinned make-up bag. 'Turn round to the light.' She waved a finger over a little book of soft brushes, making her selection.

'Patricia?'

'Mmm?'

'I'm not a journalist.'

'Mmm, I know.'

'So if we lose our jobs, I'm not really responsible.'

'What?'

'If I don't get the Arts pages feature right, we're going tits-up. Jude told me.'

She stopped brushing. 'I've seen the books, Tommie. We're going tits-up sooner or later.'

'But Devine Energy's money will keep us going for a while?'

She shrugged. 'It'll keep the creditors at bay for a month or two. And the commission will be good for Bill, I suppose. If he gets it.'

We looked at Bill, hunched over the phone. Now talking to a client, his posh selling voice tortured his vowels. I had met his daughters. They were tall, blonde and had been given everything their parents hadn't. They were terrifying.

'Jude will have something up her sleeve,' Patricia said. 'She's a good businesswoman.'

'She has no soul.'

'Anyway,' Patricia said, putting her brushes away. 'It wouldn't be hard for you to get another job.'

'Or you,' I said. I didn't look at her and she didn't look at me.

She held up her compact and said, 'Well, what do you think?'

I studied my reflection. Winter Barbie had been usurped by brand-new-just-out-of-the-box-super-plastic-shiny Barbie. Although it was much heavier make-up than I would normally wear, it worked. Not only did it cover the bruise, it made me look and smell like someone who had her shit completely together. 'Thanks, Patricia.'

She gave me the concealer and an old compact for touch-ups. 'Whatever happened, or whoever happened, I couldn't have you walking about like that. I'm going to get some lunch. Want anything?'

I gave her money for both our sandwiches.

The office was empty when I took out Diane's address book and flicked through the pages to the Fellowes Agency. I picked up the phone and called Liam.

The phone rang for a long time and I swapped the receiver from one hand to the other as I waited. Maybe he wasn't there. Out to lunch, probably. I chewed my hair and then stopped myself. It was the wrong time to call. I'd ruin my gloss.

I could tell he was smiling when he answered, as though he was chatting when he picked up the phone. After nine years, his voice was the same. Stupidly nasally. And yet my heart clattered along like someone running upstairs.

'Liam?' I said.

There was silence.

He sounded confused. 'Tommie?'

'Yes. It's me.'

More silence. We both spoke at the same time.

'I'm—'

'You—'

'You go first,' he said.

'This isn't what you think it is,' I said.

'What do I think it is?'

'This is a business call.'

He laughed. 'Alright.'

'I know we probably have a lot of other things . . .'

'Yeah.' He sounded bewildered.

'I work for a magazine. I need to set up an interview with one of your clients.'

'Oh. OK.' I could hear him breathing. 'Well, let's meet up.'

I fanned my face with Post-it notes.

'When are you free?' he said. 'Today?'

I turned pages in the desk diary I never used. 'Er, no, I have an appointment.'

'Tomorrow?'

I turned lots of empty pages. 'Meetings all day.'

'Friday? Three o'clock?'

I needed his help. Not only that, I owed him. The entire contents of his flat, to be precise. But then he did cheat on me when I was miscarrying his baby, so quite probably, he owed me.

'OK,' I said. 'Where?'

'You remember Moby's?'

'Yeah, but it's—' Not there any more, I tried to say. But before I could finish, he said, 'Perfect. Excellent. I'll see you there.' And hung up.

He never did bloody listen.

7.

Devine Energy's modern glass façade was clamped between thick cement walls. The building was set on an industrial estate next to a dump and the automatic front doors spread methane through the building with every sweep. I gave my name at reception and sat in a Wassily-style chair, playing with my pencil and staring at my notebook. I tried to look informed, possibly even inspired.

Kevin's rumble-voiced assistant escorted me upstairs and through an open-plan office, where phones rang but voices were muted. On the walls were large framed photographs of wind farms and solar panels, and under each photograph was a paragraph of text, which I assumed described the model pictured. Cubicle-bound workers stared as I walked by. The assistant opened a door at the end of the office and showed me in.

'Wait here, please,' she growled, and retreated, leaving me alone in the long meeting room. A massive, gleaming board table sat across the room at an odd angle. I walked around it and assumed a journalistic pose by the window. Kevin Loane loped in and navigated round the table, his hand extended. His hips dipped with each long stride and he looked like he was tacking in a strong swell.

'Tom,' he said. 'Have a seat.' He snorted back nasal gravel and held out an arm to indicate the room. 'Welcome to Devine Energy.'

'Thanks. I was wondering if—'

'You were wondering why the board table is set like this. Why the unusual layout? Why not have it parallel to the walls, like other businesses? Well, we're not like other businesses, Tom. It's all part of our ethos. We have a different . . . angle on things.' He crossed his thin legs and leaned back with a smug smile, waiting for my response.

I couldn't find one.

'We do things differently at Devine Energy,' he intoned. 'We bring imagination to our work, every day and in every way. You could say we are divinely inspired . . .'

Eventually, feeling obliged, I said, 'A-ha!'

'As Blake said, "Imagination is evidence of the divine."' Sniff.

I nodded and shook my head. 'Yep.'

'You don't take notes?' he said. 'You remember everything?'

'Oh yes, sorry.' I flicked through the rude doodles in my notebook to find a clean page.

'It's about innovation, Tom. In every area of the business, from technical development through to marketing and telesales, creativity is key. We encourage all our staff to get involved in the arts and try new things in life. We want them to explore what success means, to discover new ways of getting there, to share in the value of creativity.' Big wet sniff.

'So all staff have shares in the business?'

'God, no.' Kevin shifted in his seat.

'I'm not with you.'

'Staff are happier, Tom. More motivated, more productive. The MD drives a bigger car. Don't write that down. The point is – write this down – Devine Energy is different. Come with me, let me show you.' He pushed back his chair and I followed him into the open-plan office. No one looked up as he led me to the first framed photograph.

Kevin snorted mightily. 'This is our first installation on the North Coast. And below, see? If you look around the room, indeed the entire building, you'll see that all our installations, original blueprints, even large industrial customers have had poems written in their honour. Each poem is reproduced alongside a dramatic shot of the subject. The photographs were taken by one of our own staff. Where are you, Damian?'

In the distance, a hand appeared above a cubicle.

'And who writes the . . . er . . . poems?'

Kevin lowered his eyes modestly.

'You?' I asked.

In a loud singsong voice, Kevin read:

> *White winged giant, the power is thine,*
> *The glory of thy music rhymes:*
> *Shuff, shuff, shuff*
> *Fuff, fuff, fuff—*
> *Sound forth, ye mighty grand turbine.*

Big wet sniff.

'My God,' I said.

'Exactly, he said. 'And I have some further items you may find useful. Follow me.' He led the way up to the next floor, where the space was divided into large offices, each with a glass wall facing a central corridor. Kevin showed me into one of the offices. Files were piled neatly on every surface and on the windowsill was a framed photograph of two skinny children and a round woman. Above the wide desk, a noticeboard fluttered with posters, notes and leaflets. Looking like a child playing at being dad, Kevin sat behind the desk.

'I thought maybe you could share a little on how you see the feature taking shape,' he said, opening a drawer and sifting through papers.

'Er . . . well . . . there would be a section on the company and its ethos and your board table and so on. And a profile of you, to introduce the interview with Rory McManus.'

'I think it's essential that all the major poets at the festival endorse Devine Energy,' Kevin said. 'You write quotes for them and then get their sign-off at the festival.' He set a thin folder on the desk between us.

'I'm not sure they'd be—'

'Find a way. You can do it. You're creative, like me.'

'Not exactly like you.'

'What else do you have planned?'

'I . . . sort of . . . thought it might be nice to have a picture page, you know, of people who attend the event—'

'I like that.' Big wet sniff. 'What else?'

I felt an urge to chew my hair. 'To be honest, Kevin, we're not due to have our brainstorm until—'

'You don't know.'

'We're still—'

'There are eight pages to fill,' he said.

'There are? There are.'

'And I can help,' he said, leaning forward.

I felt my head tilt like a dog.

'Take those,' he said, looking at the thin file on the desk. 'Just a few things I've put together.'

I gripped the spine of the file and thumbed through the pages. Not staff profiles. Not company information. But poems. Lots of them, by Kevin Loane. Oceans of metaphors, long running dribbles of purplicity, tormented rhymes and way too much of this! and that? mid-sentence.

'If I need to fill space in the feature, I could put them in,' I ventured.

He walked round the desk to stand beside me. 'You're smart, Tom. Sensitive, tuned-in.' Snort. 'The ad agency we use are looking for a writer. Their last one left to marry an Inuit. I could put in a word for you. They're very receptive, very responsive to my needs. They're making an ad for me at the minute, using my concept. I would be very disappointed if *Bellefast* magazine couldn't find room for my contribution.'

In the silence, I could hear bin lorries reversing.

'We could print your poems alongside work from other, lesser known poets?'

His fringe moved as his eyebrows rose.

'It just seems a bit unfair . . .' I said. 'You know . . . er, when you're paying for the space.'

'My poems should go in *because* I'm paying for the space. I'm prepared to overlook your lack of acuity, Tom, and remind you of the effect this will have on your own reputation. You discovered me. It's win-win.'

I backed towards the door. 'Well, I suppose I better get back, to get started then, a lot to do, you know, and thanks for all this.'

'Perfect, Tom.' He followed me, adenoids rattling. 'Send me the quotes for the poets and let me know when you're interviewing McManus. I'd like to meet him. Tracy will see you out.'

At the door, his assistant joined me like a shadow. Kevin shook my hand again.

'Don't forget to write,' he said, and laughed in reverse, 'Ah-ah-ah!'

To: Margaret Warren
From: Tommie Shaw
Subject: Your Editorial

Hi Margaret,
Please find below the editorial for your store, which will go into next month's issue of the magazine. Because you took out a single column centimetre, the amount of text you get is limited, but I think you'll be surprised by how much you can get across in 14 words. I hope you like what I've put together for you. If you want to make any changes, please let me know as soon as possible.

Kind regards,
Tommie Shaw

'Venus — Turn on, strap on, drop 'em.
Bondage heaven for goddesses with devilish desires.

To: Tommie Shaw
From: Margaret Warren
Subject: Re: Your Editorial

Tommie,
There appears to be some mix-up. This is a dog grooming service.
Where is this Venus place?
Margaret

To: Margaret Warren
From: Tommie Shaw
Subject: Re: re: Your Editorial

Hi Margaret,
Sorry, I got my press releases mixed up. It's been a bit of a stressful
week. Your editorial is below. Hope you like it.
Apologies once again.

Tommie

P.S.
Venus is behind the shopping centre on Victoria Street.

Pluto—It's the mutt's nuts!
Pamper your pets just like the spoiled bitches of Hollywood!

up his hands, grey with dust. His skin was roughened and bloody and his nails were ragged and ripped.

'I'll go to the shop tonight,' I said, sitting up. 'You have a shower. Give me your money.'

Blob stood unsteadily, his back clicking. 'If there's nothing in my pockets, use your credit card. I want the chef's special. And more cigarettes, you thieving whore. I like your new face. You look human.' He shuffled into the hall. 'I am *so* suffering for my art.'

'Me too. Without the art.'

After clearing away the leftovers, we practised the walks we would do to collect our Oscars, but plummeting temperatures forced a retreat to the settee. We turned the electric fire on full, filled hot-water bottles and sat under blankets and throws, but my teeth chattered, my chilblains nipped and Blob's glasses steamed up every time he took a drink. We were on our second bottle. I topped up his glass.

'Thanks, Fatty.' He wilted like an Alcott heroine. 'I'm so weak.'

Blob had once made me a cassette of David Bowie songs and was delighted to find I'd held onto it. It still smelt of the yellowing Scotch tape he'd stuck the label on with and we played it low, pulling back the plastic sheet on the wall so we could see the stars. It was cloudless and brittle outside. I brought the blanket up to my chin and sipped from my glass.

'How much debt do you think you've worked off?' I asked.

In the dim light, Blob tucked his blanket under his legs. 'I don't know – Chris didn't come back. And the Polish lads weren't very friendly.'

'They didn't have any English,' I said.

'They didn't have any lunch.' He pushed up his glasses. 'Even my glasses ache.'

We stared at the tiny red lights flickering on the stereo.

I huffed under the blankets to warm the air. 'You know how, when we were kids, we used to think that no matter how bad things were, they would always get better?'

'Yes,' he nodded.

'You have so much time, you know things will improve.'

'Yes.'

I looked at him. 'We're not young any more.'

'We're not old.'

'That makes us middle-aged.'

He pulled his hat further down over his ears. 'May says she's twenty-two.'

'Shouldn't something better have happened by now?'

'Well, *you* haven't been anywhere or done anything.' He brought his wine glass inside his blanket. 'At least I get points for effort.'

'I can't help thinking it might be nice to come home to a house with walls.'

His glasses misted over as he drank. 'You're blanding out.'

'I like to be warm and comfortable.'

'You have a drip on the end of your nose.'

I blotted it on the blanket. 'Thanks.'

'You'll be buying Ecover and squeezing out progeny next,' he said.

'It's not an unattractive idea, faced with frostbite.'

'Wait a minute.' He raised his head out of his blanket. 'Are you *settling*?'

'Having a home and a partner and kids wouldn't be so bad.' I blotted my nose again. 'It's not like I set out not to do it. Wouldn't you like to meet someone?'

'I did meet someone.'

For a moment, I forgot how cold I was. Blob rarely spoke about London and didn't tell me anything about his relationships. 'So where is he now?'

He shrugged with one shoulder.

'Didn't it work out?'

'No.' He drank quickly, without tasting.

'What happened?'

'What's with all the questions?'

'I'm interested. You're the one who brought it up.'

His jaw was on edge. 'He came into the shop. He liked raclette and I didn't. *Jesus.*'

I pulled my blanket up defensively. 'Jesus, yourself.'

We stared at the lights on the stereo in silence.

'Listen,' he said eventually. 'You're going to be famous and I'm going to be in a TV ad. Things always get worse before they get better. Darkest before the dawn. Tomorrow is another day. Other platitudes.'

'What makes you so sure you're going to be in this ad?'

'Conceive, believe, achieve.' He waved his glass at me. 'I learnt that in the call centre. The day I left. I didn't know how to apply it to pet insurance.'

'What happened to "it's who you know in this business" ?' I blew on my hands and tucked them under my arms.

'If I have to resort to contacts then I must be totally talentless, don't you think?' He huffed down his nose, steaming up his glasses. 'And I don't believe I am.'

'You certainly set my world on fire,' I said. 'Anyway, it's not always who you know. Sometimes it's who pays the bill.'

'What does that mean?'

'Oh, I don't know.' I picked at my blanket. 'Work is complicated these days.'

He looked like he'd just smelled a fart. 'Don't inflict your little office dramas on me.'

'Do we still have to go to the CAC reunion, then?'

'Of course. I'll have something to boast about to that bitchface Alice Malice. We might even enjoy it. Imagine that.'

I held my hot-water bottle out to him. 'This needs topped up.'

He hit his hot-water bottle against mine. 'To us.'

'No,' I said. 'To you. Tomorrow. Break a leg.'

He hobbled to the kettle with his blanket humped over his back.
'I hope I never have to do an honest day's work again.'

9.

The air smelled different. There was something earthy about it, even in the city. Frost dusted the car but it wouldn't last long in the morning sun. I ran the engine and blasted the heater. The night had not been kind to Blob. Unused to physical labour, his muscles had undergone some kind of temporary (or at least we hoped it was temporary) atrophy. He shuffled like an old man, slowed by stiff, aching limbs.

In the time it took for him to call Chris, excuse himself from that day's work, and hobble from the house to the car, I was able to apply my entire make-up the way Patricia had shown me. But I didn't have her touch and no amount of dabbing, smearing, powdering or wishing could disguise my black eye. I put on the sunglasses and flicked up the mirror. There was sure to be something on the internet about the instant healing/disguising of bruises before meeting up with ex-boyfriends.

Blob opened the car door and let in a wave of icy air. He bent his knees slowly, lifted one foot into the car and dropped the rest of his body into the seat. The car rocked and twanged. Blob's low groan grew to a roar as he leaned outside to grab the handle and pull the door closed. His hair was flat and pushed back, the way he wore it for castings.

'I'm ready,' he said, exhausted. His skin and hair were ingrained with plaster dust.

'You smell nice,' I said, encouragingly. 'What's that?'

'Air freshener. I'd give the bathroom a wide berth if I were you. Nerves.'

I threw my bag and make-up into the back and turned the key.

'Fuck!' Blob jerked suddenly.

'What's wrong?'

He looked at his crotch, which was buzzing. 'My phone. Get it.'

'I don't want to fumble around in your groin.'

'Help me, woman! My arms don't bend.'

Turning my face away, I worked my hand inside the warm vibrating pocket of his jeans and pulled out the phone. He took it and looked at the screen.

'Eugh, it's Donkey Breath,' he said. 'Tell her you can't talk.'

I snatched the phone and answered. 'Georgie. Everything OK?'

'I wish you'd get your own phone,' she said. I could hear banging in the background. 'I don't like having to call *him* when I want to talk to you. I tried phoning your work but the receptionist wasn't sure if you still worked there.'

'Where are you?' I asked. 'It sounds like you're on a building site.'

'Workmen are taking out the old bathroom suite.'

'Come on,' Blob said, nodding towards the road. 'We'll be late.'

I turned away.

'What's the squeaking noise?' I asked her.

'Don't you ever clean the phone?' she said. 'You should try it. You'd be shocked. Anyway. Any luck?'

'None. And I didn't get the book either.'

'Why not?'

I told her about the embargo and the problems it posed with getting a preview copy. The cleaning sounds became more frenzied.

'I spoke to Mo too,' I said. 'And it's not good. Gloria was at the farm. She took the old photographs of us.' I closed my eyes. 'Mo told her everything. She didn't mean to, she didn't think Gloria would be, you know, like that.'

The cleaning stopped and the phone creaked in her grip. 'I'm going to have to tell Darren and Joe,' she said. 'I'm going to have to tell them before they hear it from someone else.' Her voice was hushed. 'Oh my God.' I could hear every breath she took.

Blob lifted his arms in a theatrically Gallic, if slow, way. He reached for the phone but I had plenty of time to get out of the car. I closed the door and stood on the path, watching the deserted morning street. Between the fading dawn and the red bricks, everything glowed, even the skip.

'Don't do anything yet,' I said. 'Give me a few days. There's someone else I can try.'

'Who?' She sounded hoarse.

'Liam.'

Her breathing was fast, forced. 'You know what I think of Liam.'

That tone always brought out the worst in me. 'You never even gave him a chance.'

'Listen, you silly bitch. He slept with your flatmate while you . . . he has a lot to answer for.'

I held the phone tight. A few weeks after the miscarriage, I'd had to go and live with Georgie and Darren, and not for the first time. I'd dismissed the signs as grief, and when I realised it was more than that, it was too late. I was crumbling and a strong wind would have scattered me like sand. I couldn't get out of bed. I couldn't stand to be awake. It was unfair that Georgie had to put up with me, and I thought switching myself off would be the best option. But she'd cleared the house of sharp things and locked away the drugs.

The window rapped. Blob's face loomed. He pleaded and when that didn't work, he mouthed profanities.

'I have to go, Georgie,' I said. 'Give me a few more days. Let me at least try Liam, he has real contacts.'

'Don't get involved with him again.'

'I'll give you a call.' I opened the car door to get in.

'Like you gave me this one?'

'I'll ring you, I promise.'

'Have you cleaned out your car?'

I hung up and crunched the car into gear.

We sat facing the advertising agency. The heater was set to max and we blew smoke through the open windows.

'What time is the casting session?' I asked.

'Ten,' Blob said.

'What time is it now?'

'Quarter to.'

'You said we were late. I drove like a maniac.'

'I didn't notice any difference.'

The agency was in the middle of a shining white Georgian terrace, a mile from the city centre. The building was tall and symmetrical with a polished glass front door. My car looked like acne beside it.

Blob wound up the window, his hair flicking manically, cigarette between his lips. 'Right.' He swung himself round and froze. 'Oh God, I can't.'

'What do you mean, you can't? This is *your* ad, you said it yourself.' I stretched across his pine-fresh bulk and opened the door. 'Give me a call when you're done. You can do this, I know you can.'

'No, really, I can't. I've stiffened up. I can't get out.'

With considerable effort, he pushed the door open with his foot and gripped the door frame, cigarette still in his mouth. I heaved from behind. Slowly, cussily, he emerged, as other actors began to arrive. None of them looked under fifty.

Blob stood beside the car, a Kubrick ape in the beautiful white street. The cigarette tumbled from his mouth.

'Bye then!' I honked the horn and took off, trusting physics to close the door. I wasn't waiting around for his rant or his retreat.

Heading towards the city centre, I thought I saw Kevin Loane driving past in the opposite direction. I checked my mirror. The roads here were packed with expensive cars and any might or might not be his. I was paranoid. And that wasn't a great sign.

8.

Even in the dark, I could see the grey dust and debris that lay outside the house. The skip was filled with rubble, ripped lino, rubbish and squawking children playing on someone else's settee. I held up a hand to say I came in peace and sidestepped the trench leading up to the door.

There was no music, no light and it felt colder inside than out. I flicked on the light to find Blob lying on the settee.

'Are you dead?' I asked.

He stirred. 'What have you done to me?'

'Where are your cigarettes?'

'I could boke in a bin,' he said. 'You said it would be enlightening.'

'Just goes to show, you can't believe everything I read.'

I surveyed the day's damage. The yard was separated from the kitchen by a plastic sheet and a trench ran from the back to the front and beyond. The stereo was covered with a dustsheet and the cooker had been detached from the wall.

I lifted Blob's cigarettes and lit up for both of us. 'Poetry is coming to get me, Blob.' I fell into the other settee.

He groaned as he swung his legs round and put his head in his hands. His hair was flat and stringy and his glasses were splashed with something unidentifiable.

'Why is there so much poetry in my life?' I said.

'That would be beautiful coming from someone else.'

'Why me, Blob?'

'We're still talking about *you*?'

'What happened to you then?' I asked.

'Asbestosis, probably. And I'll never be a hand model.' He held

Diane had had a considerable following, as it turned out. I drove to the funeral after dropping off Blob, and sat with Patricia, Bill and Seamus at the back of the crematorium while eulogies were delivered and respects were paid. The seats at the front were lined with children, grandchildren and great grandchildren. Every row was filled and the sides of the room were lined with mourners too.

Having served in the RAF, secured a commercial pilot's licence, run a dog training school, married twice, had three children, adopted two, earned a doctorate, written two biographies, been in local politics for a time and survived two heart attacks, Diane had many friends. She took on the arts as something light to see her through her sunset years. And our ignoble expectations had killed her. That and central sleep apnoea. Some friends we were.

When the service was over and the casket removed, we followed the crowd into the hallway, past flowers and wreaths stacked so far back it was impossible to read all the cards. We drifted towards the door behind slow-moving clusters and suddenly the place seemed very hot. Then I remembered we were in a crematorium. I didn't say it out loud, though, which was a breakthrough. Patricia spoke to the family on behalf of the magazine and we headed back to the office not saying much.

We worked quietly, even though Jude wasn't there. It wasn't her style to attend the funeral of a freelancer. Or maybe it was the threat of religious symbols that had kept her away. Bill chewed vowels on the phone, Patricia punched in numbers and Seamus clicked at his keyboard, chin in hand. I found a potion on the internet that could clear bruises for £125, but in the end I decided Liam wasn't worth it. I read through brochures Kevin had supplied and jolted awake when my extension rang.

It was Blob, charged with adrenaline and booming down the phone: 'I need a lift. Forthwith.'

I waited outside the advertising agency, basking in engine heat. The glass door opened and Blob hobbled out, head held high. He lifted one regal hand when he saw me and maintained a stately limp over to the car. A handful of grey-haired men followed him out and he waved to them. Behind them came a huge, pot-bellied man in a kaftan with flowing silver locks, an ebullient red-haired woman and a small, scrawny man with a floppy fringe.

Blob fell into the car beside me. 'That's the Commercials Director, the one in the tie-dye.' He lit a cigarette before handing the pack and lighter to me. 'The doll is the Creative Director, she's Austrian or Australian or something. They're making the ads for the skinny little man. He's their client.'

Kevin Loane stared at me in surprise and went back to his conversation. I rammed the car into gear and felt Kevin watch me as we pulled away.

'You'll never guess what the role is,' Blob boomed. 'They need someone with maturity and gravitas.' He bounced before grimacing in pain. 'I have maturity and gravitas coming out of my ass today. Someone with a hint of whimsy. Look at my whimsy. Look at it!' His cheeks were flushed. 'And they want presence. Presence, babes. I have more presence than fucking Christmas.'

'So what was the role?'

'God.'

'What?'

'They want someone to play God.' He beamed. 'The shoot starts next week. I'll hear by Monday. It's for a company called Devine Energy.' He tried folding his arms, gave up and grinned into the road ahead. 'I'm confident, babes. Confident.'

Maybe it was a small world, as Chris said, but I didn't believe it. It was a painfully, criminally small city. Blob was glowing. Acting, even at an audition, brought him to life. It was kinder to say nothing about knowing Kevin.

❧

A shop that sold support underwear, and not the fashionable kind, had sent me a three-page press release to condense into fourteen words and I wondered if it was an act of genius or barbarism to rhyme lasses with asses. I sat at my desk, staring blindly at the wall. My extension rang.

A bubbling sniff resounded down the phone.

'Hello, Kevin. How are you?' I doodled a heavy black cloud in my notebook.

'I'm well, thank you. Making much progress?'

'Oh, loads.' Below the cloud, I drew a sinking ship.

'I spoke to the advertising agency about that job,' he said.

'Did you?' I drew some stickmen drowning.

'The job is yours.'

Lightning struck the stickmen.

'Thanks, Kevin. I appreciate it . . . but you know . . .' – I scribbled more clouds – 'there are so many opportunities here, I'm not sure I really want to move.'

A real job? In the real world? The very idea made me sweat. The magazine might be going down the pan but I planned to cling to the rim for as long as I could.

'If you change your mind, they are holding the position for you. Just let me know.' He snorted, long and leisurely. 'Interesting, your friend hoping to be in my TV ad. God moves in very mysterious ways.'

My scribbles drifted to a stop. 'Er . . . OK.'

'I'm sure you would wish Robert every success.'

'I would. I do.'

'He has a very *distinctive* look,' he said. 'It can't be easy finding work. I'm sure he would be disappointed if he didn't get the role.'

'Yes, he would. Very.'

'Then help me to help him, Tom.'

'OK . . . ?'

'God is creating the conditions for success,' he said, delivering every word as though on a cushion.

'Sorry, what?'

He sighed noisily. 'Do you want your friend to be in this TV ad or not?'

'Yes, of course . . . oh, right! All your poems are in, Kevin. All of them.'

'Well, it's a no-brainer then, as you young people say.' I figured Kevin was about four or five years older than me. 'So we'll have the section on me and the company,' he went on, 'the Rory McManus interview, testimonials from the poets who will be taking part in the festival and the picture page.'

'That leaves four pages for your poems.'

'I'm delighted with the service, Tom,' he said. 'Delighted.'

I covered my eyes with my hand. 'I'm delighted you're delighted.'

'And keep this under your hat. We wouldn't want people to think this was nepotism.'

'Isn't this God's workings?'

He was quiet for a moment. 'Are you being sarcastic, Tom?'

'I won't say anything.'

'That's a good girl.'

I cut him off. Maybe it wouldn't be so bad. I chewed my hair. Things would finally happen for Blob, not exactly the way he would've liked them to, but there was no reason he should find out. It was what he wanted, what he needed. And he'd get paid, which would help with the rent. Maybe God did move in mysterious ways, and who was I to get in God's way? Particularly when I didn't believe in him. The Arts pages would be an abomination, but as Blob always said, integrity wasn't my thing.

10.

By the sink . . . What did you . . . wake up whisper . . . avocado bathroom.

'Did you take something?' He made me sit up.

Empty bottle and glass and foil pack. 'To help me sleep.'

We had gone out for a drink, walked, danced, slim hips under Blob's hands, Gluteus — maybe, maybe not. Hours in the dark and I had slept for ten minutes.

Blob was in T-shirt and boxers, face lined. 'How many?'

'Two. Or one. I'm fine.'

He put his hand on his head. 'Don't take sleeping pills with gin, Fatty. Jesus.' He lifted the pack. 'I didn't think they'd give you these.'

I fought with heavy clouds. 'Patricia gave me them.'

'Sure just one?'

'Yes.' *A little lie down . . .*

'. . . like that on the floor.' He was sitting beside me on the lino, hand on head, elbow on knee. He wanted to talk. I could only deflect.

'Looking for contact lens.'

'You don't wear contact lenses.'

'That's why I couldn't find them.'

'You're such a fuc—'

Slip-slept.

11.

I turned old handbags upside down and pawed through drawers looking for foundation, concealer, eye shadow, liner, lipstick. Old, new, donated – anything that might make me look normal, possibly even attractive in a 'wish-I-hadn't-slept-around-on-my-ex-girlfriend, she's-so-together-now' kind of way. From the perfumed pile on the bedroom floor, I made my selection the way a surgeon might choose his instruments.

I had slept until midday and woke to hear Blob and the Poles downstairs. My head had fogged over and gravity seemed to be pulling harder, but I knew it would lift after a shower and some tea and a bit of a sit-down. The radio played in the yard and I could hear a jumble of shouts. I opened the window in the bathroom to see Blob, in old jeans and dirty shirt, leaning on a shovel, his face flecked with dust.

The Poles were holding intense discussions concerning the walls, the ground, the sky and Blob. They gestured, pointed, shook their heads and nodded. Blob watched them with unrecognisable mute patience. He reminded me of a mule being used to ferry tourists up a mountainside. There was no end to his torment, but he had no escape. He looked up and stared at me for a second. He wagged his finger. I closed the window.

My memory was piecemeal. The night had started well. Blob was on a high and after a few drinks I forgot about Kevin. In a bar somewhere, we joined a group of people Blob knew from a call centre and ended up in a gay club, but I didn't remember coming home and wasn't exactly sure who had been in my room. Later, lying in bed, thoughts spiralled into noise and hitting my head off the wardrobe again seemed like a good idea. I left my bed to look for sleep. I must have found it on the bathroom floor.

Leaning close to the mirror, my eye looked like a shiner from a silent movie. Slowly and with concentration, I had a shower, exfoliated, moisturised, then needed a bit of a sit-down. I slid downstairs in my dressing gown and put the kettle on, waving a shy hello to the builders and Blob. I gripped my hot mug, lit a cigarette and sat on the settee under a blanket, surrounded by dusty coats and dirty plates.

Blob ducked under the lintel from the yard. 'Hello, bitch.'

'Want tea?' I asked, springing up, eager to please.

He leaned against the sink and folded his arms. 'No milk for the brothers Grimm.' I felt him watching me as I busied myself with mugs, spoons and teabags.

'What time is it?' I chirped cheerily.

He pulled out his phone and looked at the screen. 'Almost one.'

'Oops. Could I text Jude from your phone? Tell her I'll be a bit late?'

'I already told her. I said you had women's problems.'

'Er . . . thanks. What did she say?'

'She said LO fucking L.'

I spooned out the teabags, chucked their dripping remains at the sink and turned the handles of the mugs towards him. He watched me in silence. I had been stupid and unfair last night. I offered him a feeble smile.

He pushed his backside off the sink. 'To quote Morrissey, "that joke isn't funny any more".' He took the teas outside.

I slunk upstairs and sought Zen in the application of make-up. I got his point. That joke had never been funny.

Moby's, the cramped and smoky Bohemian coffee shop where I would drink sugary Americanos while Liam talked tattoos with the staff, was now an outsize shoe shop. It was at the furthest end of a narrow diesel-grey street, overshadowed by the backsides of large chain stores. Shoppers and office workers clashed umbrellas as they passed under its awning. I approached through the heavy rain, gripping my umbrella. The cold damp air had flushed away most of the fog in my head, but I still had a low-lying hangover, not helped by a nervous, jittery stomach.

Even Blob approved of the make-up, although I'd had to read between the lines because the word he used was 'harrumph'. After thirty minutes in front of the mirror, I had perfected the look of a sleep-deprived air hostess. It wasn't me, but it was an improvement. My stomach lurched as I neared the shop. I couldn't see him. He was late. Maybe he wasn't coming. I slipped under the awning, resolving to give him sixty hippopotamuses before I fled. A short, dumpy man in a grey cap and red scarf came out of the shop. I looked at his feet. They seemed average to me.

'Tommie,' he said.

'Liam!' My umbrella hit him in the eye. 'Sorry! I didn't recognise you.'

He clamped a hand to his eye. 'Well, you haven't changed a bit in nine years. I mean it.' He leaned in and brushed one cheek, then the other. His smell, woody and warm, made me think of kissing on a doorstep, tangling in the dark. We moved away, looking elsewhere.

Below the unfamiliar cap, his dark curls had been shaved and I could see silver at his temples. The round gold-rimmed glasses had been updated to the newest retro look, and he wore cord trousers. Corduroy. He once scoffed at corduroy. Now corduroy was his friend. His face was fuller, but his tanned skin still had the healthy flush that scuppered his Kurt Cobain wannabe phase.

'Have you got a black eye?' he asked, looking concerned. 'How in God's name did you get a black eye? Wait, you don't have to tell me. You look really good anyway. Still got the little gothic thing going on. Why didn't you tell me Moby's was closed? Where do you want to go? I noticed a Starbucks round the corner, will that do?'

He looked up and down the street.

'There's a café a few doors down,' I said.

'New, is it?'

'Not really.' It was a dark, old-fashioned café where the tablecloths were plastic and salad came with chips. Blob gave their 'breakfast pizza' five stars. Liam wouldn't like it. 'It's just over here.'

He insisted on walking at the edge of my umbrella, even though it kept poking him in the head. The fact that he neither protested nor moved away made me feel quite vindicated. We stopped at the steamy door of the café. I pushed it open. Heat and noise engulfed us. Dumping my umbrella in the rack, I slid behind a table by the window where rivulets of water streaked the condensation. Liam sat opposite, looking around. Mucky babies, rheumy old folk, snappy mothers and lax dads in football shirts were having a late lunch or an early tea. We would smell of fried fish when we left.

I waited for him to comment on the place, but he said nothing, just took off his coat and scarf and pulled at his collar. Underneath, I noticed small faded beads. He leaned forward and put his elbows on the striped plastic tablecloth. I leaned back.

'Tommie, it's . . .'

'What can I get you?' the waitress woofed, leaning on the back of my chair. She was short and round, in a black blouse and skirt. Her voice was like a construction site two streets away.

'Black coffee?' Liam flicked his eyes at me before looking up at the waitress. 'Black coffee. Earl Grey for me.'

The waitress's fluffy gold hair had white roots. 'Did he do that to you?' she asked me.

I held my fingers to my eye. 'No, it was an accident.'

She winked at me. 'My neighbour shot her husband.' She looked at Liam. 'We only have Tetley, love.'

'I'll have tea, please,' I said.

Liam nodded. 'Same for me.'

'Anything else?'

'No, thank you,' said Liam.

'Could I have some toast?' I asked. I wasn't sure when I'd last eaten.

'Want anything with it?' she said. 'Scrambled eggs? Beans? What about a wee chip buttie?' She nudged me, eyebrow arched. 'Go on, milk him, now you've got him out.'

Liam's smile was thin but holding up.

'Just jam,' I said. He at least owed me toast and jam.

'With you in a jiffy.' She shuffled back to the kitchen in what looked like men's bedroom slippers.

Liam leaned forward again. 'Tommie, it really is good . . .'

A small boy pushed past Liam's chair and, singing to himself, began drawing cocks in the condensation on the window. His mother pushed past and pulled the boy away by the wrist. We were left with the cocks.

'I'm just trying to say it's good to see you,' he said with a defeated smile.

I arranged my coat on the seat with unusual care.

'I couldn't believe it was you on the phone,' he said, his brown eyes intense. 'I've been thinking about you for so long. I Googled you but couldn't find anything. I thought you had moved away.' He tried another smile. 'I'm living in Belfast again.'

In my head, Liam and Marie-Claire, the flatmate who introduced us and ruined us, sat cosily in a Victorian villa in a leafy Belfast street, drinking Earl Grey in their green and garlicky kitchen. My hangover welled up.

'Marie-Claire and I split up,' he said.

'Excoozeh mwa.' The waitress unloaded teapots, teacups, milk jugs and a sugar bowl from a tray. 'Don't mind me,' she said, withdrawing.

He turned his cup in its saucer. 'She's staying on in Downpatrick. She's keeping the kids.'

No one could see, but there was a knife in my chest. 'I didn't know you had kids.' My pregnancy had lasted fourteen weeks. It was long enough to imagine holding the baby, smelling it, singing and whispering all my love, swearing to be everything my mother wasn't. It was the baby who never was. I still missed it.

He moved his cup around, stopped and looked up. His eyes searched mine. 'We were only twenty-one, Tommie. Still kids ourselves. I was scared.'

'Of course. You fucked my friend out of sheer terror.'

'I know, I'm sorry. No excuse is good enough.'

I poured tea and looked out through the rivulets on the window to the grey street beyond. The streetlights were on already. They looked shattered through the wet windows.

'I think part of getting older is knowing what you've lost,' he said. 'But I'm not so old that I have to accept it.'

I drank scalding tea. 'You don't seem to have any idea what you've lost.'

He gave me the coy smile I remembered, the one I thought was so cute, the one that distracted me from all indiscretions.

'I finally got that tattoo,' he said.

'Oh, for God's sake.' This wasn't what I had come for. 'I'd like to set up an interview with one of your writers, Liam.'

He was quiet for a moment, searching my face. He sat back. 'Who?'

'Rory McManus.'

'Oh right. Still not talking to your mother?' He was one of the few who knew about her. And about me.

'I want to be professional about this,' I said.

He looked sheepish, boyish. 'Actually, you've already been discussed.'

'What do you mean?'

'You came up in conversation. Rory and I were talking about Gloria and I mentioned that you and I had . . . and that you, you know . . . that it runs in the family.'

'That what runs in the family?'

'You know—' His voice was low. The waitress set down my toast. 'The appetite,' he said. 'The, er . . . enthusiasm.'

'You said fucking *what*?'

The waitress gave him a look.

'It's a compliment,' he protested. He watched as the waitress scuffed away, dear-dear-dearing to herself. 'You were much more responsive than Marie-Claire. More, you know, full-on.'

'What makes you think I want to hear something like this?'

'But it's a good thing.'

I buttered the toast roughly. Our relationship was blighted from the start. Everything that could go wrong, did. If we went to a good restaurant, we'd get a table between the toilet and the till. If we went for a picnic in the park, we'd be joined by a glue sniffer with Tourette's. If we kicked through autumn leaves, I'd kick a dead dog. I fell pregnant and things couldn't get any worse. Then I miscarried. Events always conspired to fuck us up. I looked at the giant cocks on the window. We were just not meant to be.

'I'd say he'd be quite open to meeting you,' Liam said.

'I bet he would.'

'I'll give you his number,' he said, feeling around in his pocket. 'What's your number, I'll send it to you.' He thumbed at his BlackBerry.

'I don't have a phone.' I licked my jammy knife and bit the toast.

'You don't have a phone? How do you live? How do you work?'

I didn't do much of either. I didn't tell him that.

He searched his pockets for a pen and wrote Rory's number on a business card. 'Not everyone gets to interview Rory. And no one gets his number. You're privileged.' He slid the card across the table.

I dropped it into my bag without looking. 'I'm ever so grateful.'

I watched the rain hitting the window, rivulets inside and out. I was hungover and angry and despite everything, I still fancied him. I wanted to throttle him, or at the very least, huff long and hard. But I still had to ask if he could get Gloria's book and I wouldn't get anywhere by being . . . well, myself. I ate the toast, wondering how best to frame the question.

He spoke first. 'I wish you'd told me you had psychotic episodes.'

I immediately started to choke. He stood up in alarm and thudded my back. Families looked round as blood vessels burst in my neck. Eventually the toast dislodged and I wheezed noisily.

He sat down. 'Alright now?'

I nodded, trying to catch tears before they dropped.

'The thing with the flat,' he said, chewing the side of his mouth, exactly how he used to. 'You know, if you'd told me how bad your, you know, illness could get, I really think things would have been different.'

He didn't get it and I realised he never had. I was prone to depression. It was a war wound that could make me think with a limp or knock me off my feet. Psychosis was the mental equivalent of having your legs repeatedly blown off, while Lemmy from Motörhead runs away with them under his arm. The two years I'd spent with Liam were probably my happiest, my most settled, my most balanced. I was in love with him and he reopened the wound. The fire was an accident. But it was one he deserved.

Everything had smelled different when I was pregnant, even Liam, but I had put it down to hormones. After the miscarriage, my sense of smell returned to normal and, waiting for him in his flat one day, I understood that the different smell was Marie-Claire. All over his things, all over him, all over the pillows. I walked round and round, unable to sit, stand or think. I kicked over the coffee table, which knocked over a candle, which set fire to the curtains. He came home to a blackened, flooded flat, and I left him to it.

But a lecture on the various ways of losing your marbles wasn't going to help me now. He wouldn't listen anyway. 'Who knows?' I shrugged. 'Maybe you're right.'

He nodded earnestly. 'I know. But it's OK, Tommie. It really is OK.'

'Liam . . . ?'

'Yes?' His eyes were bright, expectant.

'There's something I need to ask.'

'Yes?'

'I wouldn't normally ask . . . it's just, I'm stuck. I need a favour.'

He sat up. 'If I can help, I will.'

By asking for a favour, I was letting him back in and he knew it. But it was all I had.

'I need to get Gloria's book.'

He looked pained. 'Tommie . . .'

'I've got to see it, Liam. Is there anyone you can try? Rory? Another agent? Anyone?'

He passed a hand over his chin. 'I'll ask around, see what I can do.' He paused. 'I could speak to Gloria, if you like.'

'No! No. Think about your relationship with Rory. It would look like you're taking my side.'

'You think so?'

'Oh, definitely.'

'OK, I'll do what I can. What's your email?' He entered my email address into his BlackBerry. 'You're with *that* magazine?'

'Yes, I'm with *that* magazine.'

'I'll tell Rory you're with, I don't know, the *Irish Cultural Review*.' He tucked his BlackBerry into his pocket.

'The *Irish Cultural Review*?'

'I just made it up. Even fiction's better than *Bellefast* magazine.' He grinned at me, my ally. 'You want a good interview, don't you?'

It didn't matter how good the interview was. It would wither and die next to Kevin's poetry. 'You're right, Liam. Thanks.'

He moved his hand nearer mine. 'I'm glad we're talking.' I could feel the heat from his skin. 'Where are you living these days?'

'Not far from here.' I stood up.

'Can I give you a lift?' He moved fast to follow me.

'No thanks, I'll walk.'

'What direction is it?' He pulled on his coat as I wriggled into mine. 'I don't mind,' he said.

'Near the motorway. I'll walk, it's not far.'

The waitress began clearing our table. 'Just pay at the till, love.'

He hurried to the till, looking back, mouthing, 'Wait.'

'He knows how to spoil a girl,' the waitress said. Hands full of cups and plates, she added, 'My neighbour didn't really shoot her husband. She stabbed him. But that's not funny, is it?'

Outside, the street pulsed with buses, voices, distant sirens. The rain had stopped and the wet pavements shone under streetlights and glaring shopfronts. We stood in the yellow glow of the café window.

He offered me the coy smile again. 'I'll be in touch, then.'

'If you can get the book. Thanks for Rory's number.' I stepped away, feeling around in my bag for cigarettes. I'd started buying my own.

'Tommie,' he said.

I turned back, my hand still in my bag.

'I just w—'

'I have to go, Liam.'

He nodded. 'OK. I'll talk to you soon.'

'Email's fine. Email soon.'

'I will. I'll do that,' he said. I felt his eyes follow me as I walked away.

12.

It was almost half four and Jude was gone, but her Friday smog meant she was not forgotten. Returning after a long pungent lunch, she had dozed off at her desk before waking suddenly, stalking round and hovering over me. I flinched and closed one eye. She dug her fingertips into my shoulder, put her skeletal smile and grey gums in my face, and nodded at my screen.

'Devi engy tea an arj je fantav nevm,' she said. She moved a long, bony finger between her nose and mine and cackled, 'Ah? Ah? Ha ha ha!' and I nodded vaguely, trying not to inhale. I guessed she was pleased with progress on the Devine Energy feature, although how she got anything from my screen, which was opened on my horoscope, I'm not sure.

Traditionally, I was under no pressure to perform and she was under no pressure to pay me a decent wage. But this was new. She appeared to be expressing approval and suggesting that she and I were—what? In this together? Kindred spirits? My integrity had proved much more elastic than Diane's. In a sour little epiphany, I realised I didn't hold the moral high ground any more.

Jude straightened up, lifted her faux fur from her chair and bounced off the doorframe on her way out, saying, 'Hahneh nij ken fux.'

The spell broken, the others lifted their heads and breathed. On Friday we went to the bar, but as the others switched off their machines, chatty and buoyant, my extension rang.

Seamus stared at me warily. Bill swore.

'Don't answer it,' Patricia whispered.

Taking a call late on Friday afternoon was stepping into the abyss.

A mistake, a misquote, a missed payment – we might not get out alive. Or at least, we might not get out early. I stretched my hand towards the phone. Their faces twisted in horror. I picked it up.

'Hello . . . ?'

'You were supposed to ring me.' It was Georgie. Not Liam. I stood up and sent my computer to sleep, annoyed at her, annoyed at myself. Patricia drooped with relief. Bill swore happily.

'So?' Georgie asked me.

'So what?'

'Have you got it?'

'Don't you think I'd call if I got it?'

'I knew Liam would be useless.'

'He said he'd try to help.'

In the hour since I'd seen Liam, I'd deconstructed our conversation and beat myself up with the pieces. 'Sorry', followed by direct access to the country's fustiest, perviest poet, plus toast and jam, surely that was enough? I was an ex. And a psycho. What did I expect? Amends? Don't be stupid. A special effort? Deluded. And I hated that I wanted to hear from him.

'I really thought you'd have it by now,' she said. There was an odd noise at the other end of the phone, like a pig snorting and a piglet squealing.

Swapping the phone from hand to hand, I shrugged on my coat. 'What was that noise?'

'I got the settees cleaned,' she said, 'and sealed in plastic. They're a bit noisy but it's worth it. They're cleaner than new. The dust is driving me crazy, though. You can see every speck on this plastic cover. I spend all day lifting dust. And the tumble dryer has broken down. I have washing hanging up all over the house and it drops dust everywhere. I can't sleep for thinking about it.'

I sat down at my desk again. 'Hasn't Darren noticed anything?'

Her voice was muffled, as though her fingers were at her lips. I could hear each breath. 'He keeps asking me what's wrong. I don't know how much longer I can hold it in, Tommie.'

'Don't tell him,' I said quietly, doodling black spirals in my notebook. 'Don't risk everything for her. The extract this Sunday will probably be about the people at the farm.'

'What if it isn't?'

I glanced at the others as they headed out to reception, bantering and laughing. 'If I were the editor of a newspaper,' I said, 'I'd pick something newsworthy, juicy, something that'll sell. All the famous people at the farm, they're much more interesting than we are.' I scribbled fiercely.

'I don't know, Tommie.'

'Don't tell Darren anything until we know for sure she's written about us.'

Seamus leaned back into the office and flicked the lights, like it was last orders in a bar.

'I have to go,' I told her. 'They're turning off the lights.'

'You always have to go,' she said. 'Is this the night you go to the bar? What's the point in spending your life avoiding stress when you invite depression with drink?'

'They're setting the alarm, I have to go.' I threw down my pencil and stood up. 'I'll call down on Sunday and we'll talk then. Just don't tell Darren, not yet.' I hung up, looked at the phone, then followed the others into reception.

She'd spend the next day and a half Mr Sheening the ceilings and Ciffing the driveway. My mouth was watering at the thought of my first gin. At least my way of coping could be enjoyed with other people.

With both hands gripping the top of my head, I eased myself down into the kitchen on Saturday morning. I couldn't stand erect and my own breath made me sick. Blob was on the floor, a blanket over his shoulders, sorting through the box of vinyl Orbital had bequeathed to us at the farm. Wind blew in from the yard, rattling the plastic sheet and shifting rubbish round the room. Beside the hole in the wall, Blob looked like a disaster victim.

'Krautrock,' he said, without looking up.

I lowered myself onto the settee. 'Same to you.'

He turned a record over in his hands. 'Good night then?'

I shivered and sweated and tried not to retch. My memory was a series of disconnected blots. Seamus, Lisa and I in the bar. A DJ, more people, our heads together. It was so loud, I just nodded. Something about eating or dancing. His nose on her neck. Then blank, then blank blank. 'Yes.'

He slid the record out of its sleeve and set it on the turntable. 'I put you to bed, in case you're wondering why you didn't wake up on the stairs. You had a kebab in your pocket.'

I didn't like kebabs. I did like the name Abrakebabra though. I closed my eyes. The floor had developed a dangerous swell.

He set the needle on the record. 'I'm not going to be the one wheeling you round Poundland when you have a stroke.'

Sound rose from the speakers, rattling, tinkling, howling like a Hammer horror.

'That music is making me sick,' I said.

He lifted the needle. 'I think you should cut down on drink.'

I opened my eyes and looked at him. 'I'll give up drink if you give up takeaways.'

'It's not the same thing.'

'Well, that's the deal.' I leaned forward but the sudden movement was more than my stomach could take. I lurched across the room, pulled aside the plastic sheet and vomited into the yard.

He made me some Resolve and I took it back to bed. The covers were still warm and it was a relief to be horizontal again. I melted into darkness.

He leaned his head into my room. 'Nighty night, Fatty.'

'Go away.'

'You sleep it off and we'll go for a walk.'

'You? Walk? Where to?'

'Burger King. Sitting in is not taking away.' He closed the door gently and I surprised myself by sleeping.

We picked up wine and gin on the way back from Burger King. We weren't the kind of people to welch on a deal, so it was to our credit that preliminary negotiations failed. Once home, we made hot water bottles and settled down under the blankets to wait out the weekend. Blob was tired from the unaccustomed labour and fell asleep a few drinks in. I drank my wine and when Blob's unpleasant folk album ended, I listened to his snoring and looked at the books I'd picked up in Oxfam. But my eyes kept straying off the page.

What if the first instalment was about us? I didn't want people to know about us, but Georgie had much more to lose than I. We used to catch the bus to the estate where Blob lived with May. Sometimes I took speed with Georgie in a flat full of older men but mostly I drank in the cemetery with Blob. When Georgie slept on the flat's steps or was picked up by police, a friend from school would take her home. The friend was Darren. She started sleeping with him as soon as she knew she was pregnant and when she moved in with his parents, I was left at the farm with Gloria, Mo and the last of their hippy friends. That was when it went wrong for me too.

Without Georgie around to not give two fucks, I had spent nights poring over *In Utero*. When I tried to sleep, words dislodged from the poems and chased around my head. Gloria railed against motherhood as a kind of death. We took away her life, and her dreams were bloody with rage. She basked in the controversy, and I tried to laugh it off with Blob. His impersonations of her were startling and spiteful, and our mocking laughter sounded across the cemetery. He had no idea I was unravelling behind the jokes. I was a better actor than he thought.

I understood why she would write about us again. I was growing more like her every day. I too was capable of shedding everything that made me decent and could see the commercial potential in an instant. Sex and scandal sell, and now that my mother was Rory McManus's muse, she had more leverage. Even if we weren't in the first excerpt, before long she would work her way through her famous connections and arrive at us. I lifted Blob's phone and sent Georgie a reassuring text, but she didn't reply. I didn't believe it either.

I wished Blob would wake up. I nudged his thigh with my foot but he stayed where he was, chins pouring over his hand and glasses perpendicular. I was bored and cold enough to think about going to bed when I heard a knock at the front door, a familiar knock that sounded like a question. I almost fell into Blob as I made for the door. He huffed but didn't wake up. I had downed as much as I usually had by the time Gluteus Maximus arrived, but my head was still disappointingly clear. I opened the door and he stepped inside, kissing my mouth. His eyes were pale grey. I had never noticed them before.

From the bedroom door to the mattress to the floor, I was lost at last. When lucidity tried to creep back, I redoubled my efforts and the woman next door banged on the wall. He got in everywhere and stopped at nothing, so why did I keep thinking about my mother? What Freudian fuckery was this? I concentrated. Sex was not about thought. If I had to think, I would think about – what was his name, what was his name? Oh God. He pumped at me at the edge of the bed, What-was-his-name, but I wasn't there, I wasn't here, I wasn't anywhere. And then she was back.

He pulled me up onto the bed and I put my head against his neck as he moved his arm around me. He smelt of Christmas cologne. He tidied the condom away in a tissue, tugged the covers up and kissed my head, the way he always did. He would fall asleep and I would join him and he would be gone when I woke up. Except this time my eyes wouldn't close. His breathing slowed but my breasts shook with the force of my heart. His wedding ring didn't usually bother me, but tonight – what if? I was about to lose my anonymity, what if I came under scrutiny? What if someone spoke to the neighbours? His wife could find out in the most humiliating way. I left his arms and sat up, looking for a T-shirt.

He leaned on an elbow and watched me, cheeks flushed and fair hair flattened under my fingers. 'You throwing me out tonight?'

I focused on finding my knickers. 'Just think it's better if you go.'

His eyebrows shifted in brief confusion.

I sat behind him on the bed and watched him pull on his clothes, my face, chest and legs burning from his stubble. Muscles moved under the skin on his back and I stretched out my hand. Sex was nothing personal – for him, a quick appreciative shag, for me, another way of escaping myself. Without him I would be alone, thinking my way into grey, steely stasis. I didn't want him to leave his wife. I was just a vessel into which he dipped his dick, but that's not how other people would see it. His wife had everything to lose. It was my mother's fault. No, it was mine. I took my hand away.

He kneeled beside me on the mattress and kissed the side of my face, holding his breath by my ear. 'I won't come if you don't want me to.'

I closed my eyes and guided his hand down. We were breathless and mindless again.

13.

In the light of a dirty wet dawn, I flip-flopped up the short path to Georgie's front door and pressed the bell. Despite my best efforts, Sunday morning had arrived. The doorstep had been bleached and scrubbed with Georgie's usual ferocity, and the thick plastic door glowed under the damp, bluish sky. The mornings were getting brighter, which always gave me hope, however groundless.

Inside, Georgie thudded down the stairs, screaming, 'It's OK, I've got it, it's Tommie!' Through the narrow slot of stained glass, I watched her move quickly to the door. She opened it and I stepped into a choking scorch of Febreze and bleach. I ducked to avoid boil-washed whites that hung on a clothesline running from the stairs to a hook screwed into the kitchen doorframe.

The front door closed with a gentle kiss.

'Did you *see* it?' she hissed, eyes sucking me in. Her hair was alive with static.

I held up a thin plastic bag bearing the newspaper and my gift of bleach.

'Do you have a black eye?' she fretted.

'Do you have a newspaper stuffed up your jumper?'

She looked down at her lumpen top. 'We get it delivered.'

'Down there?'

'I didn't want Darren to see it.'

'Of course.'

'Come up,' she whispered, turning for the stairs. I was viciously sleep deprived and the early-morning adrenaline hit had worn off. I trudged in her fluffy, white-slippered wake, my feet sinking into spongy carpet.

'I'm just showing Tommie the new bathroom!' she screeched as we climbed.

I tapped on her hip and mouthed, 'Where's Darren?'

She pressed her hands together as if in prayer and tucked them under her ear before thumbing at their closed bedroom door. Outside the bathroom, she lifted a draft excluder from the bottom of the door, showed me in and set the draft excluder back against the door on the inside. I shivered in the sudden mortuary chill.

Pieces of her new white bathroom suite were posed in place but had yet to be fitted. Behind the toilet, complicated new plumbing was underway and a fresh hole had been knocked through to the outside. The tiles had been torn away and every wall was naked and scarred. Along the windowsill, an arsenal of cleaning products awaited the call of duty.

'You've lost weight,' she said, fishing the newspaper out of her top.

'You've put on—' It probably wasn't a good time to bring up her comfort eating. 'A polo neck. It's nice.'

She placed a hand on her chest. 'Wasn't sure if it was really me.'

Her tits looked like two buckets on a rope and it wasn't her at all. But I understood. She was hiding. 'No, it looks good.'

She sat on the closed toilet lid and spread the newspaper on the floor. 'You've read it then?' She rattled through the pages.

I perched on the bath. 'Yes.'

'And? What did you think?' She stopped at the picture of Gloria.

Our mother was kneeling behind the chaise longue, her chin resting on her plump, dimpled forearms, her eyes downcast, a master class in Photoshop. The headline read:

SOWING THE SEEDS OF LOVE

I held onto the bath, letting the usual sick, cringing dread pass. Georgie pulled her collar away from her neck.

Opposite the picture of Gloria was a photograph of the farm, looking like somewhere Brontë heroines went to die. Next to that was an old photograph of Mo, skinning up beside the kettle. There was a shot of a much younger, slimmer Mo beside my fresh-faced, bookish father. They were engineering an elaborate bong with diligent focus, accompanied by some student friends and a blueprint, which had been kindly posted to them by some friends in Amsterdam. There was a much later picture of a bare-chested man with lank blonde hair, his arm around a giant papier-mâché phallus. I recognised him from the news. He was a former member of the Tory cabinet.

Gloria didn't namedrop as much as I thought she would and I supposed it was the newspaper that was being cautious, rather than her. She hinted at the positions later held by the people who lived at the farm and the high-profile organisations they were connected with, but the feeling was that there was much more to be found in her book. Housemates were described as 'gifted' and 'brilliant' and the banal became 'extraordinary' and 'conceptual'. Besides the brief caption, 'One-time housemate Hugh Phillips', the former cabinet minister wasn't mentioned. The photograph was extraordinary and conceptual enough.

'Other papers will pick up on this,' I said.

Georgie wound her fingers into her hair. 'No, they won't.'

Gloria said that she joined the farm just as the housemates were growing out of free love and into a commune that supported itself by growing vegetables and using the outbuildings to teach. She described it as 'sexually open, a place that welcomed new ways of thinking and living, in direct opposition to the horrors outside'. She often quoted another 'former housemate' and I wondered who her source was. Whoever they were, they seemed to agree it was Mo who killed their idyll. According to Gloria, Mo was an obsessively controlling matriarch who used drugs to manipulate relationships, and whose jealousy drove a wedge between Gloria and her lover, my father Pete, ultimately causing his death.

'That's bollocks,' Georgie said.

'Mediocre tabloid fiction.'

'That's what I meant.'

'I was agreeing with you.'

'So was I!' Her chin crept forward and I shrank back. I didn't have the energy.

We stared at the paper.

Next week's second and final instalment promised more on the 'end of the dream' and Gloria's newfound happiness with literary messiah Rory McManus.

'It could have been worse,' I said.

Georgie pulled at her collar. 'You mean it could have been about us?'

'No, they could have printed her poetry.'

She didn't return my grin. I hung my head.

'Do you think the "end of the dream" means us?' She fanned herself with a hand.

My teeth began to chatter. 'I don't know.'

'Why don't you get some proper shoes?'

I looked at my grimy blue Dickensian feet. I had lain without sleeping for so long after Gluteus Maximus left, I was unprepared for waking. With no time to psyche myself up or plan my approach, I had opened my eyes, sprung into the shower and bolted from the house without checking the clock or the mirror or my feet. Sitting outside the newsagents on the empty road, listening to jazzy doumbeks on a fuzzy radio station, I chewed my hair, argued for and against, smoked, chewed my hair and pleaded with the universe for us to be left alone to get on with our faux lives. I had been much too busy to think about pedestrian practicalities like my feet.

Georgie took her hands from her hair, leaving it chaotic. 'I can't go through another week of this. I've started thinking about how I'm going to tell Darren.'

'But we still don't know if she's written about us.'

Georgie pulled her collar from her neck and coughed.

'If we're in the book, we probably have a right to read it,' I said. 'We could go back to the publisher and just say who we are.'

Her voice had a high-pitched edge. 'And have her think we're scared?'

'Well, we *are* scared.'

'I can't see a way out of this.'

I chewed my hair. 'We could talk to her.'

She cleared her throat, staring at the floor, my feet, the door. 'I'm not going to her to plead for mercy.'

'It's not about mercy,' I said, trying to sound sensible through my rattling teeth. 'It's about being . . . grown-up.'

'It will just be the same and she'll still have to win.' Her eyes fixed on mine as breaths fell over one another. 'I'd rather lose it all than go to her now.' She stood up, a fist on her rapidly rising chest. 'Oh no!'

I swallowed, nonchalant. 'Are you—'

She twisted away. 'Oh shit, oh no.'

I sprang up and looked around as she wriggled, pulling her top over her head. Did she use paper bags? I couldn't remember. I'd brought a plastic bag. But I didn't want to kill her.

'I'm too . . . oh God . . .' she panted. 'I have to get out, I have to, I have to—'

'But Georgie, you're . . .' An agoraphobic who hasn't been further than the bottom of the driveway for eleven years, where are you going to go? But I didn't say that. I said, '. . . in your bra.'

She paced the bathroom. I glanced at the door, sure Darren or Joe would hear her. She swore, struggling against torrents of shallow breaths. Fiery blotches had broken out across her neck. She gripped the edge of the sink.

There was a knock at the door. 'You OK in there?' It was Darren, his voice deep with sleep.

Georgie's frightened eyes pinned mine. Her top lip was lined with sweat.

I spun round. 'Yes!' I watched with horror as Georgie panted and swayed. She looked like she was going to faint. 'We're just . . . interior designing!' I grabbed Georgie as she leaned forward. But she pushed me away and grasped the plastic bag I'd brought.

'Sure?' Darren said.

Pulling the bleach from the bag, Georgie unscrewed the lid.

'We're fine!' My voice cracked as Georgie sucked bleach fumes through her nose and blew a long breath out through her mouth. I tried to yank the bottle away but she gripped it like an angry toddler.

'What's that noise?' Darren said.

'I've got a cold!' I said, trailing Georgie, still attached to the bleach, away from the door.

'That's a *cold*?'

Opening the window, I leaned Georgie out. 'Catarrh, I always get it!' I scanned the windowsill: Glade, Flash, Cif, Mr Sheen, Mr Muscle, Domestos, Dettol. I opened the Dettol and wafted it under Georgie's nose.

'What's going on?' Darren said.

'Nothing! Everything's fine, everything's fine and normal!'

Georgie's nose followed the Dettol. I eased the bleach away.

'I think I should come in,' Darren said.

'No!' I screamed, as Georgie sucked up Dettol fumes. 'I have no clothes on!'

'What? Why?'

'I have a rash. I wanted Georgie to check it.' Georgie stared at me with watering eyes.

'Tommie, you need to see a doctor,' Darren said.

'I know. But I'll be fine.'

'Sure?'

'Yes!' I leaned in and sniffed the Dettol too.

'OK . . . well . . . Do you like the new bathroom suite?'

'It's fabulous.'

'Did Georgie tell you we got it from a skip?'

Georgie honked at the Dettol.

'I'm going to make a cup of tea. Do you want a cup?' Darren said.

'Love a cup!' Surely then he would go away. But Georgie shook her head. 'I mean, no!' I yelled. 'We don't want tea! We'll make *you* a cup!' Georgie pushed me hard, snorting the Dettol. 'No, we'll make some later, forget the tea!' I yelled desperately. 'We don't want tea, you go ahead!'

Georgie and I gesticulated at one other.

'It's no bother,' Darren said. 'I'm boiling the kettle anyway.'

'No we're fine, thanks!' *Please* go away.

'Are you sure?'

Dear God. 'YES!'

'Alright. Don't get snippy. It's just a cup of tea.'

'OK, sorry. Thanks.' Please, please go.

My knees were like water as Georgie breathed Dettol, counting to five each time she inhaled and exhaled. The stairs creaked as Darren walked slowly down to the kitchen. I wilted and leaned out the window beside Georgie, wiping feverish sweat from my forehead. Her skin was goose-pimply but flushed. She counted Dettol-assisted breaths and I leaned in for the occasional sniff.

I couldn't remember when she'd last had a panic attack. They started when Joe was a baby and she had learned breathing techniques to control them. When Joe was three, she had a major one pushing him round the shops. Breathless, suffocating, she was sure she would die and imagined Joe left bewildered and alone. The thought tripled the power of the attack. She collapsed in the chemist's and never went out again. Now, with the internet, she could work, shop and redecorate her home without having to face or talk to anyone. Snorting bleach was a new development but I supposed it made sense, given her other habits.

We stared out the window without speaking and I held my cigarettes in my pocket like a talisman. In the garden below, the new patio furniture was covered in plastic. The impossibly level grass appeared plastic too but only because Georgie liked to feed and weed and trim it with scissors. You can always find something to do if you're stuck at home for eleven years. This house was her world. But it was Darren's house and if he wanted her to go, it wouldn't just be the end of her marriage, it would be the end of her everything.

'Have you picked towels yet?' I said. Her control-freakery was as comforting to me as it was to her.

She breathed in for five, out for five. 'Taupe,' she said eventually. 'And camel.' In, out. 'And beige.' In, out. 'To break it up.'

'And are you getting those heated towel rails?'

She breathed in. 'His . . .' She breathed out. 'And hers.'

We stared at the pristine garden and talked quietly about the bathroom's new colour scheme and the blinds and how she couldn't wait to Cillit Bang it all. Now the panic attacks had returned, I didn't think she would last another week either. When at last she seemed calm, I brought out my cigarettes.

Her voice was low, drained. 'I knew you were smoking again.'

'I know, I'm weak. Do you mind . . . ?'

She watched closely as I drew a cigarette from the pack. I expected her to stop me but she said nothing as I lit up and inhaled with relief. I blew my smoke as far from the house as my lungs could manage, glancing up, waiting for the reprimand.

But she said, 'Can I have one?'

Smoke hiccupped down my nose. She had been a central figure among the smokers at school – she got me started – but she smoked because she was cool and hard, not because she loved it. It was easy for her to stop when she was pregnant.

'Are you sure?' I asked. 'What about the smell?' I waved at my smoke, ushering it out.

'Right now, I couldn't give a fiddler's fuck.'

Still holding the Dettol, she took a cigarette from my pack and touched my hand as I held up the lighter. She inhaled lightly and we puffed our smoke across the garden. The damp smell was ugly but it felt like a victory. This was the old Georgie, the cool one, the one who would kill, or at least, bitchslap any threat.

She pushed her fingers into her curls. 'So how did you get the black eye?'

'It's not what you think it is,' I said. 'I tripped over my bra.'

She straightened. 'Oh God, it *is* what I think it is. Your house is a mess, isn't it?'

'It's not that bad,' I said.

She coughed breathlessly and covered her face at the thought of having to live with me.

'The place looks fab,' I said. 'We've got a new loo. And the landlord is renovating the place. I'd give it a really good clean, not that it needs it. Blob would help.'

She whispered expletives. She disliked Blob as much as he disliked her. He had a thing for Darren, but not only that, he knew what she did that summer. His loyalty and integrity made him the best kind of friend, but few people could live up to his standards.

She wound her unruly hair around her fingers. 'So, when do you think Liam will get the book?'

'Soon,' I lied. 'A day or two.'

Her jaw slid forward and she stubbed out her cigarette on the windowsill. I took a few quick puffs before stubbing out mine. With no bin, I threw both butts onto Gloria's article, rolled up the newspaper and put it back in my plastic bag. Georgie pulled on her top and wafted the Dettol under her nose, each breath bringing new bliss to her face.

'Ring me every day,' she said. 'Let me know how Liam's getting on.'

'He's acceptable now, is he?'

'Just ring me.'

'I will.'

'If I don't answer, keep ringing,' she said. 'I'm going to steam-clean the walls. It gets noisy.'

She put her copy of the newspaper into my bag and opened the bathroom door. She peered left and right before leading me out to the warm landing. We crept past the washing to the front door.

'Can't I even have a cup of tea?' I whispered as she hustled me into the mizzle. Her tea was worse than mine, but hypothermia was setting in.

She glanced back at the kitchen. 'He's already suspicious,' she whispered. 'You never visit two weeks in a row.'

'Nothing to do with your snorting Domestos?'

Her face was pink and grey in patches. 'Just ring me, Tommie,' she said. She stared for a moment. 'Give me another cigarette.' She held out her hand, wiggling her fingers, and I fumbled at the packet before handing one over. She tucked it inside her top and closed the kissing door. Through the narrow slot of stained glass, I watched her move quickly away. I flip-flopped back to my car, squelching through the rain.

The brief reappearance of the old Georgie was encouraging, but there was only so much relief the occasional Marlboro Light and snort of Dettol could offer. The final excerpt in next week's paper would probably focus on some other drama in Gloria's life and, unless she'd been sleeping her way through all the nation's favourite poets, there was a good chance it would be us. And thanks to Hugh Phillips and his giant papier-mâché dick, everyone would know about it.

Driving back to the city, my car's heater blew hot air for two minutes and then stopped completely. When swearing at the dashboard didn't work, I wiped away condensation with my sleeve. I held the freezing steering wheel with numb fingertips and tried wriggling my dead toes. On the radio, the jazzy doumbeks had been replaced by lisping Englishmen and I turned it off, listening to the slash of tyres on tarmac. I moved into the lane heading south, the one with the sign for Dublin, although I was only going as far as Orbital's café. I wanted to ask him how Mo was.

No matter how badly Gloria behaved, Mo was right. Talking to my mother was the grown-up – the only – thing to do. If Gloria wrote about us, Georgie would have to talk to Darren, and I would have to talk to Gloria. I couldn't stop her, but I could at least face her. But what did I know about being 'grown-up'? The one parent I had had wasn't the best role model. Mo was the only grown-up I knew and she wasn't exactly a model citizen either.

The seats and steering wheel shook as I raced towards Dublin. I could at least pretend to run away.

14.

The door was closed but not locked. I pushed it open, rattling the string of bells inside. The smell of garlic, lentils and old cold bricks reminded me of the farm. The shabby café was empty; it was too early for the foreign nationals and scholarly types who usually ate there. At the far end of the room, a figure appeared behind the counter. It was Orbital's partner, Betty.

'We're not ope—' she began. Her greying hair was in a ponytail and her lined face make-up free. 'Oh, hello,' she said tartly, recognising me.

'Hello,' I said.

'Orb's upstairs,' she said, swishing back to the kitchen. I waded after her, through mismatched chairs and scratched thrift shop tables.

Behind a partition, Betty prepared vegetables at a wooden block while a young Audrey Hepburn look-alike in bright lipstick wrote specials on a small blackboard. An extractor fan hummed as pans smoked, pots steamed and the oven sweated garlic, cumin and tomatoes.

'He's working on menus,' Betty said, so devoted to her chopping, it seemed, that she couldn't look at me. 'Go on up.'

Audrey Hepburn watched as I climbed the creaking staircase at the back of the kitchen, passing above crates of potatoes and vegetables.

I stood in the dark doorway to Orbital's office. The walls were dull and layered with smoke. Cabinets, folders and boxes lined one wall and Orbital sat by the window in the pale light. On the desk was a computer, pens, a calculator, the newspaper. He stared out the window. His skin was saggier and more sallow than I remembered.

I shrugged, almost curtsied. 'Sorry.'

He looked at me briefly and went back to staring out the window.

'How's Mo?' I asked.

His reedy voice was flat. 'As you might expect.'

'Well . . . I just wanted to say . . . sorry.' I turned away. I hadn't spoken to Gloria for more than fifteen years but I was still too close. Too much of a reminder. I was contaminated. I couldn't blame him. I started for the stairs.

'Tommie,' he said.

I peered into the room again. He beckoned loosely, indicating a folded chair on the other side of the desk. 'Come back, sit down.'

I unfolded the chair, watching his half-smile appear on his face like a curtain.

'I appreciate your coming,' he said.

I pulled the chair close to the radiator. 'Have you spoken to Mo?'

'This morning. She read it online.'

'Is she OK?'

'She says she's fine.' He pressed a hand to the back of his neck. 'But you know what she's like.'

'Couldn't she come and stay with you for a while?'

'Well, the police will be round . . .' He looked at his watch. 'Oh, any minute now, I would imagine. Why do you think she's in Donegal?' He went back to the window and I followed his gaze: wet slates, vents, chimneys with weeds.

'I'm shocked,' he said, shaking a foot so that his whole body moved. 'I shouldn't be. But I am.'

He took a breath and whistled tunelessly as he lifted a tin of tobacco from a drawer. Downstairs, someone turned up the extractor and I felt it rattle through my flip-flops. I heard the front door jingle. Hunched over his tin, Orbital arranged tobacco on papers.

'Did you know Gloria called herself a war poet?' he said.

I shook my head.

He licked the papers and smoothed the seam. 'But she wasn't a war poet; she was a thrill-seeker. I think that's partly what Dad liked about her. That and her big tits. She drove him round the bend.' He leaned across and pushed open the window. 'Although to be fair, he was already on his way there.'

The roll-up flared as it lit. Thick, damp cold moved in through the window. I could hear voices downstairs.

Orb studied his emaciated cigarette. 'It wasn't your fault, Tommie.'

The stairs creaked with determined footsteps. Movement in the doorway made us turn.

'There's a man downstairs,' Betty said, eyes sliding from Orbital to me and back. 'He says he's from a newspaper.'

'Shit.' Orbital drew hard on the roll-up and folded it into the ashtray. Standing, he said to me, 'If anyone asks, you work here.'

Hoping to escape before it came to that, I followed his clattering clogs down to the kitchen. I waited by the partition as he approached a red-faced man with a pre-disease nose who stood by the till, reading peeling posters on the walls. Scanning Orbital's nicotine hair, washed-out shirt and scuffling clogs, he lifted his lips to reveal long brittle teeth.

'Orbital Benedict?' He held out a hand to shake. 'Jim Harland. *Northern News.*'

I wondered if I smelled as strongly when I'd been on the juice.

Harland tugged at his worn cuffs and spoke as though there had been a death: 'Your sister, Astra? She called me, arranged to meet me here. Said you wanted to talk about Gloria?'

'Oh, did she?'

Harland caught the sarcasm but continued with practised diplomacy. 'I won't take up much of your time.'

Orbital folded his arms. 'Astra didn't tell me you were coming.'

'She did say she'd call you.' Harland was deeply, painfully earnest. 'I'm sorry to land on you unprepared. But I'm sure you have something to say,' he said. 'Gloria said some very strong things and

Hugh Phillips's book will be out in a couple of weeks and it looks to me like they've got some sort of publicity deal going on. It's only fair you and your family get a chance to speak.'

I wondered if Phillips was the 'former housemate' who had backed her up. This was bigger than I thought. I needed to get out. I needed to have a little panic attack of my own. I looked round for the back door but Betty stepped in front of it, eyeing me with the vegetable knife in her hand. Studying my flip-flops, I moved out from behind the partition. The front door was my only option.

'That's the veg chopped,' I murmured. 'Bye.'

The front door jingled and I looked up. It was Astra, whisking through the door in a flurry of colleen. By the time she saw the three of us together, Orbital was already on his way to head her off. They stood at the door, exchanging vehement whispers. Astra's cheeks were blotchy and the skin around her eyes pink and swollen.

Harland turned to me, using his time efficiently. 'You look familiar,' he said.

I babbled weak denial.

'Do you know the Benedict family?' He poked a finger round his molars.

I shook my head, trying to look like an oniony vegan of no importance.

'How well do you know Mr Benedict?' he said.

'Who's Mr Benedict?'

Orbital and Astra's voices rose. Harland dropped tooth mush on the floor. 'Well, you must know Gloria,' he said.

All my internal organs prolapsed.

'Come on. Everybody knows Gloria Shaw. She has a memoir coming out?'

I shook my head.

'Poet in the Community? Writer-in-Residence at the Hirsute Women's Conference?'

I went on shaking.

113

'Reports for an Arts show? No discernible talent?' He squinted at me. 'Sure I don't know you?'

I swallowed. '*Nein.*'

'How'd you get the black eye? Just curious. Excuse me.' He pulled an ageing digital camera from his satchel and began clicking at Astra, who was gesticulating with hands like fins. Orbital's voice was high with exasperation. She prodded Orbital's chest, Orbital caught her finger and she covered her eyes with her hand. Orbital patted her shoulder like he'd never touched her before. Harland scrolled through the pictures on his camera.

Orbital and Astra spoke quietly for a moment, then joined Harland at a table by the till. Astra dabbed her mascara with a tissue and Orbital wiped his hands down his shirt, his mouth a grey line. Harland introduced himself with wet sincerity and I slunk towards the door.

'I'm sure this is very upsetting for you both,' Harland said as I tried to flip-flop away in silence, 'but you're right, Astra. People should know the truth. And we can and will set the record straight. This is about presenting a balanced view, that's all. So what's really going on? Is Gloria the psycho I think she is?'

'Why not ask *her*?' Astra's voice wobbled with tears. 'That's the bitch's daughter.'

I sucked in a breath. All three looked my way – Astra accusing, Orbital aghast, Harland fumbling for his camera. I watched my hand pull the jingling door as Harland's camera clicked.

'Wait!' he called.

The bells clashed as I clambered out to the mizzly street and launched into a run. Hearing the bells clash again, I looked back. Harland was following. Squelching perilously, I ran to my car and forced the key into the lock, but, knowing I was under pressure, it refused to open. I didn't have time to negotiate. I ran on, past shuttered boutiques and charity shops and into a narrow residential street. Cars were parked nose-to-tail outside red-brick terraces. Behind me, closer than I hoped, Harland shouted, 'Wait, please!'

I squelch-slapped past the houses at speed. Blob and I used to dream of this sort of thing. Now it was happening, I was gripped by a stitch, close to vomiting and limping like Charles Laughton fleeing a Parisian mob.

I skidded across the wet road and shimmied between two cars on the other side. Swinging round, my flip-flops gave out on a greasy manhole cover and faded purple beach flowers rose before my eyes. I thudded onto my hip with a comic-strip 'oof!' Shockwaves rattled through me, every muscle turned to water. Shaking, I scrambled under the car for my Judas shoes and turned to get up. Harland stood over me. Heaving and sweating, he extended his hand and I took it.

'Are you . . . OK?' he gasped, hauling me to my feet.

'Are *you* OK?' I said, as he leaned forward to grip his knees, wheezing, his face a worrying shade of yellow.

He pressed his hand to his chest and, with what sounded like death rattles, said, 'What . . . were you . . . running for?'

'You were chasing me.' I leaned on a garden fence and squirmed gritty feet into flip-flops. A small dog popped up at the window of the house behind and ate the glass with rage.

'I—' Harland tried to talk but the urge to survive was too strong. He appeared to be drowning.

'Do you need to sit down?' I asked.

He shook his head and held up a hand, gulping air noisily. I waited, looking up and down the street. Finally, he straightened and smeared a sleeve over his forehead.

'Jeeeeeeesus!' he said. 'Who gave you the flip-flops? Usain Bolt?'

The dog in the window turned inside out with fury.

'Look, I don't want this, Mr Harland.'

'Call me Jim,' he said. He was younger than I first thought. Not young, but the washed-out purple at the ends of his reddish hair suggested he was too rock and roll to be old.

'I don't want this, Jim.'

'Everybody wants this.'

'No, they don't.'

115

'Not even a few words?' His sprouting eyebrows wriggled in emphasis.

'Preferably not.'

'So you condone your mother's behaviour?' It wasn't a challenge, more a theatrical, eyebrow-centric expression of his confusion, disappointment, pain.

'Oh, come on,' I said. 'This is why I ran. Talk to Astra.' I edged backwards and, in a shabby tango, Harland followed.

'It could look bad if you don't want to talk to me,' he said.

'It could look bad if you want it to.' I turned towards the café and tried to pick up speed but my legs shook from the unaccustomed exertion and I slowed despite myself. Harland limped beside me, his coat brushing hedges and fences as we squeezed past parked cars.

'Thank God we're not running, eh?' He shammed a chummy smile. Having dispensed with offers of fame and passive threats, now he wanted us to be friends, united by our lack of physical prowess and our shared inability to catch a bus. When I didn't respond, he dropped the olive branch.

'It's better to have me on your side, you know.'

I looked around. If only someone I knew would drive by and pick me up, or shoot him, but all the nice, normal people were having a lie-in. I opened my mouth to speak, but froze when Astra appeared at the end of the street. She decelerated quickly, lifting her chin and assuming a wounded but dignified promenade.

Harland leaned in. Last night's alcohol was pungent. 'Wouldn't you rather control what's said about you?' he said. Close up, his nose looked irretrievable. '*She* doesn't seem to have much love for you.' He nodded at the advancing Astra. 'And as for your mother, well, I just hope you're on good terms. Although you being here this morning makes think . . . ?' He watched me carefully and despite my attempt at oniony vegan, a kick of realisation passed over his face. He'd scored a point and he knew it.

I was at Gloria's mercy and he was offering me an out. He was giving me the chance that Mo never had – the chance to pre-empt her. Harland was from a daily newspaper, albeit a local one with limited reach, but his story would be published before Gloria's next excerpt. I could say how Gloria's cold parenting drove Georgie to do anything for love and how her awful poetry drove me to . . . No, I couldn't. Georgie wasn't ready. And it wouldn't look like self-defense; it would look like fifteen trashy minutes of fame.

I shook my head.

Harland pushed his hands into his pockets and smiled bashfully. 'You know, I'll be honest with you.' He looked at his scuffed Oxfords. If there had been sand, he would have toed around in it. 'I've never had a scoop before. I haven't even used the *word* before.'

'Oh, please stop.' I looked past him to where the houses led. Probably an inescapable warren of identical terraces but now that Astra was coming to take back her thunder, getting lost was probably the best option. I stepped away. 'I really have to go.'

'No, wait!' He held up a hand as Astra's solid heels bore down on us. He rummaged in a pocket and, holding my gaze, waved a business card like he was coaxing a cat with scraps. 'I'd make it worth your while.'

His pitted nose and worn suit, my slab feet and smoky guts, everything made me sick. The street, the road, the cement sky, it all made me sick. I needed to get away. I put my hand out for the card.

'We haven't spoken for fifteen years,' I said, hearing revulsion in my voice.

Acquisitive glee flitted across his face before Astra slotted between us. She wore her perfume like she was flying a flag.

'Mr Harland, if you're not interested, I can call another paper.'

Harland twisted in contrition. 'Of course I'm interested. I thought you wanted me to talk to Gloria's daughter? When you pointed her out?'

Astra paused. 'Yes,' she clipped. 'Mr Benedict and I are very busy people, Mr Harland.' She guided him away with a hovering hand and I wrapped myself in a soothing shroud of smoke when they turned the corner. The cigarette left me lighter but no less shaky.

117

Hollowed by nausea and fatigue, I squelched back to my car.

The café door was quiet as I tried the car lock. I tried it slowly, quickly, violently, tenderly, but the car would not oblige. I leaned my elbows on the roof, watching blank faces drive to church or the newsagents. I wished I had somewhere to go that required such zoned-out commitment. Or at least, I wished I had something to go there in. The door of the café jingled and my ankles twinged with dread.

'Let me have a go,' Orbital said, taking the key from my hand. I almost buckled with relief.

He slid the key into the lock and pulled open the door. Dead air seeped out as I dropped into the driver's seat. He handed me a takeaway cup of coffee and I gripped the scalding sides.

'Thanks, Orb.'

His knees clicked as he sank to his haunches. 'Sorry, Tommie, Astra was upset—'

'It's fine,' I said, letting the coffee burn my gullet. 'I'd be the same.'

'I doubt it.'

I rubbed my feet on the mat, the friction warming them.

'Harland can't have had many exclusives in his career,' Orbital said, his half-smile creeping back. 'I had to make him sugary tea.'

'Better warm up the defibrillator,' I said. 'I took his business card.' Because he offered it and we owe two months' rent and we don't have enough walls and we need the money, but if it makes me sick enough, maybe I won't be able to go through with it. But I didn't say any of that. I had my excuses but I was still selling my story and Orbital already thought there was too much of Gloria about me.

'You OK?' he said.

'Just a little existential angst, nothing serious.' I laughed like Peter Sarstedt.

'The Highway Code suggests pulling over and taking a nap.' His half-smile broke into its full, freakish Phantom of the Opera glory. Then it fell away. He pressed a hand to his neck and his vertebrae creaked. 'At least Harland's not a fan of Gloria's,' he said.

'He's not a fan of anyone's. He'll print whatever he thinks will sell.'

'Then we need to keep him onside.'

'Let's run away, Orb.'

He looked thoughtful. 'I have friends in Sweden.'

'I always wanted to play chess with death.'

'You sure you're OK?'

'I'm fine.' I set the coffee in the holder and turned the key, shaking the engine awake. The wipers squealed across the windscreen. Orbital stood up, clogs rattling.

'I'll let Mum know you were asking about her.'

'Thanks. Thanks for the coffee too.'

'And be careful, for God's sake,' he said, rubbing his neck. 'Don't think I didn't notice your black eye.'

'I have a black eye?'

'Keep in touch, Tommie. Call by during the week, you and your big friend. You look like you could do with a decent meal. So does he.'

He stepped back and I set off for home, pulling into the path of a bus. It screeched and puffed to a halt and I saluted a polite apology as Orb covered his eyes with the hand he was waving.

15.

The drizzle turned to fog near home and moisture followed me inside when I opened the door. The house was silent and hung with damp. The plastic sheet covering the hole sagged under the weight of droplets, but nothing else had changed. The kitchen was the way we had left it the night before, a squall of ashtrays, blankets, bottles, books and glasses, ugly in the wet light. I assumed Blob was still in bed. He was generally tidier than I was, although I suspected that his urge to clear away the mess had more to do with denial than good housekeeping.

I took a blanket from the settee and pulled it round my shoulders before hauling myself upstairs. I hoped Blob was awake. My head spiralled with little tornadoes and he'd help me get some perspective. He'd belittle everything and everyone and quell the tornadoes before they could grow. I knocked softly on his door, giving him a moment before I leaned in. The ageing double bed took up most of his room. It came with the house and smelt of years of bodies. The curtains were closed, but even in the darkness I could see the faded covers had been pushed back and the bed was empty.

I chewed my hair.

I trudged downstairs and had a glass of water at the sink, staring out at the wet earth and rubble in the backyard-cum-bathroom of the future. A thought bubbled to the surface. Chris wanted to make things so unpleasant for us we would either pay up or leave. Pay up *and* leave. God, I was stupid, why hadn't I seen it before? I was usually good at figuring people out. He wanted his pregnant girlfriend to have the house. Why didn't he just say he wanted us to go? This was the ultimate in passive aggression. I finished the water and thumped the glass into the sink. Chris was so pleasant, so chatty, so underhand.

I pulled the blanket over my head. I was nuts. I had enough experience to know:

$$drink + stressful\ week + insomnia = \frac{headcase}{paranoia\ ^{\infty}}$$

I was dangerously tired. Assertively, I told myself I had to go to bed. I boiled the kettle, stirred a teabag into a mug and brought it up to my room, closing the door against the light. My bedroom curtains hadn't been opened for days and the room's syrupy darkness blurred every edge, including my own. Setting the tea beside my clock, I dropped blanket and clothes to the floor and struggled into a fresh T-shirt. I fell onto the bed and pulled the covers up to my ears, breathing in soft sweat and cologne from last night. A nest. I could stop here. I closed my eyes.

Tornadoes.

I was committed. I would have to tell our story, the story we wanted to forget. We would look cheap and grasping. Fifteen minutes. Georgie would lose her husband, possibly her child. It ran in the family, there would be kiss-and-tells, neighbours, Gluteus Maximus's wife. I should have sent him away long ago. I could have helped Mo. I still could. Maybe I could give Mo's side of the story instead of ours. That's what Astra was doing. I couldn't get out of it that easily. Silly bitch. Sly bitch.

Under the quilt, I covered my head with my hands. Stop thinking, you idiot. Concentrate on breathing, in for five, out for Orbital, poor Orbital, related to me when I was related to her. How selfish to inflict myself on him. What was I thinking? *Northern News*? She gets the Radio 4s and broadsheets of this world, we get a local rag nobody reads. She'd laugh at us. She didn't usually laugh like Baby Jane, but she would now.

How long can I stare at the colourless plaster on the ceiling, hating every lump and crack? I cover my eyes with my arm. I'm just tired, that's all. There is a bang on the landing, so loud it bursts my temples. I look at the door. That's the danger. I smother fear with logic. It's not real, I know it's not real. It just happens sometimes but it's not serious and sleep will sort it out. I could look for sleep in the bathroom but I'm too tired to get out of bed. I'm pathetic. I wish Blob was here.

I push myself up, reposition my pillows and take a swig from the cold mug. The tea is like coal dust round my teeth, and I don't do it again. I lean over and feel around in my pocket on the floor for my cigarettes. I let smoke drift from my nose and mouth. I should get up and open the window if I'm going to smoke . . .

I wake up and bat the smouldering quilt with a frantic hand, catching it before flames can take hold. I throw the cigarette into the tea and laugh, sort of. Blob would find it funny. Or possibly not. I slump onto the bed and look round the misty room. I really should get up and open the window, the fumes are probably deadly. I should get up and clean the house in case Georgie . . .

Gone.

The clouds had cleared while I slept. Low sun splayed into the yard and the rubble blushed. The plastic sheet was loaded with water and the inside was slick with condensation. With no sign of Blob, I shook the water off the sheeting, emptied the ashtrays and cleared away the glasses and bottles. I turned on the lamps and electric fire, tossed the blankets and throws artfully over the settees and fluffed up the cushions. The place still looked like Sodom laid to waste. I dropped some bread into the toaster and set the kettle to boil.

After a decent sleep, the tornadoes were under control, the phantom sounds were gone and Chris was back to being impulsive. And coming from the hysterically fearful Chicken Licken worlds Georgie and I lived in, impulsiveness was a good thing, if a little impractical. The hole in the wall was inconvenient and nothing more. The toast popped and I ate where I stood, guiding crumbs into the sink. I really would have to clean the place. Properly. This time next week, Georgie could be here.

I surveyed the crockery, cutlery, dust, crumbs and various, precarious clutter. A bottle of Febreze and a pack of baby wipes would take care of it. And upstairs, maybe Georgie and I could share the double and Joe could take the single and Blob and I . . . I was being ridiculous. It would never work. Chris would know the cleanest hotel in town and I'd put it on my credit card. I was cheered to learn housework wasn't all bad – thinking about it had sent me to sleep. But tackling this place would induce a coma.

The lock rattled, the front door whacked back to the wall and Blob whisked in, raincoat flailing, flat quiff flapping. Apparently seeking a response from the gallery, he said, 'I'm going to follow your gin and Ready Salted diet, bitch.'

He whammed the door closed, dropped his coat on the floor and crossed the room, spine so straight he appeared to be leaning backwards. 'Can I have toast?'

'You wouldn't like it. It's not deep fat fried.'

He was wearing the shapeless black jumper he wore when he was having a fat day. Beside me at the sink, he smelt damp and smoky and slightly medicinal. His beard was sprouting like Play-Doh.

'You're sweet for trying to help, but just fuck off,' he said. He took my toast and bit into it, closing his eyes and sighing, 'I hate myself.'

I slotted more bread into the toaster. 'You're not fat,' I said. 'It's just the pleats in your trousers.'

He tapped the kettle to see how hot it was, then hijacked my mug and poured in water.

'Why can't I just forget to eat?' he said, dunking the teabag with a spoon. 'I might forget I ate a packet of Hobnobs or something but I don't . . .' He thunked the teabag at the plughole and turned, leaning on the sink, feet crossed at the ankles.

'What's wrong?' I asked.

'What makes you think something's wrong?' He chewed joylessly.

I leaned on the sink beside him. 'Because you sound like you're in a teen soap.'

He tutted. 'It's just May.'

'What happened?'

He whirled his limp quiff round a finger. 'She's in hospital.'

'What happened?'

'She had a stroke. Last night. Eleanor and Sharon are still there.' I remembered them as Blob's aunts. The medicinal smell was hospital soap.

I touched the sleeve of his jumper. It felt hard, greasy.

'I think I'll be coming into some Frank Ifield records soon,' he said, tearing off more toast.

'Oh no.'

'Exactly. At least I could sell Elvis.'

Steam fogged his glasses as he blew on the tea. He set down the mug and put his arm around my shoulders. His profile reminded me of Churchill, with toast instead of a cigar.

'Let's get pissed,' he said. 'You owe it to May. She introduced you to it.'

'She introduced me to some dodgy sangria stored inside the body of a stuffed donkey and, come to think about it, I don't think she knew it was there.'

'Then you saved her from it. Come on.' He squeezed my shoulder. 'I can always rely on you to stoop to the lowest level.'

I concentrated on swilling a teabag round a mug. I shouldn't really. Drinking didn't help. I was in much better shape without it. Mondays were hard enough. But Blob's family had always been kind to me. Surely I could show some solidarity?

'Just one or two,' I said.

❃

Two trenches.

Four settees.

Two Blobs pole dancing round two bannisters *chick-a-ching-ching.*

This is my life.

Screaming like a girl, *big fish little fish, glowsticks glowsticks glowsticks glowsticks,* let's do a snake, Tommie come on come on come on, *cardboard boxes cardboard boxes, stacking shelves in Crazy Prices.*

They're banging the wall.

They're all bastards.

16.

Sunglasses. The winter sun would lift my soul if only I could open my eyes wider than slits. I sucked in newly verdant air and floated by the university gardens, feverishly pink, too drunk to be hungover. I drifted through reception on the breeze from the door.

Lisa perked up. 'Good morning! And you're here for . . . ?'

'My sins. I work here.' I wafted towards the office.

'Tommie!' She slapped her hands to her mouth, her perk melting. 'I didn't know you in those *amazing* sunglasses. Vee Hollywood. Did you get home OK on Friday night?'

'No problem.'

'It was such a good night.' She grinned and leaned forward, beckoning. 'Listen—'

'I have to—' I held up a hand. I had to sit down.

I seeped into the office. Jude was wearing clean tights. Hooray for Monday. And new, unpolluted shoes. Huzzah for her capitalist whims. She stared blackly at her laptop. Bill's pink-shirted back was taut and curved tight, Patricia's '80s' yellow bouff was angled away from everyone and Seamus's fuzzy hair fell almost to his desk. The electric heater plinked and hummed and the radio muttered on the floor.

I eased into my seat, comforted by the new and luxuriantly verbose press packs Jude had flung at my desk. Her head swivelled round like a ventriloquist's dummy.

'You.'

The others ducked by millimetres.

She folded her arms, red leather jacket squeaking. 'Gloria.'

I felt like the wavy mirror at the funfair.

'I told Kevin Loane we'd get an exclusive,' she said, tendons in

126

her neck writhing. 'And now that fucking woman is fucking everywhere. They're calling them fucking Roria.'

My floating brains couldn't keep up. *Roria*? They'd given them a name. She'd been welcomed into pop culture. Oh the horror. But at least Jude hadn't discovered I was the spawn of the devil. She had been my friend last week. Was she angry because she was sober and I was obviously drunk? I attempted sobriety.

'The feature is completely under control,' I said, straightening my sunglasses.

'How, exactly?'

'Kevin and I have agreed structure and content. And content of structure. And all that.'

'And what about Gloria?'

'I have done considerable background research.'

'Make sure you *talk* to her.' She jabbed her finger on her desk, shiny plum fingernail tick-tick-ticking. 'And think of a good angle. We want this to sell.'

My heart yammered along on gin calories. I nodded. 'I will. We do. Will do.'

She eyed her computer like it had killed her horse and rattled at the keys. I sank back in my seat as my email dinged. It was from Patricia.

To: Tommie Shaw
From: Patricia McNeill
Subject: Admin

It's not admin at all!!!!!
You wont believe it!!!!!!!!!!!
Seamus handed his notice in!!!!!
You look awful!!!!!!!!!!!
P

To: Patricia McNeill
From: Tommie Shaw
Subject: Re: admin

Fucking fuck! Where is he going?
Just a bit tired. Busy weekend.
T

To: Tommie Shaw
From: Patricia McNeill
Subject: Re: re: admin

Hes starting his own business!!!!!!
What will we do without Seamus????!!!!!!!!!
I have paracetamol, Resolve, Proplus, Gaviscon, Imodium!!!!!!!!!
P

To: Patricia McNeill
From: Tommie Shaw
Subject: Re: re: re: admin

She must think he's setting up a rival magazine!
Ha ha ha ha ha ha ha ha ha ha!
Ha ha ha ha ha ha ha ha ha!
Ha ha ha ha ha ha ha ha!
Excuse my schadenfreude.
T

To: Tommie Shaw
From: Liam McMullan
Subject: Update

Hey Tommie!
Hope you're well. Lovely to talk to you last week. I've been thinking about you and hope we can get together again soon (and I mean that).
Just a quick email to let you know Rory is expecting your call so feel free to contact him. He'll be out of the office most of this week so you're most likely to catch him today. I also told him about our 'predicament' (ie you and me, then and now) and he was actually pretty insightful. He's very interested in meeting you.
No news on the you-know-what but I'm still trying. A friend of mine from uni knows a guy whose sister is married to someone who works for the you-know-what so fingers crossed!

Take care
L
xxx

Sent from my BlackBerry

To: Patricia McNeill
From: Tommie Shaw
Subject: Re: re: re: re: Admin

I need the Imodium.
T

To: Tommie Shaw
From: Patricia McNeill
Subject: Re: re: re: re: re: admin

So that's what schadenfreude is.
P

After swallowing Patricia's prescription, I surrendered to the haze of press releases – slashing, burning, rejecting and injecting my way through trichologists, dental hygienists, escapologists, gutter special-ists, dog handlers, ship chandlers, wedding singers and suppliers of all-purpose, quick-inflate gazebos. I broke into an involuntary stretch and groan and slapped one hand to my head, the other to my mouth. A headache was looming like a tsunami.

My email dinged.

To: Tommie Shaw
From: Liam McMullan
Subject: Rory

Hey Dollface!
You there? You didn't call, you didn't write . . .
Was just talking to Rory and he said you haven't called yet? Hope everything's OK. I suppose you're just busy but I have primed him to receive your call so if you could give him a call as soon as possible, then I won't look like a big fat idiot, lol!

Love ya!
L
xxx

Sent from my BlackBerry

Having bolstered my resolve with Resolve and a quick cigarette on the loo, I returned to my desk and dialled McManus's number. Bill talked toff to a saddlery about a new monthly equine feature he'd just made up and thankfully his phone-posh voice dominated the office. Still, Jude was listening to me. She targeted her computer with extreme concentration, which never happened when she was working.

I reached a secretary at a Midlands university.

'Hello, can I speak to Rory McManus, please?' I giggled coyly.

Oh no.

'Could you repeat that please?' the woman said in flat, Yorkshire tones. 'I don't quite understand your accent. Where are you from, if you don't mind?'

'Northern Ireland.' I smiled sweetly, forgivingly.

'Indianapolis?'

'Northern Ireland,' I said, with a giggle that skirted hysteria.

Breathy, simpering girl was back! Noooooo!

But of course she was back. I didn't know this woman, I didn't know McManus, but I wanted them to like me. I was eleven years old. I was pre-cool music and pre-life-changing books and I was ugly and smelly and without love.

'Irish-American,' I breathed in upstate New York.

'Oh, how exciting. Who do you wish to talk to?'

'Rory McManus please.'

'One moment.'

Cast into the oblivion of a phone transfer, I let my hair fall over my sunglasses. Jude leaned over, ear blatantly cocked.

'Hello?' McManus's voice was deep and warm. He sounded at least 6' 3" with lots of hair.

'Hello!' I peeped, pressing my nails into my palm. *Talk like a normal person, talk like a normal person, talk like a normal person.*

'Hello.' He sounded amused.

'Hello!' I tittered.

'Is that Thomasina? Tommie?'

My chin hovered above my keyboard. I poked pencil lead into crumbs and split ends. 'Yes,' I breathed.

'Liam said you'd call.'

'Well, we do have a bit of a history.'

What had that to do with anything?

'People are rarely so duty-bound,' he said.

'Well, you see, I still sort of fancy him.'

Whaaaaaaaaaaaat?

'I imagine,' McManus said. 'Things can't be easy.'

'Oh, well, you know how it is with exes . . .' I went on. Simpering Girl looked round. The hangover tsunami was approaching the beach. It was getting cold and dark.

'What with,' he said, 'your mother.'

I opened my mouth but nothing came out. The tsunami breached the beach, flooding up from the back of my neck, over my skull, through my left eye and down into my cheekbone. I worked a finger down behind my sunglasses and pressed my eye.

'Hello?' he said.

'Hello, sorry, sorry, got distracted there!'

'I'm sorry, Tommie, I . . .'

'No no no, it's fine really, we just, you know, things aren't really, we just don't, I can't . . .'

He said nothing.

I filled the space with a sissy giggle. And a long, disappointed sigh.

'We can't really avoid her,' he said.

I gripped the handset, chewing my hair. I needed every medication Patricia had in her drawer. Slowly I spilled over the desk.

'Without her, we wouldn't be here,' he said.

Standing behind Simpering Girl and Hungover Wretch, Literary Critic raised an eyebrow.

'But *with* her, Tommie,' McManus said. 'With her, sex was a . . . new thing. Experienced through a new lens. Without her, I'd still just be an award-winner.'

I drew squares, feeling sweat break out on my neck. 'Amazing.'

'I'm sorry, is this awkward?'

'It's fine.' Smile, smile, smile.

'Sure?'

'Consummate professional.' I doodled handles on the squares, turning them into cleavers.

'You know, I'm very interested in meeting you,' McManus said.

'Me?'

Jude loomed.

'In terms of Gloria,' he said.

I tittered miserably. My Resolve rolled over like doldrum swells.

'I think we'll have much to talk about,' McManus said.

I spoke helium high. 'And that's why I rang, believe it or not!'

We laughed, oh ho, ho, ho, how we relished the jollity.

Jude sat on her desk.

'You're appearing at the Poetry Festival in Belfast this weekend,' I said. 'I was hoping I could interview you then?'

'Liam showed me your photograph,' McManus said. 'You look slightly . . . tubercular, which I've always liked.'

'Gloria was a departure, then.' It came out before I knew it.

'Now, now,' he smiled.

How we chortled.

'Perhaps I could meet you at my reading?' McManus said.

'Perfect!' I wrapped my arm over my head. 'Fabulous. Amazing. I'll see you then.'

'I look forward to meeting you, Tommie,' he said.

'OK!' Droplets of blood fell from the cleavers. 'See you soon!'

'Goodbye,' he whispered.

I set down the phone and let Simpering Girl dissolve into my hangover. I covered my sick head with both elbows.

'Oi.' Jude pulled back her cheeks to flash her rictus grin. 'Now if you could fuck him, *that* would be an angle.'

We joined a queue of office workers seeking comfort at a Chinese buffet. Bill, Lisa and a buoyant Seamus tucked into plates piled high with steaming yellow stuff. Patricia pecked at glistening chow mein and I trembled over a bowl of soup. Lisa made an effort to include me as she pressed Seamus for details of his resignation but ever the gentleman, he would not divulge the horrors. Their knees touched as they flirted, which reminded me of my conversation with Rory, which made me feel like a heel.

Bill and Patricia wrung their hands over Seamus's departure, or desertion as Bill called it. They fretted over what would happen to the magazine without him as lynchpin and what they would do if the worst happened. Bill, walking his hand over his stringy comb-over, considered topping himself for the insurance money. Patricia said she was sure they'd find other jobs but she looked over her shoulder like she expected a predator. We toasted Seamus's imminent escape with Cokes and optimistic smiles, but I'm not sure everyone meant it.

As the day wore on, my Resolve wore off. By late afternoon, I lay over my desk, boiled and reduced to pure essence. I longed for death, although a taxi home would do just as well. My extension rang and I grunted hello.

A great watery snort, like trash washing up on a beach.

'Hello, Kevin.' I planted my hand in my hair.

Jude looked up. I looked down.

'Only four more days till the Festival!' Kevin sang, with a huge, wet sniff.

'Goody,' I said.

'Written the testimonials for the poets yet?'

Shit, fuck, bollocks. I'd forgotten. 'Just finishing them off.'

'I've had a go at them myself actually, Tom. I'm going to email them through. Run your eye over them and let me know if they float your boat.'

'Aye aye, captain.'

'And Tom?'

'Yes?'

'I think they're shipshape as they are.' He laughed backwards – ah ah ah. 'That's a good girl.' Sniff. He hung up.

Jude narrowed her eyes. 'What was *that* about?'

'He was just ringing to say how happy he was. With everything.'

She pinioned me with a glare before hammering at her keyboard.

My email dinged and I looked down to see a message from Kevin. I opened the attachment. His testimonials were on headed paper with Devine Energy's logo in the top right-hand corner – a fat old man with a beard and massively inflated cheeks.

I looked through the quotes Kevin had written for the poets: six in total. The first was for Helen McGonagle. I Googled her. She turned out to be a shaven-headed and occasionally homeless star of the slam poetry circuit.

> *'I share so much with Devine Energy. They uncover the profundities of the prosaic, as I do. They are inspired by the wondrous and endless power of nature, as I am. And they believe in excellent value for money, which is something I insist on. In fact, you simply won't find a better quote (than this one!)'*

Kevin had inserted a comment alongside the text: 'Too emotive perhaps?'

I scrolled down to the next page to see a quote he'd written for

Orla Connolly. I Googled her. She had been a contender for Poet Laureate last time round.

> 'I have shaken and quaken at the roar of captured waves and the power of trapped wind. I fear the might of Mother Nature but Devine Energy alone has tamed her. The possibilities are endless. As is their choice of solar panels and turbines.'

And Kevin's comment: 'Did you see what I did there?'

I scrolled to the next page where he had written one for McManus.

> 'Devine Energy is the power behind every artist. It takes deliberation, inspiration and determination to create something of value, and that's what Devine Energy is all about. Their new solar-powered garden lighting range is sublime.'

Another comment from Kevin: 'Will revert with more "ations".'

I skimmed through the others with growing alarm. Chewing my hair, I sent Kevin a reply.

❀

To: Kevin Loane
From: Tommie Shaw
Subject: Re: Poet Testimonials

Thanks for these, Kevin.
Perfectly punctuated, very impressed.
T

❀

To: Tommie Shaw
From: Kevin Loane
Subject: Re: re: Poet Testimonials

Tom
I thought you'd approve.
Regards
Kevin

P.S. Do you know what time the bar opens at the festival?

By five o'clock, I had been trampled by the horse that carried me round seven circles of hell. I filled my chair like a wet towel and closed my eyes behind my sunglasses. Kevin Loane wanted to kill me. He wanted to humiliate me to death. How could I ask anyone to put their name to his testimonials? But I'd have to find a way. I couldn't let my friends down.

17.

On Monday night I drove Blob to the hospital to see May. She was in intensive care, breathing through a machine. Behind tubes, wires and tapes, she looked angular and misshapen. I didn't recognise her.

We stood beside the bed, listening to scuttling nurse feet, electronic beeps and deep rhythmic breaths, our fingers touching her white sheet. Someone had brushed her frothy white hair. It was grey the last time I had seen her.

Blob kissed her before we left, and stayed silent on the way home. When I got up on Tuesday morning he was on the settee with his phone in his hand. He'd already got the news.

We toasted her with tea and smoked at the hole in the wall. Work had resumed and the Poles would arrive soon. I took the echoes of my hangover back to the magazine, hugging Blob before I left. I wished he could have a better day.

Jude's mood persisted through Tuesday and to make matters worse, she was wearing last season's shoes. It was early in the week for that kind of stench and I wondered if she was trying to punish us. By five o'clock, I was almost seeing stars and my shoulders felt like they'd been run through with blades. I wriggled to shake off the tension as we left, avoiding eye contact with my colleagues for fear it looked like collusion.

Outside, the streetlamps flickered on and the sky was pale in one corner. A blackbird fought to be heard as the city scrambled for home. Bill limped beside Patricia as she bustled toward the bus.

Seamus and Lisa left together, he walking backwards. The earthiness was back in the air, sifting through exhaust fumes. I lit up and headed towards home.

A car pulled up behind, tooting its horn. Chris, I thought, come to throw us out. Oh, stop it. It was just a hole in the wall, evidence of a very positive thinker, nothing more. I turned to see an old BMW I half recognised and ducked to see the driver. It was Darren. I dropped my cigarette and got in.

Car air fresheners seized me by the throat and I coughed and sneezed at the same time. With car perfume on my tongue, I said, 'Thanks, Darren, I could do with a lift.'

His hair, cropped weekly to ensure minimum mess, was longer than usual. There was a little brown stain on his T-shirt. He moved his jaw around, grinding his front teeth. Sudden sickness spread through me.

'Everything OK?'

He rubbed his eyebrows with a finger and thumb. 'It's Georgie.'

'Oh, God.' She'd told him. Why did she tell him when she didn't need to? Shit, shit, shit.

His eyebrows struggled, his chin crumpled.

Thoughts spun. When I got home, would she be there, bleaching, scrubbing and Ciffing my house? And Joe. Did he know yet? Poor Joe. Georgie was another mother from hell. Now there was nothing to stop our story coming out. But it wasn't fair to hurt them just to pre-empt Gloria. If we had to tell our story, we'd change their names. No one really knew Georgie anyway, not even her neighbours of twelve years. If we concentrated on me, we could limit the damage to them. I swallowed and opened the window.

He let out a long shaky breath. 'She's having an affair.'

I blinked at the traffic. 'What? How?'

It could be someone from the chatroom. It could happen. He could come to the house when Darren was at work and Joe was at school. Maybe it was the milkman or the postman or the window cleaner or someone else from a 1970s' British porn movie. She'd kept this so quiet. But why do it now? When so much was at risk? Maybe she'd been doing it all along.

He smeared his hands down his face. 'She's been acting weird and I keep asking her what's wrong and she just gets really angry.' He turned his stricken eyes on me. 'Did you know about it?'

I puffed a stream of indignant consonants. 'Of course not.'

He put his hands on his head. 'I don't want to lose her, Tommie. I can't believe this is happening.'

'But what makes you think . . . ?'

'I checked her phone. There's a number she keeps calling.'

'Did you call it?'

'Yes.'

'And?'

He clamped his teeth. 'A man answered.'

A little light turned on somewhere.

'What did he sound like?' I asked.

'What do you mean, what did he sound like? He sounded like a man. A bloody big man. With a big, deep voice.'

'Darren . . . I think I can explain . . .'

'You mean you did know?' His eyes were torn by betrayal.

'No, it's not . . . She's been ringing my housemate, he's g—'

'He's fucking dead, that's what he is.' He turned the key and forced the car into gear.

'No, listen, she calls his phone to talk to me because I don't have a mobile.'

'Oh, come on. Who doesn't have a mobile?'

'I don't.' Because I'm an idiot on the phone. Because I don't have a life. Because this is what happens when you have a life. It falls apart. I have successfully avoided having a life for quite some time. And anyway, I only have one friend and I live with him.

'She's been phoning him to talk to me because . . .' This would need to be pretty truthy. 'She hasn't been . . . feeling well.'

He left his hand on the gear stick but let the engine idle. 'What do you mean? What's wrong with her?'

'I think . . . maybe she needs some help.'

'You mean like a cleaner?'

'No, more sort of . . .' If I pushed over a single domino, the rest would fall in turn.

'You mean . . . like *you* had?' he said.

I shrugged. 'It does tend to run in families. . .'

Georgie would be outraged. But it would buy us time.

'Do you think I should have her sectioned?' he said.

Stop the dominos! 'Er, no. But I do think you should try talking to her.'

He pushed a hand over his head and I got a whiff of Dettol. 'But why wouldn't she tell me?'

'It can be hard for people to talk about . . . it.'

He dried his face with his T-shirt. 'She could tell me anything, I wouldn't care.'

'She didn't want to worry you.' My chest cramped at the accumulation of lies. I kneaded it away.

He gave me a soggy little smile. 'I really don't mind if she's nuts.'

'That's great.'

He let out a moan of relief. 'OK, I'll talk to her.'

He offered to drop me home and I made an effort to keep him talking on the way. On the subject of Joe, his chat flowed. He told me about Joe's GCSE choices and how Joe and his friend had formed a band and how I should put them in the magazine, they really were very good, if you liked that sort of thing.

I made approving noises, all the while berating myself for telling massive whoppers, manipulating him *and* consigning the unhappy/unfaithful woman to the asylum. How Victorian of me. It seemed like a good idea at the time, and it might even help, but it didn't make it any more acceptable. Feminism, sch-eminism. Shame on me.

Darren pulled up outside my house and I flung off my seatbelt.

'OK, so remember, just talk to her and . . . be patient,' I said.

He sucked in a lungful of air and smoothed his hands down his thighs. 'Suppose I should've known.'

'Sorry, Darren, I have to rush. I'm going to a . . . thing tonight.'

'Tommie?'

'Yes?'

'Go easy tonight?'

I smothered a burst of irritation. He was just a nice guy. He wasn't trying to hit a nerve.

Getting out, I could hear the house grooving to a familiar twang. I waved at Darren until his car turned the corner, then I ran inside. The Smiths' 'This Charming Man' was playing at stadium volume.

Blob seized me by the shoulders. 'I got it!' he screamed, swinging me round, swaying in a delirious Morrissey dance. 'I got it! I am *so* God!'

'Congratulations. Give me your phone.'

After an alarming five minutes listening to Georgie honking between a paper bag and a bottle of Dettol, she agreed to stick to my story. We would phone each other less and email more and she would delete everything sent and received. She said she looked forward to punching my lights out, which I took as a good sign.

18.

Blob was to appear in three TV commercials which would run throughout the year. The shoot would take two days, and he would be needed for another day for radio commercials and overdubbing, which we didn't understand but liked the sound of. That meant he would miss May's funeral on Thursday.

He twirled his greasy quiff as he spoke to Eleanor on the phone. She seemed sympathetic, supportive even, but something about the way he ate his chicken Balti, kebab meat on chips and king pepperoni pizza suggested he was still upset. When I said I'd go to the funeral, he let me have some of his chips.

The cemetery was close to the housing estate in the north of the city where May lived, and it was where Blob and I used to lie and drink and dream. The long soft grass around the cemetery's perimeter was perfect for hiding bottles of White Lightning and the gradient was made for Byronesque loafing.

The rain had returned, a soft grey drizzle, and I stood under my umbrella, one of forty or so people. After the coffin was lowered, mourners shuffled forward to speak to the family, and I moved with them. Now in their fifties, Eleanor and Sharon were wider than when I last saw them but little else had changed.

'Are you coming back for the wee tea?' Eleanor asked me. She'd said it to everyone. She was the older and taller of the two sisters, with thick grey-black hair in the same square style above her square jaw. Her freckled skin was wet and puffy.

'No,' I said. 'I've got to . . .'

'Tommie?' She clutched my arm in sudden recognition. 'My God, Tommie, you're very glamorous.'

'No, it's . . .' I pulled off the sunglasses, suddenly aware how 1980s' American oil heiress I must look, standing there at the graveside.

Eleanor noted the bruise and squeezed my hand. She touched her sister's arm. 'Sharon, look who it is.'

Releasing a bewildered woman from a hug, Sharon turned to face us. She had pale red hair, white blonde eyelashes and a bountiful nose. Her long black cardigan fell over her lumps and bumps. Both sisters had always seemed on the verge of a cackle and it lingered in their crow's feet, too deep to be shifted by grief.

Sharon moved closer and we bunched in the rainbow shade of our umbrellas.

'Tommie?' She peered at me. 'Och, love, thanks for coming.' She gripped me in a hug. Mourners ducked to avoid umbrellas. 'Are you coming back for the wee tea?'

'Sorry, I—'

'You have to come back for the wee tea,' she said. 'Come on, we're all going back. It's in the flat.'

I had only meant to come for the funeral. Eleanor held my hand as the last of the mourners paid their respects and headed to cars. A plump blonde in her early twenties, decked out in jeans, heels and a black strappy top like she was going to a club, linked her arm through Sharon's.

'Ready, Mummy?' she said.

'See you at the flat then?' Sharon said to me.

I nodded.

May's flat, on the ground floor of a small, utilitarian block, was Eleanor and Sharon's base, if not their home. It was where they and the family left things off, picked things up, took a break, had a sandwich and talked about nothing before moving on. The exhaust fell off my car as I left the cemetery and I arrived at the flat like the onset of the apocalypse. Squirming, I left the car at the end of the street. The door of the flat was open and I stepped inside.

My feet were silent on the soft, smudgy carpet and a sudden light-headedness reminded me to breathe. It was the smell. Of cigarettes she gave up years ago, of carpet, polish and ornaments, tights on a radiator and potatoes and Bisto. It was vegetables cooked to mush and stuck in the plughole, jokes about everything and no one mentioning that I never went home. I didn't leave home outright when Gloria's first little book of literary horrors was published. I just gradually stopped going back.

The family's voices had been loud enough to drown out the noise of my car. I stood beside the radiator in the hall, as mourners filtered through the front door and in and out of the tight kitchen, shaking hands, accepting drinks, uncovering sandwiches. Children waved biscuits and spilt orange juice. Like Blob, the family were tall and loud. They were dressed soberly and laughed persistently.

'Smells like egg and onion in here.'

'That's how you know somebody's dead. The sandwiches.'

'Thought you were meant to have tea at funerals.'

'We'll have tea at your funeral, I'm having a beer.'

A man I half recognised leaned round the door of the kitchen. He was short and balding with a wide neck and an overhanging belly in a thin white shirt. His face glistened with sweat. 'What do you want to drink, love?'

'Tea?'

He disappeared into the kitchen. 'Another tea.'

I heard a man's voice: 'Fuck's sake, could they not just have a beer?'

Stepped on, bumped into, smudged with toddler biscuit and tea-less, I wandered into the living room. The air was sticky and hot. I moved through thickets of people:

'. . . couldn't pass up on a unicycle . . .'

'. . . Teletext holidays . . .'
'. . . up his own arse . . .'
'. . . John Denver . . .'
'. . . sod brought Werther's Originals . . .'
'. . . never knew what camel toe was . . .'

The wallpaper had changed and the furniture was new but it all sat in the same place. By the wall, the settee where Blob and I had practised smoking languidly in case we had to do it for a movie; in the middle, the coffee table where we would roll joints and play hangman; in the corner, the TV, which we frowned upon as cretinous, viewed from our cerebral heights. The TV was now a giant widescreen. Imagine Blob on that. Widescream, ha ha.

In the opposite corner, Sharon sat on an armchair with her shoes off, a glass of Coke on her knee. Her cardigan lay over the chair and her bumpy arms were bare and blotchy. Her daughter sat on the arm of the chair and struggled to wipe a toddler's face as it wriggled and whined to be allowed to join the children spinning noisily through the flat. Extra chairs were lined up round the walls and older in-laws and neighbours had settled for the day, leaning, chatting, bantering. I knelt on the floor beside Sharon.

'Hello, love,' she said. 'Did you get a drink?' Back from the cemetery, she seemed flat and dazed. She tipped back her glass as her daughter drained a peacock blue alcopop.

There were no introductions in Blob's family, no reminders who everyone was. You were expected to know, or learn by osmosis. I couldn't remember the daughter's name but I knew she had a brother. As kids they were unusually laid-back, sharing their stuff without a fuss.

A cheer went up from the kitchen. Sharon's daughter stood up. 'That'll be our Adam back with the drink.'

Adam. That was Sharon's son. The daughter was – think think think – Emma.

'Do you want a drink?' Emma asked me.

'I'm fine, thanks.'

'Sure? There's plenty.'

'Just tea, if there's any going?'

'Back in a minute.' She stalked through the thickets, catching banter, her heels trailing the flattened carpet.

Sharon pushed herself up on an elbow and I smelt rum.

'Well,' she said. 'Good news about our Robert, isn't it?'

'He was gutted he couldn't come today.'

'Sure, he's wanted this a long time.' She hung with fatigue.

'He's really happy,' I said. 'Well, apart from being really . . . sad.'

She finished what was in her glass. 'I'm glad you and our Robert are still friends. He doesn't usually hold on to friends. I'm surprised you can stick him.' She dusted at her trousers.

'He sticks me.'

Her cheeks were flushed with heat and drink. She touched my arm. 'It's nice to see you again, Tommie.'

Emma returned with another alcopop, another rum-and-Coke, and a bottle of beer which she handed to me.

'They happen in threes,' Sharon said, shifting uncomfortably. 'Funerals.'

'I was at one recently,' I said. 'Does that count?'

Emma stared across the room at the old folks. 'We could always leave a toy on the stairs for her from number five. That would be three.' Her deadpan was frightening. I felt a rush of affection.

'Wasn't somebody close, was it?' Sharon asked me.

'Someone I knew through work.'

'Oh.' She rubbed her face. 'Where are you working?'

'I work for a magazine.'

'Still doing the writing then?'

'You could call it that.' If you had a generous spirit or were easily misled.

She studied my face, curious about my eye. 'And have you got a . . .' – she searched hard for the right term – '. . . partner these days?'

'No. And this was an accident. I fell.'

She leaned on her elbow, drink almost spilling. 'You were always having accidents, Tommie. I remember our Stephen had to take you to hospital.'

'Yes,' I said, getting to my feet. 'Well, I better go, Sharon. I just came to say how sorry I was about May.'

She squeezed my hand, her smile fading as it formed. 'Thanks, love. Sorry if I seem a bit out of it. I took a Diazepam there.'

'With Bacardi?' I chided. 'I think it might be bedtime.'

We shared an awkward shoulder hug, me up, her down, all rum and perfume sweat, and I broke away to sidestep through the living room.

The hall was jammed with kitchen overspill, drinks close to chests. I heard Eleanor's unmistakable laugh and peered into the packed kitchen. She stood by the fridge with another woman. They held onto one another, laughing into the backs of their hands. With a stream of 'excuse me's and 'sorry's and 'if I could just's, I wormed my way in. Three mountainous men, not having seen each other for years, hugged like footballers and I was walled in. A hand caught my wrist and Eleanor pulled me through.

'How've you been, Tommie?' She caught tears on her knuckles. 'Sorry. Have you been alright?'

'I've been fine. What about you?'

She gripped her temples with a finger and thumb and her features crumpled. I put my arms around her.

'I just keeping thinking about our Robert,' she said into my neck.

'Why? He's OK, isn't he?'

'He was only a wee boy when his mummy died.' She sobbed into my shoulder until my bra was damp.

'Had Bl . . . Robert's mum been ill?' I asked, trying to be tactful. I never knew what happened to her.

Her wracked smile ripped into me. 'No, she fell down the stairs drunk.'

All the times he'd picked me up when I was pissed. All the things I'd done. All the things he'd said. This room was stifling.

'But he's alright now,' I said, breath catching on heat. 'He's going to be really successful.'

She smoothed her hair. 'He thinks everybody's out to hurt him, Tommie. What if he never meets anybody? *We* won't be around forever.'

'He will meet somebody. And he'll always have his fag hag.'

Her crow's feet deepened.

'And you wouldn't believe how many men are in love with Morrissey,' I continued. 'I beat them off with his man bag.'

'Och, love.' She put her arms around me. 'I'm glad yous are alright. Here look, you won't need a shower now.' She smoothed my wet shoulder, cackling loudly. It was as good as crying.

The short, pot-bellied man in the thin white shirt put his hand on Eleanor's arm. 'Shift yourselves, I'm putting the sausage rolls in.'

Eleanor moved one way and I moved the other as he opened the fridge.

'Sorry, Eleanor, I have to go,' I said. 'I have to get back to work.'

'You and Robert look after yourselves.' She released me with a squeeze of my hand. She looked down at the man who pushed things around inside the fridge.

'Not in there, Fatso,' she said. 'That's the freezer.'

'Yes, dear,' he mocked.

Outside, I breathed grey, damp air. May's garden was a small patch of paving with empty pots under the window. A small group stood outside smoking, chatting, joking, and among them I could see Stephen, Eleanor's son. I remembered him as tall and thin with wispy bristles and rock and roll hair. He was heavier now, with short hair and a goatee beard. His crow's feet extended into his cheeks.

I hadn't seen him since I was fifteen, since the day he took me to hospital. I hadn't seen him *on* the day he took me hospital. I should say thanks at least. He raised his cigarette in a wave before going back to his conversation and I headed for my car. We wouldn't talk about it. For all their noise and natter, Blob and his family didn't talk. They glossed and distracted and made light of things. Coming from a home where feelings were let like blood, I was an easy convert. Blob and I built our friendship on it and I couldn't have been more comfortable.

But every time I got drunk and fell over, I rubbed his face in his past. Every time he put me to bed, I reminded him of it. Maybe, sometimes, we both needed to hear the truth.

19.

To: Tommie Shaw
From: Liam McMullan
Subject: News

Babe
There has been a positive development.
Meet me at Dock tonight at 7. I've booked dinner.
Wrap up warm.
À bientôt . . .

L
xxx

Sent from my BlackBerry

To: Tommie Shaw
From: Mature Lady
Subject: I HATE YOU

OH MY GOD, THIS IS THE WORST IDEA YOU EVER HAD. HE
WON'T STOP GOING ON AT ME TO SEE A DOCTOR. HOW
CAN I SEE A BLOODY DOCTOR? I CAN'T GO TO SEE A DOC-
TOR AND ANYWAY, I'D BE FUCKING LYING, WOULDN'T I? I
AM GOING TO KILL YOU. WHAT A STUPID BLOODY MOVE.

WHAT ABOUT THE BOOK? WHAT'S HAPPENING?
YOU SAID YOU WOULD LET ME KNOW.
G

✿

To: Mature Lady
From: Tommie Shaw
Subject: Re: I HATE YOU

I told you it would buy us time and it's working, isn't it? And it
wouldn't do you any harm to see a doctor. You have anger issues.
Take a deep breath. And another one. And a couple more. Liam has
the book – I'm getting it tonight. Is it safe to call when I have it or
should I email?
Is this your work email?
T

✿

To: Mature Lady
From: Tommie Shaw
Subject: Re: I HATE YOU

Did you get my reply?
Where did you go?
Are you OK?
T

✿

To: Tommie Shaw
From: Mature Lady
Subject: Re: re: I HATE YOU

YOUR EMAIL BROUGHT ON AN ATTACK AND HE CAME HOME
IN THE MIDDLE OF IT. HE'S WORRIED NOW BECAUSE I'M
HAVING PANIC ATTACKS AGAIN AND *I HAVE DEPRESSION*.
THIS IS AWFUL. AS IF ONE BIG LIE WASN'T BAD ENOUGH.
I WANT TO RUN AWAY.
RING ME WHEN YOU HAVE IT. I'LL KEEP THE PHONE ON
SILENT AND I'LL GO TO THE DOWNSTAIRS LOO WHEN
YOU RING.
YES, THIS IS MY WORK EMAIL.
THE BATHROOM'S LOOKING NICE, THANKS FOR ASKING.
ARE YOU DELETING THESE??
G

To: Mature Lady
From: Tommie Shaw
Subject: Re: re: re: I HATE YOU

By tonight, we'll know what to do, OK? So don't panic, ha ha (sorry).
Yes, I'm deleting everything.
Do you moderate the chatroom in that font?
T

To: Tommie Shaw
From: Mature Lady
Subject: Re: re: re: re: I HATE YOU

YES. WHY?
G

❀

To: Mature Lady
From: Tommie Shaw
Subject: Re: re: re: re: re: I HATE YOU

No reason.
T

❀

To: Patricia McNeill
From: Tommie Shaw
Subject: favour

Do you have a few minutes after work tonight?
To do my face?
T

20.

I took my shit-together face shopping on Thursday evening before meeting Liam. Unnerved by Blob's growing panic over what to wear to the CAC reunion the following night, I thought I'd look for something new. But the overheated shops blazed with premature spring and summer collections. I looked out at people trudging wet streets, heads bowed against fuming rain. I couldn't imagine how the sun felt on my skin. I fingered through the sale rail of winter clothes and found a black top that covered me from neck to hips. It was perfect. In fact, I had another one just like it, in charcoal.

I checked my reflection before setting off for the restaurant. My shit was still together, in a Barbie-attends-a-business-meeting-in-the-Underworld kind of way. Patricia had more problems covering the shadows under my eyes than the fading bruise, and donated more sleeping tablets when I asked. She looked uncertain though, and advised me to see my own doctor, if only for my skin's sake.

It was a short walk to Dock from the city centre. It was on a narrow, cobbled side street in the Cathedral Quarter, where nineteenth-century warehouses, banks and merchant buildings sought atonement through food and culture. I had slashed a press release to pieces about the restaurant and knew that it was one of the city's newest and its chef had won awards, but that's all I could remember. I would have preferred a street corner. A restaurant would be wasted on my tight, nervous stomach, but Liam wanted more and I understood why. He'd done the seemingly impossible for me. Surely I could afford him an hour of my company.

Outside the restaurant, the narrow grey entry was lit by repro gas lamps and a few diehard smokers shivered under an awning that

155

gushed rainwater at both ends. I needed two hands to lift the iron latch and push open the door. The noise inside was like every nation, tribe and language, and the smell of fried liver was eye-watering. The place was lit by gas lamps and candles, and three long bench tables ran the length of the room, packed with noisy diners. At the far end was a huge open fire with a chimney breast wide enough to accommodate five or six children.

A maitre d' approached, wearing a long white apron tied round the middle. His hair was slicked back and shiny and he had the moustache of a circus strongman.

'Welcome to Dock,' he said. 'Do you have a reservation?' His Belfast accent had undergone a tortured process of poshification.

'I'm meeting a friend here. Liam McMullan?'

'This way, please.'

I followed him along a dark furrow between benches. People chatted and guffawed over splashy food in what looked like tin plates and tankards. The maitre d' stopped and hovered near the middle of a bench. The gap looked like the personal space between two diners, who themselves were sardined against others. It would take a co-ordinated effort to work our elbows.

Liam smiled and tried standing but his knees were trapped and he semi-squatted. I apologised to my neighbours as I clambered onto the bench, stuffing my bags below and retracting my elbows.

But Liam was still standing, still leaning in my direction. I stood up, pissing off the neighbour to my right, and brushed Liam's cheek quickly. I moved back but Liam stayed where he was, wanting to do the other cheek. I rose again, pissing off the neighbour to my left.

'Amazing place, isn't it?' Liam said, sitting at last, straining to be heard.

'Yes,' I yelled back. I took in the high vaulted ceiling with its heavy lamps, pulled my scarf tighter and shuddered involuntarily. 'Is the heating broken?'

'No, it's always like this. The place is inspired by old Belfast. No mod cons.' He leaned over the table. Under his raincoat, his black polo shirt was a cool brand but he was heavier now and it gave him moobs.

'The menu is incredible,' he said. 'It's on the blackboard behind us.' He offered up the first coy smile of the evening and I summoned silent venom in defence.

'God, it's good to see you,' he said. 'I think your black eye is starting to fade.'

I felt the neighbours' eyes slide in my direction. I fixed Liam with a stare, which he missed.

'I just thought that, you know, after that,' – his nose wrinkled – 'little café the other day, you might like to try something a bit, you know, a bit more contemporary Belfast?'

'A bit more what?' I looked at my neighbour's plate. His pie had chicken's feet sticking out of it.

'It's quite loud in here,' Liam said. 'Lean in a bit, so we can talk.'

'I'm happy to shout.'

He rallied. 'It takes weeks to get a table. But I know the chef. He's written a book about the history and richness of local food.'

'I hope he put that little café in it.'

He laughed awkwardly.

A waitress with a billowing nineteenth-century bun appeared behind Liam. She wore the same full-length apron as her colleague, tied in the middle. 'Are you ready to order?'

'I think so.' Liam swigged from his tankard. 'You first, Dollface.'

I winced. I might develop a tic before the meal was over.

On the wall behind us was a blackboard with a short but energetically scrawled list, featuring trotters, tongue, sweetbreads and various entrails that had been pinioned, harassed and generally abused. My stomach contorted, killing the butterflies.

'Are they the specials?' I asked.

The waitress, unmoved by human frailty, said, 'Chef creates a daily menu based on fresh ingredients. That is what we have today. He is Michelin-starred.'

'What are the sides?' I asked.

'Colcannon. Cabbage. Marrowfat peas.'

'I'll have colcannon. And a large glass of red wine.'

'In the nineteenth century, ordinary folk had no access to wine. Will stout suffice, madam?'

'As long as it has lots of alcohol in it, yes.'

'And for you, sir?'

Liam ordered oxtail accompanied by something awful, in a reduction of something deeply disturbing. The waitress whisked away and Liam fiddled with his fork. I concentrated on taking off my scarf. Sitting so close to fellow diners rendered heating completely unnecessary, I realised. What fun for us all. How clever. How cynical. I wished we'd met at a street corner.

'Did you get the book, Liam?' I asked. 'Can I see it?'

'The book?' He stopped fiddling.

Knots formed and reformed in my gut. 'Yes, can I see it?'

'I don't have the book.' He gave a confused smile.

'What do you mean, you don't have it?' I gripped the table.

A waiter slopped down a tankard of headless unappealing stout.

'You said there had been a positive development,' I said, feeling my ankles twinge. I finally understood the feeling. It was like a cliff crumbling under my feet.

'I've tracked down a copy,' he said. 'But I don't have it yet. I just thought it would be nice to . . . where are you going?'

Neighbours harboured noticeable grudges as I extricated myself from the bench.

'Cigarette,' I said.

Outside, I shivered and watched water pour from the awning. Liam joined me, hands in pockets, shoulders up. He took off his scarf and put it around my neck. I resisted its warm woody smell.

'The book's on its way,' he said. 'That's what I wanted to tell you. It's in the post.'

'*In the post?*' Three little words for the desperate and the damned.

'We just have to be patient.' He brought a hand out of his pocket for emphasis. He was wearing chinos. Maybe he got them free with his cords. 'The guy is putting his career on the line. And I had to promise to take on *his* book. It's about docking dogs' tails, for God's sake.'

I chewed my hair. That sounded genuine. Ish. But I could imagine Georgie's reaction.

'It's the embargo.' Liam shrugged. 'They do it with high-profile books, if they're likely to be controversial.' He tried the coy smile again. 'Or if they suck.'

'When will it be here?'

'Saturday probably.'

'Probably?'

'Saturday definitely.'

That was the day before Gloria's last excerpt in the paper. The week before her book launch. The day after the reunion. The day of the poetry festival. I'd have to read it in between poets and, if the reunion fulfilled Blob's hopes, probably hungover.

He stepped closer, as if it were a dare. His eyelashes were thick, like his eyes were lined with kohl. I used to lick his face. *Don't think about it.*

'Can I have a cigarette?' he asked.

I handed mine over and he lit up self-consciously.

'You don't smoke any more, do you?' I said.

'Not really,' he said, looking at his cigarette. 'But I like doing this with you. It reminds me of when we used to go to gigs.' He exhaled slowly and jammed a finger in his eye as smoke drifted in his face.

We had gone to see live bands all the time when we were together. It was how we met. It was our thing. We must have seen hundreds but our heads were at a permanent love angle, nibbling, nuzzling and touching, and really we saw none.

I pulled the plug on the reverie. 'Don't call me pet names, Liam,' I said. 'I don't like "Dollface". It makes me sound empty. It makes you sound like a twat.'

He rubbed his eye. 'I always called you that.'

'I always hated it.'

'Why didn't you say?'

'You're right. I should have told you I'm not a doll. It's my fault.' I watched rain bounce off the cobbles.

'Well, I'll try to be more gender-aware, babe.' His low laugh in the dark made me think of snogging on a doorstep. It had been a while since I had snogged someone I loved on a doorstep.

Noise tumbled out of the restaurant and a raucous party bustled onto the cobbles, all Barbours and boots and rah-rah-rah.

'Where to next?'

'Where stays open late?'

'The rain! My hair!'

'Come on, Jude, get us a taxi!'

Jude hobbled by on pinnacle heels, dwarfed by the jumbo green leather bag she chased around in, cigarette dangling from her lips. I stepped back, cursing this town for being too small to have more than one fashionable restaurant at a time.

'Oh let me have a fucking smoke, will you?' she muttered. 'Aoife, order a fucking taxi, for fuck's sake.' She squinted at us. 'Got a light, chum?' Her face lit up, as though Jesus himself had broken through her clouds.

'Fuck me.' She staggered forward. 'Look who it fucking is. I didn't think this was your scene. Not very C2DE, this place. Is this the man then?' She sank her talons into Liam's arm. 'You and her, I know about . . .' She tapped her suspiciously fine nose and tried whistling through her dry tortoise lips.

Liam's shoulders were stiff enough to repel bullets.

'Come on, Jude!' The men clattered down the entry. 'Aoife's got a cab!'

'Better go.' Jude stepped away, her huge shopping bags jostling. 'Entertaining the new fucking clients.' She drew a small whip from a bag and threw her big grey gums in our faces. 'Equine feature.' She ripped the whip through the air. 'Ha ha ha. Ah? Ah?'

She lurched along the cobbles, shopping bags on her shoulders swaying like the wings of a dead pterodactyl. One of the bags was from Venus. Dear God, she worked hard for her money.

'What the hell was that?' Liam asked, shaken but recovering, as though from a minor car crash.

'My boss.'

'*That's* your boss? Oh, Tommie, come on.'

I'd forgotten how patronising he could be.

'Let's go in,' I said, handing back the scarf. Let's get this over with.

We resumed our places, neighbours bristling with tight-lipped irritation as we knocked gruel off their spoons. Our plates had arrived and the sight and smell of the bony swill on Liam's tin plate had me diving behind my tankard. He pointed at his food as he ate, rolling his eyes, emitting grunts. He offered to let me try and I waved no thanks. I forked at the super-salty colcannon and took refuge in the stout.

Liam mopped his plate with hunks of soda bread and then froze mid-swipe. 'I just had a thought,' he said. 'You haven't turned vegetarian, have you?'

As a child, I ate the vegetarian food Mo made for the house and my first sausage roll was like someone else's first spliff. I ate meat but in polite and guilty amounts.

'No,' I said, poking at the marshy food. 'I think I'm just a bit stuck in the present for this place.'

He sucked marrow from an oxtail, chin shiny with grease. 'Sometimes I think it's good to revisit the old.' He wiped his face with a napkin. 'To experience with fresh eyes, if you know what I mean.'

I watched him closely. 'Rehashing the old doesn't take you anywhere new.'

'So much for Darwin.' He grinned.

I hoisted up my cheeks in my most hollow smile. 'You know what I mean.'

He set down his napkin and sat back. 'You know, ba—Tommie. You know how I said yes to this guy about his dog tail book?'

'Yes?'

'Well . . .' He chewed his cheek. 'It could be hard for me to sell something like that to a publisher.'

Suspicion flickered. 'So . . . ?'

'But if I had a bit more leverage, you know, if I was to offer them something really interesting at the same time . . .'

'Like what?'

He leaned in. 'I think you should write a book about . . .' He glanced left and right and mouthed, 'You know who.'

'Voldemort?'

'Don't piss about, Tommie. This is a real opportunity.'

'Sorry, Liam, is that the time? I have to go.' I lifted my scarf and bag and clambered out, the people next to me protesting loudly.

'Tommie, wait—'

'Thanks for the lovely . . . yes. Thanks, bye. I'm just tired. Bye. Thanks.'

'Wait! Shit—' His voice was swallowed by din as I made for the door.

I quick-marched over the cobbles, head tucked tight under my umbrella. So that's what this was about. I should have insisted on a street corner. I could have escaped without the self-deception. I thought he wanted me, but it was the opportunity he wanted. He should have known not to propose something like that. He'd probably told other people, in anticipation of selling his 'something really interesting'. I raged red under my umbrella. Who else knew? Who had it spread to?

I slalomed through shoppers. Cars and buses snaked and braked, lighting the rain with their headlamps. And it was me who had invited him in! I started it. It was my fault. What a fool.

Out of the main shopping area, I passed blank-faced office buildings. Traffic moved freely, slashing by on wet tarmac. People queued at bus stops and headed to car parks. I heard his feet thudding along behind, his voice calling. I kept moving, umbrella held tight.

He tapped my elbow, out of breath. 'You forgot your shopping.'

The new top. 'Thanks.' I took the bag and kept walking.

He paced alongside. 'I forgot you liked to storm off.'

'I didn't storm off.'

'I felt like a dick back there.'

'Oh, fuck off.'

He stopped and I felt him watching me as I walked away.

'Do you still want her book or not?' he said.

I turned. 'I can't believe you'd threaten me with this. You can't coerce me into writing a book for you.'

'What are you talking about?' His glasses were spotted with rain and his coat was two-tone with it. 'What's coercion got to do with it? So you didn't like my suggestion, fine. But you asked for a favour and I pulled every string I could think of because I know I owe you, Tommie. If you think I've done enough, that's fine too, but I still don't know what I'm supposed to do with the book. Just tell me.'

I rubbed my eyebrows. What a leap of paranoia I'd made. I was underslept, perfect territory for overthinking.

'Yes, I still want the book.'

He approached. 'OK. So now I know.' He stood at the perimeter of my umbrella and it dribbled rain onto his cap. 'Give me a chance, Tommie.' He tugged my coat.

The venom rose up. 'To do what? Sleep with my housemate?' He wouldn't have you anyway.

'I'm trying to make amends.'

I watched traffic turn left and right at the end of the road. 'I won't be used, Liam. You should know that. I'm not an opportunity for you. For anybody.'

His cap was sodden with drips. 'This is *your* opportunity.'

'I couldn't do it.'

'If you think you shouldn't do it, that's understandable. But if you think you can't do it, you're wrong.'

He remembered I used to write. He even seemed to think I was good at it. I tipped my umbrella to the side, letting the dribbles fall onto the road.

He shrugged. 'Any dick can write a book.'

I moved the umbrella back to where it had been. It dribbled on him copiously.

'Will you think it over?' he said.

'You haven't told anyone, have you?'

'No.' He wiped his face with damp sleeves. 'Can I come under?'

I raised my umbrella and he moved in. His damp skin had barely aged. To cars passing, we would look like lovers. His stubble would feel good on my skin. *Don't think about it.*

He touched my fingers. 'Give me a chance.'

To touch him, to want him, to need his help, to look for fault and keep a distance because he hurt me and I wanted to hurt him – it was too hard.

'I better go.' I turned and walked away.

When I got home, Blob gave me his phone with just one small threat. He would get me a mobile with his first big fat pay cheque. I left him in his room, exploring yet another bag of shirts he'd bought at the charity shop ahead of the CAC reunion. Thirteen shirts had made it onto his shortlist, having met one criterion: 'if it doesn't smell like a dead man, it's in.'

I lay on the bed in my lamplit room and scrolled through the names until I found 'Turnip'. He often changed the name she was saved under but I could always guess which it was.

Georgie answered almost immediately. 'Hello,' she whispered.

'It's me.' I turned up the volume.

Her breathing was louder than her voice, and laboured, as if she was running out of air. 'Well?'

'He didn't have it.'

'Oh shit. Oh my God.'

'Georgie—'

'I just knew.' She honked as she sucked in breath. 'I've been—' Honk. 'Cleaning the downstairs—' Honk. '. . . Loo for an hour.'

Honk. 'I just knew.'

Her downstairs toilet was a converted cupboard under the stairs. I could imagine her crouching next to the vacuum cleaner, ironing board and spare light bulbs, going over the pan with a cotton bud.

'You're not using bleach, are you?' I said.

'Dettol.' Honk.

I listened to her scrub and honk. The toilet flushed. More scrubbing.

'I knew . . .' she whispered, 'he'd let you down.'

'He'll have it by Saturday.'

'Oh—' Honk. 'My God.'

'It's only the day after tomorrow. Not long.'

More frantic elbow grease.

'Georgie?'

She scrubbed and rubbed. 'Darren's driving me mad.'

'He just wants to take care of you.'

'I feel like I'm at the bottom of a well. . .' Honk. 'I can't see the top.'

I sat up. I knew that feeling. 'Georgie, maybe you *should* see a—'

She hung up.

I redialled but she didn't answer. I tried again, pacing the room, kicking knickers out of my path. Almost five minutes later, she called back. I froze, my hand on my chest.

'What happened, where did you go?'

'Joe wanted to use the loo.' Her voice was low, still breathy. 'I'm outside, sorting the recycling.'

I paced the room.

'I've been stealing Joe's cigarettes,' she said. 'I think he's started to notice.'

'Joe smokes?'

'Yes, Joe smokes. Can't tell him off, can I?' Honk.

'How's the garden?'

'Fresh.' Her teeth chattered and she ripped cardboard mercilessly.

'How's the bathroom?'

'Fine.' Honk. 'It's the rest of the house—' Honk. 'I can't stand.'

'It's only one more day,' I said, gratuitously chipper.

'Then what? I can't think beyond telling him.'

'We'll think of something,' I said. 'If we need to,' I added quickly.

'Can you bring the book when you get it?'

'I've to cover a festival on Saturday. I'll call as soon as I get it.'

Her breathing had evened out. She sounded like she was doing aqua aerobics instead of drowning.

I dropped onto my bed. 'Georgie?'

'What?'

'Have you been sleeping OK?'

'No, but I do the graveyard shift so it's fine. You?'

'Oh, like the dead.'

'Good for you.'

'Georgie?'

'What now?'

'What would you think if a man took you to an offal restaurant?'

'Awful? Or offal?'

'Both.'

'I'd think he was cheap.'

'It was very expensive.'

'I'd think he was an idiot. You went *out* with Liam, didn't you? I told you—' Honk. 'Not to get involved with him.'

'I know.'

Honk. 'He won't have changed, Tommie.'

'I know bu—'

'He loves the chase. . .' Honk. 'He can't help himself.' Honk.

'Don't worry, I'm not—'

'Get the book and leave it at that.' Honk. 'I have to go, he's coming. Bye.' She hung up.

I rolled over on the bed and looked at the dusty carpet tiles. All she had to do was last out till Saturday. She would have Darren's help and sympathy – until he had to learn about Joe not being his, *if* he had to learn about Joe not being his – then I would be there. I sent her a quick follow-up text suggesting she clean the skirting boards, but she texted back to say she already had them in the sink.

She knew me too well, she could always catch me out. But she needn't have worried about Liam. Of all the points he was making through his choice of restaurant – he had money, he was cultured, he was connected, he was deeply masculine, that revisiting what's gone before wasn't necessarily a bad thing – all I got was silk purse and sow's ear. Letting him back in would be crazy.

21.

On Friday morning, Blob and I waited for a table in Orbital's café. Blob had woken me with a mug of tea and a song at 8 AM, only five hours after I'd taken a sleeping tablet. He wanted to go out for breakfast to celebrate the end of his shoot, although I would have to pay because he had no money until his big cheque came. I suggested Orbital's place. I was in need of a decent meal and I still hadn't taken him up on his invitation. Blob protested loudly but I slept through most of it.

I had never known the café to be so busy. Every rickety chair and wonky table was filled with the usual scholarly types and foreign nationals, but now there were young mothers and children, backpackers, suits, ageing punks, cobwebby hippies, even a couple in high-vis and hardhats. All were perusing the menu, ordering and eating. The door jingled often, as people left or joined the queue. Betty, Audrey Hepburn and a waiter I didn't know waltzed through the tables, frazzled in the warm air.

Standing in the queue, I sent Jude a bleary text, saying I had no idea there were so many Irish poets and this might take a while. She replied saying she'd be in bed too if she had a man like that.

Blob was suspiciously quiet and went slightly pink as the waiter took us to a table and gave us menus. The waiter was tall and lithe with buoyant fair hair. As Blob's mood had lifted, so had his quiff and it now wobbled with indignation.

'*What?*' Blob accused me, when the waiter left.

'I didn't say anything.'

He turned his attention to the menu, his jaw on edge. 'Well, don't.'

He'd been defensive like this once before and I swam through cloudy synapses to remember. It was when I asked him about his partner in London. The clouds parted. He fancied the waiter. And when he clammed up, that meant it was serious.

I studied the menu but by the time I reached the end of one sentence, I'd forgotten how it began. I breathed deeply and blinked away blear. Driving to the café had been dangerous, as Blob had let me know with screams when I pulled out, jumped lights and alarmed pedestrians. One of my windscreen wipers had disappeared – I didn't know where – but luckily the rain was light.

I rubbed my eyebrows, wondering how I would survive work.

'There's nothing here I can eat,' Blob said. He watched the waiter move through the café. 'You never told me about the ambience.'

'That's because he's new.'

We examined the menus.

'No, really,' he said. 'There's nothing I can eat. What's asafoetida?'

'You worked in a deli, you tell me.'

'I sold the stuff.' He looked appalled. 'I didn't eat it.'

I felt someone touch my shoulder and looked up to see Orbital. He had the gleam of the enviably well-slept.

'Good to see you,' he said, settling his hand on the back of my seat. 'Hello, Blob, Robert – never quite sure what to call you.'

'God is fine,' Blob said.

'Blob just finished shooting a TV ad,' I said. 'He plays God.'

Orbital wiped his hands down his apron. 'Who's that for?'

'Devine Energy,' Blob said.

'I checked them out for solar panels. Too expensive. Now I see where the money goes.'

'I think you'll find my whore dollars are keeping you in business.'

'I think you'll find *I'm* paying,' I said.

'I think you'll find that's what I said.'

'Don't they have something to do with that Poetry Festival this weekend?' Orbital asked.

'Yes, I'm covering it for the magazine.' I bit my lip. I needed to wake up. Blob's ego was too big to see any connection between his getting the role and me working with Kevin Loane but I'd kept quiet about the festival just in case. I hid behind the menu.

'What's asafoetida?' I asked.

'You're looking at the lunch menu.' He turned it over. 'That's breakfast.'

'Oh, right.'

'That'll be a fun day,' Orbital teased. 'I know how you love poets.'

'Will there be refreshments?' Blob said. 'Wine and so on?'

'It will be a really boring day, Blob.'

'Well, obviously I'll come and support you,' he said. 'I hope you appreciate the sacrifices I make for you.'

'What did you think of Harland's story?' Orbital said.

At last, a tangent, although one I had purposely avoided all week. 'I didn't see it. How did it go?'

'I'll get it for you,' he said. He set his long hands on both our shoulders. 'This is on the house, by the way. Give me your menus. I'll sort you out with something . . .' He looked us over. 'Wholesome.' He loped back to the kitchen.

'What's the thing you're doing for Devine Energy?' Blob asked.

I rummaged furiously in my bag. 'Oh, it's just a sponsorship thing. Haven't had that much to do with it. I've been distracted, you know, what with Gloria and everything.' I found lip salve and applied it with great deliberation.

'You're not still worried about that, are you? She's your ticket to fame and fortune, Fatty. I thought you were a bit quiet. PMT?'

'Er, yes.'

His eyes followed the waiter. 'You should have said. Not that I would have cared.' He turned his attention to me. 'Oh, cheer up, little zombie.'

'Do I look that bad?'

'Don't worry, it'll be dark when we go to the reunion tonight.' He patted my arm. 'And no one will be looking at *you* anyway.'

The waiter arrived with two huge pale purple smoothies.

'Here you go,' he said in a low Scottish voice. He had round boyish cheeks, incongruous with his slim build. Blob's silence was like a hole in the room.

'I love Morrissey.' The waiter smiled.

Blob stared at his porky fingers.

'*What?*' he said to me, when the waiter left.

'I didn't say anything!'

The waiter brought plates piled high with veggie fries and mugs of steaming lapsang souchong. When he'd recovered from the paralysis brought on by the waiter, Blob segregated super-healthy super-seeded bread from eggs, tomatoes and mushrooms.

'We're going to Burger King after this,' he said.

'I have to go to work.'

He recoiled from the tea and sucked on his smoothie. 'I thought we could go shopping and you could drop me at the recording studio.'

'I got something new to wear last night.'

He shovelled breakfast in. 'Your bum will look big in it.'

'Are you working for Chris today?'

'Not if I can help it.' He scraped up eggy mess. 'This is nice.'

'Aren't you getting fed up with the hole in the wall?'

'Not at all. In summer it will be like a Roman villa.'

'If Chris lets us stay that long.'

'We can pay him back when we're rich and famous. Relax. You're going to think yourself to death.'

Orbital joined us with the newspaper. 'Here it is.' He handed me the paper, opened at the page devoted to the story.

There was an old photograph of Gloria and Mo, sitting on kitchen chairs outside the farm. Mo was smoking and patting one of the mongrels she'd adopted and Gloria was doing her usual pout. Below it was a close-up of Astra and Orbital, looking martyred. Their picture was set at an angle over a large, clear shot of the front of the café. The headline read:

HARMLESS HIPPIES SUFFER AT GLORIA'S HANDS

Harland denounced Gloria as a frumpy poetess-turned-attention-seeking-diva who spared no one in her quest to fill the papers. Mo was described as an elderly, fragile artist who helped spearhead the vegetarian movement in Ireland and used marijuana for medicinal purposes. Harland said that her son, proprietor of leading vegetarian café Orb, and her daughter, a Doctor of Divinity, were deeply saddened by Gloria's actions but, in the spirit of the hippy movement, were willing to live and let live. Gloria would find her reward in the 'karmic wheel of life'. Gloria was unavailable for comment.

'What do you think?' Orbital asked, his half-smile creeping back.

'But not everyone in here reads the *Northern News*.' I looked round the café. May used to read the *Northern News* but she'd gone to join the rest of the paper's readership. 'Where did all these people come from?'

Orbital shook his head in relief and disbelief. 'Internet. Things just took off. There's a Facebook page called Fork Off, Gloria, Leave Us Veggies Alone. One called Roll a Fat One for Mo and there's even one named Marijuana Mo for Mayor.' He took the paper and put it under his wiry arm. 'Some of them aren't even vegetarians. We're in Wikipedia, *Time Out*, the *Rough Guide*, I don't know what else.'

'And how's Mo?' I asked.

The half-smile faded. 'She's amused but she hasn't been very well. She said she hopes you're looking after yourself.' He glanced quickly at Blob, who'd surrendered to the healthy bread.

'I'm fine.'

'You look tired.'

'I'm fine, Orb.'

Betty appeared at the partition and beckoned Orbital urgently.

He held up the paper. 'Not everyone is on her bandwagon, Tommie.' He backed away, wiping his hands on his apron. 'Call in next week?'

I nodded vaguely. Like Georgie, I couldn't see next week either. I turned to Blob.

'I have a confession to make,' I said.

'You used to be a man. You used to be a woman.'

'I don't want to be famous.'

'I'm sure there'll be enough limelight to go round. You eating that?'

Orbital's fresh food helped with concentration and driving home was easier. Blob prattled on about the recording studio and the reunion, who might be there and which charity shop shirt smelt least infected, and I thought about the bandwagon Orbital mentioned. I didn't want to jump on a bandwagon going either way. Matricide was just for laughs, my way of making light. I didn't want to see anyone pilloried, not even her.

❧

To: Tommie Shaw
From: Liam McMullan
Subject: Last night

Hey Tommie
I think I probably came across as a little presumptuous last night. I hope you can forgive me. Maybe we could just go for a walk next time?
I'll give you the you-know-what when I see you at the festival tomorrow. We can arrange our walk.

Love
L
xxx

Sent from my BlackBerry

To: Tommie Shaw
From: Kevin Loane
Subject: Festival

Tom
Ideation, creation, indication, machination, fabrication, consumma-
tion, conflagration, depilation.
I've just learned that we're not the only sponsor. There are, in fact,
two major sponsors and at least seventeen lesser sponsors. I'm very
disappointed. I'll be there early to check our signage gets best posi-
tioning.
See you there.
Regards
Kevin

P.S. No one seems to know what time the bar opens. Any ideas?

To: Patricia McNeill, Bill Ogilvy, Seamus Hughes
From: Tommie Shaw
Subject: Service disruption

Wake me when Jude comes in?
Thanks.
T

22.

We stopped at the top of the stairs and looked round the bar.

'Who the hell are all these fat old people?' Blob's jowls wobbled. By the time I had got home from work on Friday, refreshed by the short siesta at my desk, Blob had worked himself into an adrenaline-fuelled, unbearably loud frenzy of anticipation. Anyone – Elvis, Gandhi, Barbra Streisand – was going to be a disappointment.

The reunion was in a part of town we didn't normally frequent, even though it was walking distance from our house. At either end of the 4x4-lined road, private schools hid behind mature gardens. Between them gleamed designer boutiques, glassy restaurants and bars stuffed with ex-rugby players insulting each other witlessly.

The bar looked Swedish, with its thoroughly designed seating and tables, and understated lights that gave drinkers a subtle glow. The reunion was in the 'VIP area' which, as far as I could tell, meant upstairs. Unidentifiable music rolled over the crowd as reunited drama queens screamed, boomed and acted out their interim years.

I touched Blob's arm. 'You're right, they're gross. Let's go home.'

I had joined CAC because I joined anything that took me away from home, as long as I could get a bus to it and didn't have to run. Over the course of my school career, I had been a euphonist, a dog walker, a reader in retirement homes, a singer in hospitals, a dancer in prisons and an award-winning speller. I was team-spirited and community-minded if it took up at least two evenings and a Saturday. The only thing I actually liked was spelling.

Behind us, I heard a woman's voice. 'Is this the CAC reunion?'

Blob and I turned to see a willowy woman in a silk jumpsuit, soaring diamante sandals and honey hair in an upscale up-do.

175

'Robert?' she said, revealing a perfect Hollywood smile. She touched her chest. 'It's me. Roberta.'

Blob screamed. 'Oh my God!' He flung his arms around her. 'Roberta!' He jumped up and down. 'Oh my God!'

Heads turned to see who was making the fuss, although if they'd thought about it, it would have been obvious. And to think I'd considered getting us some speed.

'Look at you!' Blob screamed. 'You're fabulous!'

Robert and Roberta, the yin and yang of obesity. Roberta used to be short and fat, mousey, greasy, retiring. Now, even the mole on her chin had vanished.

She batted her eyelash extensions. 'Look at you, Robert. Still a legend.' She fiddled with her clutch bag. 'God, I was so nervous about coming tonight.'

We moved aside to let others by. The bar was filling up and the noise levels were rising.

'Roberta,' Blob said excitedly. 'You know Tommie?'

She smiled politely. 'Sorry, my memory is really rubbish.'

'Let's get drinks,' Blob boomed.

The crowd parted as the mountainous man with the four-inch quiff moved through the room. We followed in his wake like quaking Israelites.

Blob took up position at the bar. 'Roberta, what would you like?'

'Mojito please.'

'You, Fatty?'

'Biggest gin in the world.'

'Money, please.'

I handed over my purse and he waved at a beardy barman.

Roberta leaned in close. 'Why do you let him talk to you like that?'

'I don't mind.'

She gave me a reproachful smile. 'You shouldn't let him, you know.'

My sense of humour was complicated and grimy. I put it away.

'Do you recognise anyone else?'

We peered around. The bar was packed and the competition between screamers and boomers was heating up. I didn't know anyone. Now that Blob had found a new-old friend, maybe I could slip away.

'Look, there's Marty,' Blob announced, passing the drinks. 'He used to be the leading man, remember?'

'I used to really fancy him,' Roberta said, sheepishly.

'He looks like a paedophile now, so you didn't miss anything.'

I touched Blob's arm. 'I think I might just—'

'Oh, wow!' A tall red-haired woman in a softly sparkling dress and discreetly expensive jewellery halted in front of us, hands on hips. 'What was it we used to call you – Boob . . . No, Blob! That was is it! Was it Marty who made that up? Oh, he was so funny! How lovely to see you all!'

'Blob' was in fact a May-ism – the diminutive of Blobert.

'What are you all up to these days?' Her eyes roamed all over us. 'Come on, spill, that's why we're here, isn't it!' She ripped the air with a brutal laugh.

It was Alice Malice, as Blob called her, the wham-bam am-dram superstar of CAC. She could crush the meek and charmless with one sweep of her nouveau-riche confidence. Having put on my Patricia face, she might not notice my bruise. Having hidden myself in Blob's shadow, she might not notice me at all.

Blob spoke in tones you could drink. 'I'm an actor and voiceover artist. Just out of the recording studio an hour ago.'

'Wow,' Alice said, eyes hard as mirrors. 'You must be talented after all. And what about you?' she asked, calculating Roberta's degree of polish.

'Just finished shooting a reality TV show.' Roberta smiled.

'Oh wow, isn't everyone doing well?' Alice's eyes were torn between curiosity and boiling hatred. 'What's the show called?'

'Big Blubber. I had a gastric band fitted. And a makeover.'

'Oh wow!' Alice screamed her monstrous laugh.

'I've never been so grateful for being fat.' Roberta's smile was as clear as Doris Day. She was too good for this world.

Alice's eyes fell on me. 'And you?' Her fine brows dipped at my blinglessness. 'Were you part of CAC?'

'For a while but I left.'

'And what are you doing now?'

'I work for a magazine.'

'Oh wow, which one?'

I felt like I was being mined. I opened my mouth but Blob chipped in.

'The *New Yorker*.'

'Wow,' Roberta said, eyelashes batting.

Alice nodded. 'Yes, I thought you looked very New York.'

'It's the city that never sleeps,' I said.

'What?' She stared at me for a moment. 'Wait, I do remember you. You were Blob's friend.' She touched her necklace. 'Oh wow, I remember now! When you didn't come back, Blob said you tried to kill yourself!' She screamed that hideous laugh. 'Trust you to make a song and dance out of a dropout, Blob!'

Blob lifted his chins and chortled, 'Bah-hah-hah-hah!'

Alice turned to me, approximating sympathy. 'Not everyone could hack the CAC.'

I looked at Blob but he perused the crowd, nose in his glass. I followed his gaze. The word 'wow' was everywhere, a Gatling gun of awe and admiration. In the hail of fakery, everything and nothing was true. I retreated further into Blob's shadow.

'And what are you doing these days?' Roberta asked Alice.

'I'm a stay-at-home mummy!' Alice's eyes glittered with bile. 'Three children and I've got them all on stage already. The eldest is sitting her first speech and drama exam tomorrow!'

Hiding behind Blob, I ordered tequila at the bar.

'Marty! Josie!' Alice shrieked. 'Wow, look at you! Come and join us! Look who's here! This way, this way!'

The beardy barman poured my drink. I downed it and ordered another.

Blob twisted round. 'What are you doing?'

'I'm thirsty.' I paid for my drinks and stayed at the bar.

'I'm not carrying you out of here.'

The gin tasted like mouthwash after the tequila. 'I can't believe you told them that.'

He looked over his shoulder and back to me. 'I had to tell them something, they were waiting on your script.'

Nudged and bumped by the heaving crowd, my gin slopped over my hand. 'You said you covered for me.'

'They thought it was a joke.'

'Who else did you tell?'

'No one. Now lighten up and join in.' He chortled into the crowd. 'Bah-hah-hah-hah!'

'I don't like these lovey types. They're fake.'

He tutted and sighed. 'Roberta's nice. There must be other nice people here. Just mingle.'

'*Nice*? You said you only came for the contacts.'

'Yes, but I'm not averse to having a good time. God, isn't there something you can take for PMT?'

'Yes, gin and cigarettes. I'm going for a smoke.'

I followed the signs to the smoking area. Which was downstairs, beside the front door. Which led to the street. Which was walking distance from home.

I walked home, picking up gin on the way.

I'm giving in.

I'm tired. I've tried.

I miss the handle, hit my face. Ow, idiot, my eye. Bag's on the floor, if I get on the floor I won't get up. Floor is fine. One with gin. Or two. Or just one. Better go bed.

Did I take one?

Ceiling is different . . .

❧

At the furthest end of a road. Up.

Wake up.

Don't shake me.

I can't, tornadoes.

'If you're not dead, wake up.'

I blinked into a blanket, brushed it off my face. I was still yesterday.

On the floor of the kitchen, Blob leaned against the settee and watched me. I sat up and leaned on the other settee. I could smell frost in the yard. I pulled the blanket up, numb and heavy with cold. The lamps were on and the stereo glowed in the pre-dawn light.

'Thanks.' I cleared my rusty throat. 'For the blanket.'

He stretched out his legs. He was still wearing his raincoat and his voice was hoarse. 'We went to a party.' He tossed flat hair out of his eyes.

Droplets of memory fell into place. 'Going to New York then?'

He took off his glasses and pushed the heels of his hands into his eyes. 'No.' He lit a cigarette and threw the pack and lighter to me.

'I can't keep doing this,' he said.

I lit up. 'You're getting too old.'

'I mean *this*. You.'

'Wh—?'

He looked at his brogues. 'Who did you think would find you? That day? In the cemetery?'

That day. In the cemetery. I rubbed sense into my face. He wanted to talk. I wanted to be sober, be awake, be ungroggy, to know how not to talk about this. But I couldn't. I had nothing to deflect with. I picked at the blanket.

'I wasn't thinking straight. That day. That summer.'

He studied his cigarette. 'I thought you were asleep. I thought you'd drunk yourself unconscious.' His voice was tired, sinking into whispers. 'But I couldn't wake you. Not even when you started choking on vomit.'

I pulled the blanket up.

'Did you never wonder?' He looked at me finally. With his glasses off, I saw fatigue, fear, grief. I pulled the blanket over my head.

'Yes,' I said.

'But you never asked.'

'I thought you were OK about it.'

'Did you? Seriously?'

'No.'

'Did you know I ran to May's to get help? Me. I ran. I was sure you'd be dead when I got back. The run nearly killed me.'

'I'm sorry.'

'I never understood why you would do that to me.'

'Make you run?'

'Take an overdose when I'd be the one to find you.' Something soft hit me on the head. He'd thrown a cushion.

'Is that why you didn't come to the hospital to visit me?' I asked.

He didn't answer.

'Or when I went into care?'

Nothing.

'Or when I went into hospital again?'

I listened to his silence.

He spoke softly. 'You abandoned me first, Fatty.'

I should fold myself up and put myself somewhere no one can find me. I'd done a terrible thing to him and now I was finding fault.

'I'm sorry,' I said.

'And you keep doing it.' He threw another cushion.

I pulled the blanket off. 'This is different, I just can't sleep.'

He put his glasses back on. 'It feels the same to me.'

We smoked in silence. I watched the rise and fall of his stomach, slowing with each breath.

He threw his cigarette into my gin, leaned back on the settee and closed his eyes. 'This isn't fun any more.'

I slept on the floor, my head on the cushions he'd thrown.

Beyond the dry, unmoving plastic sheet, the yard was sharp under white sun. I plugged in the electric fire. The floor was spread with stale drinks, scrunched magazines, mugs, cement splashes, ash, takeaways and Blob. He was in the same place, chins concertinaed on his chest, glasses on the precipice and brogues at ten to two. I tugged a blanket over him and pulled another round myself, flinching at a stuffy headache. I could hear cars passing and guessed it was late morning. The morning of the Festival. The morning of the book.

Breaths scraped down Blob's throat like bins pulled along a path. Our earlier conversation didn't seem real but there he was, sleeping it off. It lingered like mental indigestion or a reverse nightmare in which I was the torturer. I'd traumatised him, abandoned him and made him talk about it. Or had he made me talk about it? I ran my hands into my hair. He was the one who brought it up. And he never talked about the serious stuff. Next stop *Jeremy Kyle*. What had I done to us?

'Hey, Fatty.' His voice was octaves lower than usual. He flicked his flat grey quiff and pushed up his glasses. His Play-Doh beard was back. 'Something about your hair in the morning really does it for me.'

'Morning,' I said delicately. 'Tea?'

He took out his phone. 'Fuck-a-doodle-do, look at the time.' He stretched his arms straight up and his features disappeared into head fat. 'Jesus!' he puffed. 'I've still got my coat on. Make toast, Fatty. I'm going for a slash.'

By the time he returned, the kettle was on, the toast was in and I was bursting for a pee and dancing by the door. When I came down, the tea was made, the toast was buttered and he'd set mine on the floor by my usual settee.

Reclining nonchalantly with an arm over the back of the settee, he tapped his fingers like mouse feet. 'Aye, aye, aye,' he sighed. 'Know what I mean?'

I nodded, tucking into toast.

The mouse feet went on. 'So. You were, what . . . in a children's home?'

'Yes.'

'What was it like?'

Tantrums, stone throwing, gum, dope, hysterics. 'Screamy.'

'How long for?'

Indefinable, drug-misty. 'I'm not sure. I lost my marbles.'

He watched the mouse feet. 'I didn't know.'

At the time, I felt it was only right that he didn't come to see me, he was better off without me. Now, I realised, I'd probably left him terrified.

'S'okay,' I said through toast.

He nodded, chins wobbling. I gulped thick tea. He sighed melodically.

'La-la-la.'

'Out with it, Blob.'

'Did you do it again? After the first time?'

Crosses cut in pig flesh.

'Sorry, Fatty.' He leaned across. 'Sorry. Won't mention it again.'

I pushed my plate with an inchworm finger. 'No, I'm sorry. I should have said it before. I'm sorry I didn't. I'm sorry for . . . you know.'

He lifted his mug. 'A toast.'

I held up my mug.

'To not talking about it,' he said, resolutely.

'To holding it in till your arteries harden,' I rejoined.

'To the way it should be.'

'To the way it was.'

'Forever and ever.'

'Amen.'

We polished off our tea.

23.

The car rocked as Blob dropped into the passenger seat.

'It will be incredibly boring,' I said, putting on my sunglasses. The day was pin bright. The houses basked in early spring sun and children kicked a ball off the cars. Hitting my face on the kitchen door the night before had brought fresh bruising to my eye.

Blob pulled his seatbelt across. He'd showered, shaved, resurrected the hair. 'I like poetry.'

'Don't be ridiculous.'

'You don't want me to come to this Festival. You're meeting a man. A new man. An old man. A dirty old man. Let me come.'

'I don't want you to be bored, that's all.'

'There will be lots of people to talk to. I like people.'

'They're boring, freakish people.'

'I don't mind.' He gave me a beguiling smile. 'I live with you, don't I?'

'There will be a limit on the free drink.'

He tutted. 'Drop me at Oxfam, I'll do some shoplifting.' He'd spent all his money on 20p shirts but he was still wearing the fat jumper under his raincoat. He could probably fit a few albums up there. 'So, what time will you be back from this Festival thing then?' he said.

I rubbed my eyebrows. 'Why?'

He pushed his glasses up. 'I don't really have much planned today.'

He was broke, his favourite aunt had just died and I had spent a

184

proportion of the night, if not the past fifteen years, torturing him.

'Oh fuck it, you can come, alright?' I said. 'But I have to work, I can't get pissed.'

He slapped his hands on his thighs. 'Well, let's arise and go now, Fatty.'

My gloom had grown while I showered and only the thought of Patricia and Bill jobless, homeless and wedding receptionless, kept me from crawling back into bed. I was glad of Blob's company. Walking into the valley of the shadow of death, anyone would appreciate a comforting chinwag on the way. I would just have to make sure he didn't meet Kevin while I was with him. If I was vigilant and moved fast, it couldn't be called abandonment.

I turned the key. The car coughed and died.

I turned the key again. The car coughed and died.

'Come on, you bastard.' I turned the key, the car coughed, and Blob's door fell off and clattered to the pavement. Blob and I stared at the door, rocking gently where it fell.

'I think we have some parcel tape,' Blob said. He brought out his phone. 'Or maybe I'll just call Chris.'

The limo's window rolled down with a quality hum.

'Where would you two be without me?' Chris chuckled. 'Jump in. Tourists in the back, but you still have to pay. I'll put it on your tab.'

Blob opened the door and I followed him in. It was like the mobile grotto where Santa kept his whores. Pink and red leatherette seats lined one side with a gleaming chrome drinks cabinet in the middle. Trickling lights ran the length of the limo and formed a frame round a TV screen at the back.

Blob screamed. On the puffy pink seat were three other Morrisseys. They froze before launching to embrace him, laughing, clapping and back-slapping.

'Ready?' Chris chuckled over the intercom.

The Morrisseys cheered:

'Jawohl!'

'OK!'

'Let's go!'

The limo moved off and the Morrisseys introduced themselves: Jürgen was from Germany, Hao was from China, Hanneke was from Amsterdam. They were visiting a few Irish cities on their way to Limerick to attend a Morrissey Symposium.

'I didn't know there was a Morrissey Symposium,' Blob said, starry-eyed.

'Aren't you in our Facebook group?' Hanneke asked. She was tall and athletic, with Morrissey hair and glasses.

'We're getting the train there tomorrow,' Jürgen said. I'd never seen Morrissey with a moustache. It was mind-bending.

'Come with us,' Hao said.

'Should I?' Blob asked me, bouncing in his seat.

'Aren't your coffers a bit empty?'

'Oh, here's an idea!' Blob wriggled his fingers at them. 'You come with us! We're going to a Festival of Irish poetry! You'll love it!'

Jürgen shrugged, thinking it over. 'We have done the tour of Belfast.'

'I write poetry,' Hanneke said.

'Will Roria be there?' Hao asked.

Blob looked at me urgently. With Hao's heavy Chinese accent, I wasn't sure whether he meant him, her or both of them. According to the internet, Gloria was filming Celebrity Fit Club – The Relay. Blob's eyes widened, urging my response. He desperately wanted the Morrisseys to come. And they'd keep him distracted.

'Er, yes,' I said.

'Let's go,' Hao said to his friends.

Blob jerked in his seat. I thought he might be delirious with Morrissey fever but he drew out his buzzing phone, looked at it and dropped it in my lap. 'Eugh.'

The screen flashed: 'Swamp Donkey'.

I jammed my finger in my ear as the Morrisseys felt one another's hair and compared glasses.

'Georgie?'

She panted, breath trapped in her chest.

'Georgie, are you OK?'

'T . . .' Laboured squeaks.

'In through your nose, out through your mouth, Georgie.'

The Morrisseys sang, 'I would go out tonight . . .'

Chris's voice: 'Do you want the karaoke on, lads?'

The Morrisseys cheered. I forced my finger in my ear till it hurt.

'Georgie?'

'I'm . . .' Honk.

'In for five, out for five.'

'I'm . . .' Honk.

'Where's the Dettol?'

'S . . .' Honk, honk, huge snort, orgasmic hoot.

My stomach scrolled in on itself. 'Speak, Georgie!'

'Oh my God . . .' Honk.

'What happened?'

'Can't . . .'

'Count, breathe.'

'Can't . . .' Honk. 'Move.'

'What?'

'Had to run.' Honk. 'I'm stuck.' Honk.

'Where?'

Hanneke warbled into the mike '. . . jumped up pantry boy . . .' She looked more like Morrissey than she sounded. And she didn't look like Morrissey.

'I had to . . .' Honk.

'Yes?'

'Get out . . .' Honk.

'Yes?'

'Of . . .' Honk.

'Yes?'

'The . . .' Honk.

'Keep going.'

'House.' Honk, honk.

'You left the house? Where are you now?'

'Over . . .' Honk.

'Where?'

'The fence.' Honk.

The Morrisseys continued their mutual appreciation.

'The fence?'

'The garden . . .' Honk. 'Fence.'

'Next door?'

'The alley.' Honk.

'Stay where you are.'

Honk. 'Can't . . .' Honk. 'Move.' Squeak. 'Anyway.'

I hung up.

'Chris?' I spoke to the ceiling. It was like talking to the spirit world.

'Yello,' he chuckled over the intercom.

'Can we make a detour?'

Horror spread over Blob's face.

Chris chuckled. 'On the tab, my friend.'

I gave him directions to Georgie's house.

We pulled up at the end of the narrow fence-lined alley at the rear of the house. It was scattered with bins and burst rubbish bags and the fences were sprayed with artless graffiti. I walked through sunny bin stink and gusts of laundry, peering behind each bin and bag, calling my sister in self-conscious whispers. I found her, huddling next to her own sweet-smelling bin, Dettol between her knees, hands over her curls.

I knelt. 'Georgie?'

She looked up, eyes wide and unfocused, skin grey.

'You OK?' I asked.

She searched my face. 'Have you got it?'

I touched her arm. 'No, I said I would call.'

'I have to see it.' She gripped her hair. 'I have to know.'

Johnny Marr's twanging guitar drifted up the alley.

'Is Darren home?' I asked.

'Working.' She snorted Dettol. 'I had to get out. Oh my God.'

'Will I help you over the fence?' It had been a long time since we'd climbed anyone's fence. She must have vaulted using a mop. Neither of us was particularly athletic but as long as she didn't mind a broken collarbone, I was sure I could get her over.

'I have to see it, Tommie.' Misery made her wilt.

'I don't have it yet.'

'I can't wait any longer.'

'Then you are stuck, aren't you?' I looked up and down the alley for inspiration. There was warmth in the low sun. Brittle leaves skittered by. I rubbed my neck. 'I think it's better if you go inside, Georgie.'

'The house makes me sick.'

'It must be clean by now.'

She honked into the Dettol. 'Every room reminds me of feeling like this.'

I understood. I had a ceiling like that. 'But you can't stay here.'

She pulled her white jumper over her knees. 'I'll stay here till you get the book.'

The day was wearing on and Kevin would be looking for me. I took Georgie's hand. Her fingers felt light and watery.

'The bin men might take you,' I said.

She gawped down the alley. 'Is that a limo?'

'Yes.'

'Did you come in a limo?'

'Long story. Yes.'

'I like limos.'

'Come for a ride.' I tugged her hand but she stayed where she was.

'I can't.'

'It's either this or over the fence. You can't stay here.'

She stared at the limo, fighting with possibilities.

'I'm going to get the book now,' I said. 'Come with me. Then it will be over.'

'In a limo?'

'Yes.'

She took a shaky breath. 'Give me a cigarette.'

I took out the pack and handed her one, the click of my lighter loud in the empty alley. We smoked without talking. She stared at the stained path. I hoped she was summoning the old Georgie, the bitch, the bitch-slapper, the slapper.

I threw down my cigarette and stood on it. She did the same. Then she lifted the butts and put them in the bin.

'Ready?' I said.

'Oh my God.'

She snorted Dettol as I led her to the limo and stopped breathing completely when she saw Blob.

'Sit here,' I said, setting her at the furthest point from Blob and warning him with a glare. She blinked at the multiple Morrisseys and looked to me for verification. I nodded, relieved to find astonishment could sort out her breathing. I always knew there was something special about Morrissey.

Blob looked like I'd dragged in a rotting dog corpse. He turned his back on us and focused on his new friends. They looked concerned for Georgie but Blob mimed drinking from a bottle and swaying as though sozzled. They nodded a little uncertainly, and moved onto Abba hits.

I held Georgie's hand as the limo rolled along the motorway and around the Lough. We turned inland, wallowed through suburbs and climbed country roads above the city. Colourless fields slotted by until we pulled into a drive lined with high laurel hedges. An illuminated sign said *Down House* in dated letters with an illustration of the hotel. Above it was a hole where someone had thrown a stone.

We pulled up in front of a pink and white Victorian house and I showed my press pass and complimentary tickets to two women in hi-vis. A banner hung across the front of the building with the words *Belfast Festival of Poetry*, written as if by a giant ink pen. Another banner hung to the left with the words *Proudly brought to you by* and below it, the Devine Energy logo. To the right, another banner dangled by a single string and swayed in the breeze.

A windowed corridor connected a personality-free extension to the main house, which I assumed housed function rooms and accommodation. On the lawn, stalls sold food, crafts and books, and traditional Irish music floated down from somewhere. People lingered and dawdled and, noticing the limo, they stopped to watch.

I hadn't thought about this bit.

'Out of the way!' Blob pushed past and opened the limo door.

Georgie watched with horror as the Morrisseys filed out, squinting into the sun. 'I can't go out there,' she whispered.

Chris's voice came over the intercom. 'Here, Tommie, there's that woman, your boss. Must go and say hello.'

I swung round to see Jude in the garden having her picture taken with her new equine clients. She was in full riding regalia with a whip and a saddle balanced on one hip. Chris sauntered over, butch in his Terminator sunglasses.

Hearing applause, I turned to see Blob and the Morrisseys pose for photographers and punters. Eyes sorrowful, hands pleading, the Morrisseys looked winsome. Blob posed with his hands on his thighs like Marilyn Monroe.

'Everyone will look at me,' Georgie gasped.

'Believe me, they won't.' I took off my jacket and put it over her head. 'And now they're not even there.'

'I'll faint.' Her voice was muffled.

'Don't you dare.'

'I've changed my mind, I can't do this.'

'You have to.' Ignoring her panicky breathing and squeaking moans, I led her out and propelled her towards the hotel.

'Hey look, it's Gloria, isn't it?' I heard a voice in the crowd.

My legs turned to liquid. Gloria wasn't supposed to be here. I looked round but people stared at us.

'It's *her*, isn't it?'

'Which one?'

'Gloria's here!'

'Her tits aren't *that* great.'

'Which one?'

'Liposuction.'

'Hey, Gloria!'

Separately we would have been fine but the combination of my sister's bouncing Gloria bosom and my Gloria face was just too much Gloria not to be noticed. I gripped Georgie tighter and wondered frantically about the sunglasses. Should I keep them on and look like a liposuctioned Gloria, or take them off and look like a liposuctioned Gloria with a black eye? I focused on running.

'Get 'em out, Gloria!'

A door was open at the end of the windowed corridor and I shuffled at speed towards it, Georgie panting, honking, squeaking under my jacket, 'Oh my God! Oh my God!'

I pushed her in. Beyond the windowed corridor was a garden that housed a shallow fountain with a meagre jet of water, but I couldn't find the way in. I half-dragged Georgie in the direction of the main building, bestowing nonchalant smiles on faces we passed.

At the end of the corridor we stepped into what was probably the most unsuitable room for an OCD agoraphobic on the verge of a fresh panic attack. The humid air was seasoned with twenty years of sweaty functions, spilt drinks and old smoke. It was some kind of reception: waiting staff handed glasses of wine to a hundred or so people, who stood around chatting and consulting festival programmes.

Under my coat, Georgie heaved. I looked around desperately.

I'd have to get her a room. To do that, I'd have to find reception. I pulled her through the turning heads.

'Excuse me, allergic reaction, a bit John Merrick, excuse me, sorry . . .'

There were five or six doors leading off the room but none said Reception. I stopped at a group beside a nameless, signless door.

'Excuse me,' I said. 'Could you tell me wh —'

Beyond the group, Jim Harland held a glass to his lips. He moved back his cheeks to show me his teeth, looking like he'd spotted prey. He began circling, squeezing through the crowd. I opened the nameless door and pushed Georgie in.

'Won't be long.' I closed the door to her muffled peep. She would make fine material for Harland – a new angle, and ammunition if he needed it. I just hoped the cupboard was stuffed with industrial cleaning products.

'Hello.' Harland sidled up beside me. There was burnt toast in his teeth.

'Hello.' I smiled, suspiciously brightly. I toned it down.

'How are you, *Ms Shaw*?'

'Fine. You?'

'I'm very well.' His nose looked like it was pulsating. 'We're really enjoying the day. Some thought-provoking readings and now I've bumped into you. Let me get you a drink.'

'No, I'm fine, thanks.'

'It's not bad for being free.'

'No, really, I'm fine.'

He sipped his drink. 'Did you see the article?'

'Yes.' I wiped my hands down my jeans. 'You were very supportive of the Benedicts.'

'I can do the same for you,' he said. 'If we work together.'

I noticed the threat but said nothing. Depending on what Gloria wrote, I might need him.

'My offer still stands.'

'I know, Mr Harland, it's just —'

'Jim.'

'Jim, I really have to go.'

'Got my card?'

'Yes.' I smiled.

'Give me a call.' He showed me his toast. 'Any time.'

'I will.' I waited for him to move off.

He folded an arm over his stomach and tapped his glass on his teeth. 'Bye, then.'

I continued to wait.

So did he.

'Those are my friends.' He nodded at people on the other side of the group. 'Want to meet them?'

'No, sorry, I have to go.' I sidestepped him with a tight smile and weaved by the drinks table, glancing back. He saluted me with his glass. If I did a lap of the hotel, surely he'd be gone by the time I got back and I could retrieve Georgie. Providing she hadn't been asphyxiated, electrocuted or poisoned.

I heard a sniff, like a van sliding up to a pedestrian crossing on bald tyres.

'You naughty girl, you're late!' At the end of the table stood Kevin Loane, his neck blazing against his black shirt, his eyes glistening with drink. He embraced me, slopping wine down my back.

'This is fantastic,' he said, with the rapturous abandon of a man who is never normally let out. 'A great day for literature and it's all down to me, ah ah ah!' The alcohol and warm air had dried his sinuses and each sniff was cut off in its prime. 'You missed some of the best readings, you know.' He drained his glass and set it down. 'Let me get you a drink.'

'Sorry, Kevin, I—'

He lifted two glasses and handed me one.

'Now listen,' he said. 'I've spoken to a few of our poets already.' He flicked his fringe. 'To be quite honest, things didn't go as smoothly as I would have liked. Most said they would get back to me about the testimonials, which I suppose is positive.'

'Kevin—'

'Tom, if you'll allow me to debrief you, you'll find your questions answered. There are only two more to meet. It's . . . let me think, sorry, I've had a few to help the old creative juices.' Sniff. 'Yes, Helen McGonagle and Rory McManus. We can see Ms McGonagle now.'

'Kevin . . .'

At the other end of the room, four tall quiffs coasted in from the windowed corridor.

'Er, what a good idea,' I said, extending a hand towards a door. At least I'd found reception. 'After you.'

I followed him out, consoling myself with visions of Georgie exploring vats of disinfectant.

24.

With the skill of someone who could evade his wife and children and not lose a drop, Kevin took the stairs two at a time, briefcase in one hand, wine in the other. At the top was a sign for the accommodation block.

'This way!' He took off down a dim corridor lined with modern faceless doors, the carpet deadening his sniffs as he checked room numbers. At the end, an arrow pointed through a heavy fire door for rooms 401–405. Kevin pushed it open.

'Ooh, this is nice,' he said, head rotating.

We stood on a landing in the older part of the hotel. A smell of aged wood, polish and slight damp hung in the air. Grand oak doors led off the landing and an ornate balustrade swept gracefully down crimson-carpeted stairs. A vast chandelier hung level with the landing and the hall below was sunken and tiled black and white. Above us a shallow dome of blue and green glass created fresh, cool light.

'They gave me a chalet,' Kevin said in hushed but indignant tones. 'I think I'm going to have to say something.'

'Which room is she in?' I asked, stomach wringing like a rag. I hadn't been face-to-face with a poet – Kevin aside, that is – since I last threw a bowl of noodles at my mother. I tried to remember what Blob had said while we waited for Chris: poets are more scared of you than you are of them, poets are usually friendly and curious about man, fear of poets can be averted if the offending poet is put to sleep. I chewed my hair frantically.

Kevin stopped at one of the doors, drained his glass and set it on the floor.

'This is exciting!' he whispered, and knocked.

'It's open,' called a deep voice.

Kevin grinned wildly, his face flushed, and stepped inside. The room was high-ceilinged and bright, lit by two tall sash windows with glass so old it swirled and warped. On the left, a wide four-poster bed hung with heavy curtains. The furniture – dressing table, wardrobe, writing desk – was oak. We skulked across a springy carpet to studded leather armchairs, where Helen McGonagle sat next to a low round table. She was in her late forties or early fifties, muscular and masculine with a shaved head, pustule-red skin and a man's suit. She chewed gum.

'Ms McGonagle, thank you so much for seeing us.' Kevin limped with respect. 'And might I add, what a fabulous room.' Sniff. 'Much better than mine.'

'Like it, do you?' she said as we sat down. She drank whiskey from crystal. 'I think it's obscene.'

Kevin peered out the window. 'Poor view?'

'It disgusts me. All of it.' Her lip curled in distaste. 'Drink?' She gave the low table a spin and slid open a door in the side. 'Bushmills? Or Red Bull?'

'*Uisce beatha* please.' Kevin brandished his Irish heroically.

My larynx, grasp of language and sense of perspective all failed me at once. 'Plissnuh,' I whispered.

She splashed whiskey liberally and offered no water. 'So what do you want from me?'

'I'm a very big fan,' Kevin said shyly.

She tested him. 'Where did you see me?'

'At the Poetry Café, numerous times. And I even had the fortune to catch you in the city centre chalking your poetry on the pavement. I spoke to you, you might remember me?'

She studied him. 'No.' She lifted her whiskey and waved it in an understated toast before drinking. Kevin grabbed his, raised it and drank.

'So,' she said. 'What do you want?'

Kevin laughed brightly. 'Ah ah ah! Yes.' He pulled his briefcase onto his knee. 'I'm Kevin Loane, Marketing Director with Devine Energy.'

She watched him, chewing her gum.

'We're the Festival sponsors,' he reminded her, opening his briefcase. 'We've made a substantial investment to ensure every kind of poet and every form of poetry is supported, promoted and brought to the people. Indeed, we wish to ensure that every writer is appreciated the way they should be.' Sniff.

'Do you write poetry?' she asked.

'I most certainly do.'

She sneered while she drank.

'I have something here I would like you to cast your eye over, if you would.' Kevin handed her the testimonial. 'As I said, we have made a substantial investment and all we ask in return is a small favour. If you could have a read and just . . . ?'

She took out a pair of chemist-bought glasses and perused the paragraph.

'Do you have a pen?' she said.

I felt my eyebrows scrape my sunglasses.

Kevin took a silver pen from his inside pocket and handed it across as though bearing tobacco to Elizabeth I. She put the paper on the table and wrote on the dotted line. Her signature took a surprisingly long time to complete. She handed the paper back to Kevin.

Kevin smiled. 'Wonderful, Ms McGonagle, thank you so much. Wait a minute, this says "Go fuck yourself"' – he strained at the page – '"asshole".'

'Well done,' she said. 'Now fuck off out of my room, you weasel shit.'

'Wait a minute,' Kevin said with thin bravado. 'I'm paying you.'

'I don't accept fees,' she said, standing. 'I never have. They're lucky I don't burn this place down. Now get the fuck out.'

Kevin's mouth opened and closed. I got up to run.

'And you can fuck off too,' McGonagle spat at me. 'You meaningless streak of piss.'

I crossed the room quickly, Kevin close behind.

'And don't forget your stinking bourgeois pen,' McGonagle bellowed. The pen shot past us and thwacked off the oak door, leaving a stab mark.

We slipped outside. Behind us, the door rattled violently as though from a kick.

Kevin slotted together the pieces of his pen. 'I'm glad you witnessed that,' he said, breathlessly. 'Now you understand why I need you. It's the injustice of it. I'm not in the clique, you see. I'm an outsider. You and I belong together. I think I need a drink. Let's go to the bar.' Sniff.

'Sorry, Kevin. I, er, have to go to the loo.'

'Entirely understandable, Tom.' He dabbed his forehead with his sleeve. 'I'll catch up with you at the McManus reading. *You* can present the testimonial this time.'

At the bottom of the stairs, Kevin sailed off to the bar to piece together his dignity and I scurried back to the drinks reception to find Georgie. The room was empty, the table scattered with glasses and stained with spillages. I yanked the signless door open. The walk-in maintenance cupboard hummed with meters, ducts and switches. At the back was a dusty industrial floor polisher. But no Georgie.

I raced to the windowed corridor, but it too was empty. A few smokers stood in the garden but she wasn't there either. I crossed the lawn, scouring faces at the stalls. Chris had parked the limo over six spaces in the car park. More cars had parked on the path and grass. People drifted towards the front door of the hotel.

I ran back to reception. It was plain and functional with depressing orange and grey furniture. There was a banner like the one at the front of the building, alongside a Devine Energy banner and another which dangled loosely and couldn't be read. Below it, a large nose in a pinstripe suit complained to a woman with cropped chestnut hair and a long green pinafore.

'Every one of our banners is like this,' he said. 'They can't all be faulty. I think it's sabotage.'

'We'll sort it out, don't worry,' she soothed. 'Why don't you show me where the problems are and we'll do our best to . . .' They walked away and I didn't hear the rest.

A young bony man with gelled hair and a thin grey shirt manned the reception desk, his chin in his hand. His name badge said Matt.

'Excuse me,' I said. 'Could you tell me . . .' What happened to the hyperventilating woman I shut in a cupboard earlier? It needed more delicacy. '. . . if anyone was taken ill earlier?'

Matt pouted. 'Don't think so. A few pissed people but no one's been ill. Loving your sunnies, by the way.'

'Thanks. No one faint or anything?'

'Not that I've heard.' He leaned his chair back on two legs. 'Harry, you hear of anyone fainting?'

A voice floated in from the right. 'It's only poetry, for God's sake.'

'OK, thanks,' I said. Georgie had no purse with her, so presumably she had no credit card and couldn't have booked a room. Maybe she had been uncovered by a maintenance man and rescued or abducted, or worse, taken to a reading. Darren would never believe I lost in her a cupboard. He'd think I was definitely covering for an affair.

'Aren't you going in to see the big star then?' Matt asked.

'What?'

'Rory What's-His-Name. Has anus in it.'

'Rory McManus?'

'That's the one. Everyone else is going in, look.'

At the other end of reception, a long queue of pessimistic raincoats shuffled through double doors. Stragglers watched from the door of the bar, gauging the time left to drink.

I gripped the desk. 'McManus is here?'

'He's on in about twenty minutes.'

'Where is he now? I need to speak to his agent urgently.'

'I wish I got more questions like yours. If you go up those stairs, turn right, you'll see a door immediately on your right. Just knock. It's an anteroom off the main function room, usually where we store brides and grooms before guests upstand.'

'Thanks.' I hurried up the orange and grey stairs, followed Matt's directions, and knocked at another signless door. No one answered. I knocked again, replaying the directions in my head. The door was opened by a man with a long, red, wispy moustache.

'Is there a *fire?*' he said.

'I'm looking for Liam McMullan, Mr McManus's agent?'

'Mr McManus sees no one before a reading,' the man said, enjoying the rebuff.

'I'm not looking for Mr McManus, I'm looking for his agent.'

'I know this is exciting but even the partially sighted have to wait, just like everyone else.' He closed the door.

I knocked again.

He opened it, leaning back on one foot. 'I *will* call security.'

'I need to speak to Liam McMullan.'

'Mr McManus will meet and greet at a reception after the reading. Perhaps you should try listening.'

'I need to speak to *Liam McMullan!*'

'*Security!*'

'OK! God.'

'Don't swear at me, missy.'

'Sorry.'

He blinked with dignity. 'The reading will begin soon. I suggest you take your seat if you don't want to miss it.' He closed the door.

I trudged down to reception. The queue was gone and latecomers hurried through the double doors. The woman in the green pinafore stood with Kevin Loane.

'Mr Loane, I really feel you should have a coffee,' she said, blocking his way.

One of Kevin's legs was stationary, the other wandered away. 'Nope, I'm fine, Jill. Fine wi' wine.' His fiery shaving rash had spread out to his ears. 'Frisky wi' whiskey. Randy wi' bran—'

'Mr Loane, please . . .'

'Tom, over here!' Kevin beckoned. 'Bez seats in the house, come on!'

Pinafore Woman turned to me. 'Try not to let him drink any more, will you? I have to run.' She danced up the stairs, pinafore gathered in her hands.

Kevin swung an arm over my shoulder. 'Wha' a day,' he said. His teeth were purple. 'Emotional, vey emotional.' He pressed my nose with a finger. 'Friend.'

'Er, yes.'

'You see Gloria?' he said. 'I hope she be here.' He looked love-struck. 'I wan' see those zeppelin breasts. Wai'.' He scrutinised me. 'You Shaw. You related?'

I used Blob's chortle. 'Bah-hah-hah-hah! With these boobs?'

'You boobs vey nice.' He trailed his arm away and meandered into the cavernous, noisy room. 'Ahh, a bar.'

In the room, hundreds of people faced a stage with a podium and microphone in the middle and a single chair at the back. To the left of the stage was a closed door. Above the podium hung three banners, the third finally fully displayed. It was for a pet food company.

I scanned the crowd but couldn't see Liam. Unsurprisingly, there was no sign of Georgie either. Eight or nine rows from the back, four tall quiffs rose unmistakably. Kevin handed me a large glass of wine and I took it gratefully and followed him to the front, scouring the audience and allowing other people to walk between, in case Blob looked our way.

Kevin's shirt had come out of his belt and his wandering leg took him to the wall and women with blonde hair. At the end of the front row, Kevin tossed two 'Reserved' signs to the floor and sat down. At the opposite end of the row, the nose in the suit fired him a look of hostility. Between the nose and Kevin, people drank greedily. I assumed they were sponsors too.

The lights dimmed. A few people oohed. Others tutted. I looked over my shoulder to see if Liam had come in the back but the doors were closed. Nothing and no one moved. It wouldn't be easy to sneak away. Unless I feigned fainting or a fit, I was trapped. I gulped wine. What if McManus read from *Gloria! Gloria! Gloria!?* Fainting or fitting would not be beyond hope.

The door beside the stage opened and I glimpsed the man with the wispy moustache. Out danced Pinafore Woman followed by a man with a lick of grey hair over his forehead and small intense eyes. He was thin but with a small ball-shaped belly. Mossy, smoky, rumpled and nowhere near as tall as he sounded on the phone. The door closed without any sign of Liam.

The audience rose to applaud. Kevin swigged his wine and stood up, gripping his top lip with his bottom teeth and clapping loudly. Pinafore Woman stood at the podium while McManus took the chair and crossed his legs, a few slim books on his knee. Pinafore Woman's eyes sparkled and her voice was breathy.

'Ladies and gentlemen,' she said, kneading her hands. 'I'd like to welcome you to a very special evening. My name is Jill and I helped organise this, if I may say so myself, amazing event. We've been lucky to secure some incredible talent for this Festival but I'll be honest with you, when I got the email saying Rory McManus was confirmed, I printed it out and framed it – with apologies to the planet!'

The audience laughed warmly. Kevin spilt wine down his shirt and swore, dusting himself. Pinafore Woman made a half-giggle, half-sob noise.

'In fact, I have a text from the man himself, and I keep it next to my heart.' She patted her breast pocket and looked round at McManus, who fiddled with his books. She bobbed in an unconscious curtsey.

'A lot of work has gone into the organisation of this event,' she said. 'Obviously I'd like to thank all those involved . . .'

Kevin snorted as she thanked everyone she knew and loved.

'That's why this Festival has such a unique ethos, which I'm sure you've all experienced today,' she said. 'To explain more, please welcome Professor Horatio O'Neill, chair of the Belfast Festival of Poetry committee.'

The audience applauded as a bendy man appeared from the left and shuffled to the podium. He had long pale hair, pale sandals, pale trousers to his armpits and a bodhrán behind his back. The front row sniggered as he began to play.

Kevin was licking the inside of his empty wineglass when Professor O'Neill finished. The man gave an abrupt little bow and strode off the stage to fervent applause. Pinafore Woman reappeared.

'Thank you, Horatio. Wonderfully illuminating. Now I know you're all very keen to hear from Mr McManus but first, we must thank our funders and sponsors.'

The audience sighed, apart from the front row who cheered.

'Our deepest thanks go to the Arts Council, whose help and assistance have been invaluable. Thank you to all our sponsors, particularly Nutrinsic and Devine Energy. Without their commitment, we simply couldn't have staged such a quality event. Before we hear from Mr McManus, a short address from David Doran from Nutrinsic, followed by Kevin Loane from Devine Energy.'

She danced off the stage, rubbing the top of her chest.

Kevin booed as the nose stood up. A short address was probably optimistic for Kevin, but I'd never seen him 'vey emotional' before. Maybe he would surprise me.

Rory McManus swung his crossed leg, picked dust off his trousers and brushed away his lick of hair as the nose approached the podium, arms folded awkwardly.

'If it were up to me,' he said, 'sponsors wouldn't speak.'

'Hear, hear!' a voice came from the audience.

'But someone insisted.' His eyes landed on Kevin.

'Oh, fuck off,' Kevin said.

'Ladies and gentlemen,' the nose said. 'We at Nutrinsic feed animals but we appreciate that to feed people, it takes a lot more. That's why we're delighted to be involved in bringing you the UK and Ireland's most celebrated and successful poet. I'm sure your soul will be nurtured tonight. I hope you enjoy the reading. I know I will. Thanks.'

The audience clapped dutifully as the nose resumed his seat. Kevin rose and leaned into my face, a finger on his chest.

'Feez like he introduce me, hee hee!'

He wandered after his leg which explored the row behind us, the steps twice and the back of the stage. Pinafore Woman asked if he felt quite well enough to speak. He held up a hand and, making it to the podium, tapped the mike. The audience flinched under feedback. He took some sheets of paper from a pocket and took more from another pocket.

'Mr Loane—' Pinafore Woman whispered loudly.

'Yez, thank oo, Ji'.' He shuffled his sheets and squinted at the audience. 'I go' a poem abou' Devi' Engy.' He turned the sheets upside down. 'You know, I sen' my poems to pubishers bud no one wants 'em.'

A weak 'awww' went up from the audience.

Kevin took a long time to blink. 'Oo know eye?' he said. 'Coz I'm not in the click. Clique. It's who oo know. It's unjus'.' His dry sniff set off the feedback again. 'But it's who oo know.'

In her prompter's voice, Pinafore Woman said, 'Mr Loane—'

He held up a finger. 'Hang on Ji' . . .' He fingered through his sheets. The audience stared, as though watching a nature documentary on tar pits. McManus uncrossed his legs, bouncing them at the ankle.

Pinafore Woman raised her voice. 'Mr Loane, if you've—'

'Shh, Ji', please!' Kevin held up his hand again. 'Oo kin all read my poems in this month's *Bellefast* magazine.' Sniff. 'Got my poems in there. And photographs of all oo lovely nice people.' He swept an arm over the audience. 'Had to put this big fat bloke in my TV ad to geh my poems in, but thaz the worl' we live in. Iz who oo know.'

I slapped my hand to my mouth. I hoped Blob wasn't listening, I hoped he was whispering with his new friends, I hoped he wouldn't make the connection but when I swung round to look, he was rising to his feet.

'Hello?' Kevin tapped the mike. It whistled. Pinafore Woman hurried up the steps. Blob sidestepped along his row.

''S a fantazzic day,' Kevin said. 'Cheer up. Wha' abou' a joke?' He pulled out his trouser pockets, unzipped his fly and said, 'Look, an elephant, hee hee hee!'

The audience reeled with screams. Pinafore Woman dragged Kevin away and the nose sprang onstage and judoed him to the floor. Kevin's fists flailed and Rory McManus stood up. I rose to follow Blob as others got to their feet, howling in protest or clapping with delight. The deeply offended shuffled out of their rows and into my way.

'Ladies, gentlemen!' Pinafore Woman went soprano with horror. 'Plea—'

Kevin grabbed the mike and it thudded to the floor with a squeal of feedback. Kevin, Pinafore Woman and the nose writhed onstage as McManus walked past. I squirmed through the crowd and out to reception. Near the front door I saw Blob's quiff. Squeezing by shocked and amused faces, I touched his shoulder. He turned. It was Jürgen, his cheeks shining.

'*Danke*, man,' he said. 'This is fantastic. Where is Robert?'

I pushed on to the front door and took off my sunglasses. It was dark and the frost was returning. People lit cigarettes on the pebbled drive and dry leaves skipped by. The stalls on the lawn were closed, wares removed, canvas roofs rattling. They looked like plucked eyes. Blob was gone.

I turned. Liam stood behind me.

'Here it is,' he said, holding out a heavy brown envelope.

25.

'Where've you been all day?' he said, moving in for his two kisses. 'I've been looking for you everywhere.'

'I was late and . . .' His neck was warm and I wanted to hold on. My knees popped nervously. I stepped back.

'You alright?' he said. 'You look a bit fraught.'

'I'm . . . just, I've lost the people I was with.' I put my sunglasses on.

'They're probably in the bar. Everyone else is. That client of yours is full of surprises. Rory found it amusing, thankfully.'

Of course. Blob would be in the bar, holding court, freeloading. 'You're right. Let's look in the bar,' I said, moving off.

'Wait.' He touched the heavy envelope I held to my chest. 'What about this? What do you think?'

I looked at the envelope, neat, blank and anonymous. 'Thanks,' I said. 'Have you read it?'

His eyebrows dipped. 'Of course not.'

'Thanks for getting it for me.'

'You're very welcome,' he said. 'Do you want to have a quick look in the bar before you meet Rory?'

'Yes, but I really have to read this, Liam.'

'Come on. There's plenty of time.'

Beside the stairs, drinkers spilled out of the bar into reception, discussing the originality of Kevin's address. I followed Liam on a weaving circuit of the bar, holding the envelope close. I saw Harland again, squeezed into a snug and laughing with friends. I ducked and looked away. The Morrisseys ordered drinks at the bar, chatting happily with people I didn't know. Blob wasn't there. No sign of Georgie either, unsurprisingly.

Outside the bar, Liam stopped. 'Are they booked into the hotel?' I shook my head.

'Don't look so worried,' he said. 'They'll turn up. Come on, they're going to invite people back in for the reading soon. I think we may have lost some of the audience, although how they can be offended by one little man's wang when Rory's poetry is about . . .' He smiled warmly. 'Anyway, come on, I'll introduce you to Rory.'

I followed him up to the blank door where he knocked confidently. My stomach twisted. I thought of Blob and his efforts to reassure me as we waited for Chris. Poets are eaten as a delicacy in Japan, he'd said. That's all I could remember. Blob wasn't just a morale booster, he was a buoyancy aid. And he was gone.

The man with the wispy moustache opened the door.

'Hey, Stan,' Liam said.

Stan's moustache waggled as we passed.

The room had a sloping ceiling with a bank of dark windows that reflected ten or twelve people drinking tea, including Pinafore Woman and Horatio O'Neill. They nodded at Liam as we crossed the room to McManus. Four avid women stood in his thrall. One had glossy ripples of Pre-Raphaelite hair, another was older with short hair and heavy make-up, a third had a short wiry bob and rimless glasses. A blonde one was probably still school age.

'Hey, big man,' Liam said.

Blob was a big man. McManus was only slightly taller than Liam. Everything about him was recessive – smoky skin, earthy shapeless clothes, grey head – but his small blue eyes stood out. He had a hangdog way of standing that made him look at us sideways.

'Rory, this is Tommie,' Liam said. 'Tommie, Rory.'

Rory took his hand out of his pocket and shook mine. There was something tense about his expression, as though keen attention were mixed with impatience. The women watched me. I felt like a trophy.

'Mr McManus.' The woman with the bob attempted to seize back the attention. 'I wondered if you wouldn't mind answering a question about the nature of the form and how it interplays with your vision?'

'Interesting question,' McManus said. 'Email Liam and he'll pass on your query.' He looked at me in his hangdog way. 'Do you smoke?'

I nodded.

'Come outside,' he said.

I gave Liam a look. He missed it.

The harem muttered as I set off through the room after McManus.

'Could we do the interview while we smoke?' I asked, hugging the envelope. 'It doesn't have to be a long interview. It's just, I'm on a very tight schedule.'

A woman with a sheet of black hair and enormous eyes touched McManus's sleeve. She worked her eyelashes. He looked flummoxed, as though he wasn't just bothered by a fly, he was questioning its motivations, its purpose, its metaphysical ramifications.

She gushed, 'Mr McManus, I wondered if you wouldn't mind. . .'

'Can I help?' Liam said.

Her eyes slid up and down Liam.

'Take my card,' Liam said. 'You can email me with any . . .'

McManus walked on, checking I was following. At the side of the room, double glass doors led to a small, plain balcony with a high wall. I followed him into the cold, aware of being watched. He waited till the door was shut before he spoke.

'You're not how I imagined,' he said, his small eyes watching me intently as he lit up. I thought of simpering girl. She wore her hair in ringlets and had long frothy petticoats. He inhaled and sighed forcefully. 'You're much, much better.'

Simpering girl stamped her foot. I was a newer, younger, more tubercular Gloria. I took a cigarette from my pack and he moved in close to light it. He didn't move back.

'I feel you are important,' he said.

I stepped back and pressed against the wall, looking through the glass doors. Surely someone else smoked.

'There are some things about Gloria I don't understand,' he said. His eyes moved unfocused along the black trees at the side of the hotel. Through the trees I could see more lights, chalets I assumed.

'I struggle to find a way to frame them,' he said. 'It's empty when I know it should be full.'

'Can I say you felt your last collection was empty?'

'I can't rush this,' he said, more to himself than me.

I swapped the envelope from hand to hand. 'I don't mean to be rude, but I really need to get moving.'

'Liam said you were like this.'

'How do you feel about being thrust into the spotlight?'

'He called you slippery.'

'Have you started work on your next collection?'

'But you are, in fact, elusory. I must know more.'

'Just answer one question. Please. Give me anything and I'll turn it into something.'

'You don't know how deep my obsession has been.' He held a hand over his chest like a claw. 'I have been consumed.'

'You say "have been". Is it over between you and Gloria? That's a purely journalistic question.'

'You're so like her and yet the difference is . . .' He set his head at an angle, bemused by his puzzlement.

Liam pressed his face against the glass. He held up three fingers and pointed to the door. People were leaving, heads turned in our direction.

'Stay.' McManus pressed fingers to his temples. 'I have the reading and a reception. Stay with me.'

'I'm sorry, I have work to do. It really is quite urgent.'

'Come to the reading.'

'I can't.'

'Then I will go with you.'

'What?'

'I'll give you what you need, Tommie. But you must give me what I need.'

I could temp again. I would. I should. I should leave now, read the book and go to Darren and suggest his wife was in Narnia. But the look on McManus's face suggested he would come with me.

'No?' he said. 'Then come to my reading. I'm one of the UK and Ireland's greatest living poets.'

'I don't like poetry.'

He looked at the sky and back to me. 'You are amazing.'

Liam knocked again, peering curiously. Rory waved him through.

'Jill is waiting,' Liam said. 'And a few hundred others.'

'I cannot read tonight,' Rory said.

Liam looked from Rory to me and back.

'Now that I've glimpsed the future of my work, its current form is meaningless,' McManus said. 'I can't do this without her.'

'What?' Liam said.

'She must come to my reading.'

I shook my head frantically.

Liam seemed to fade in and out before my eyes. 'We can't let everyone down. They've come to see you. Jill's on the Kalms now.'

'For God's sake, Liam.' McManus closed his eyes, creases forming between them. 'This is my work.'

'Can't you just take a few notes? You can get a lot done in a minute.'

Rory pressed his forehead as though in pain. 'You're being ridiculous.'

Liam turned to me. 'Come to the reading. We can sort this out afterwards.'

I widened my eyes at him. 'I have *work* to do.'

Liam opened the door, rubbing his hand over his chin. 'OK, right. Right. Rory, you get your books. Tommie, you come with me.'

'Thank you, Liam.' McManus passed back into the room.

'I have to read this,' I hissed. 'And I don't particularly want to hear about him having sex with my mother.'

'It could be liberating,' Liam said desperately.

'That's completely fucked up.'

He was almost panting. 'Look, we'll get this sorted out later. Don't look at me like that, it's not coercion. It's . . . returning a favour.' His skin was flat with anxiety. 'Please, Tommie. Indulge him, please. He's one of the UK and Ireland's—'

'Yes, I know.'

I could hurt Liam in a way he'd never forget. All I had to do was leave. I stepped into the room.

'I'll need the biggest gin the world,' I said. 'Twice.'

'Thank you,' he whispered, smoothing a hand over his head. 'Thank you, thank you, thank you.'

In the darkness, I sat beside Liam, took off my sunglasses and drank. We sat near the front where McManus could see us. Behind, the audience was only slightly reduced. Pinafore Woman had introduced McManus with fast and fluttered apologies, passing off the earlier drama as the enthusiasm of a 'superfan'. Having had time to revisit the bar, the audience now shared much of Kevin's enthusiasm.

I stared at the envelope that held the manuscript as McManus began to read, sliding his hands into his pockets. I'd softened the envelope with my sweaty hands and it was ripped in one corner. He started with poems I remembered studying at school. His greatest hits. I felt around the seal on the envelope. The glue was the kind that needed to be wet to stick, the really effective kind that doesn't open easily.

One large gin in, I worked a finger into the rip at the edge. It tore a little. The noise was magnified in the worshipful atmosphere.

'What are you doing?' Liam whispered.

I stopped. 'Nothing.'

After a few minutes, I tried again. The couple in front turned around.

'Stop it,' Liam whispered.

I started on my second large gin and tore the envelope, millimetre by millimetre. Ten minutes later, it was two centimetres dilated.

I leaned into Liam. 'Do you have anything sharp?'

'No. Be quiet.'

I wriggled my finger in and pulled a little. It ripped through the room like a gunshot. The entire row looked round. I searched for something at my feet and found my gin. I kept my head down and drank.

Minutes passed before I began again. Concentrating, I tore slowly, steadily. It sounded like fire crackling under the floorboards.

The man in front turned. 'Jesus wept. Will you just rip it?'

I ripped. It cracked through the room like a fissure in the earth, but at last I was in.

Liam sighed, touching his brow.

A buzz rippled through the audience. A few people clapped in anticipation. McManus swapped books on the podium.

I sucked in a breath and pulled out the block of paper. On the cover was the title: *Gloria In Excelsius*. More pretentious pseudo-academic Latin, like *In Utero*. I held the manuscript and looked up at the stage. Hands in pockets, McManus was intoning over her 'butterfly'. Oh God. I stared at the manuscript. Slowly, I turned the first page. It slid off my knee and the rest followed, slithering noisily into the underworld of feet. I chased it.

'Leave it!' Liam whispered.

A woman behind yelped as I brushed her foot pursuing a page. 'Sorry!'

Liam leaned over. 'We'll be asked to leave.'

I sat up. 'Do you think so?'

'Just sit down,' Liam pleaded.

I pulled the pages together, the pile chaotic, the order lost. I scrambled onto my seat, clutching the manuscript, and took a mouthful of gin.

'Slow down,' Liam whispered.

I drank more, holding his eye.

On stage, McManus was getting worked up over something 'heaven scent'. Words on the page below caught my eye.

'. . . manhood . . .'

I scanned the page, listening at the same time.

'. . . pulsating . . .'

'. . . climb aboard, captain . . .'

'. . . all night . . .'

'. . . piscine pleasures . . .'

'. . . on and on . . .'

I held my head and looked at Liam. 'I don't feel well.'

He pushed up his glasses. 'Give it to me.' He held out his hand.

I handed the manuscript over.

'Take a deep breath.'

I took a deep breath.

'Think of Ireland.'

I stared at my lap, legs twisted, pinkies in my ears, and thought of the Newry Bypass. When McManus finally finished, there was blood in my nails. I felt nothing.

The audience got to its feet, euphoric. Liam stood too, joining the applause.

'Alright now?' he asked over the applause.

'Fine.'

He sat beside me. 'Look, you'll feel better after something to eat. There will be nibbles at the reception.' He gave me the coy smile. 'Thanks for helping me out. I appreciate it.'

The lights went up and I put on my sunglasses. 'Can I have it back now?'

He handed the manuscript over, looking uncertain.

Someone tapped me on the shoulder. 'Is this yours?' Behind us, an emaciated woman held out a page.

'Yes,' I said, adding, 'but I didn't write it, someone else did.'

'Doesn't leave much to the imagination,' she said. 'I hope the rest is like that.'

Pinafore Woman led devoted applause, encouraging cheers and whistles as McManus left the stage, looking directly at me. I stuffed the manuscript into the envelope and followed Liam to the side of the stage as the pink-cheeked, giddy audience began filing out. The door at the side opened onto a flight of stairs. At the top, I could see the bank of windows in the anteroom.

'Rory has a meet-and-greet now,' Liam said. 'It won't take long, he's not into that kind of thing. Then you can get your interview.' He turned to climb the stairs.

'Liam.'

He stopped.

'Did you know he'd do this?'

'What?'

'Fixate on me.'

'It's not you,' he said. 'It's the bits of you that aren't *her*. He's obsessed. Did you think you were his next muse? Oh, babe. You're funny. Come on.' He held out his hand and I shooed him ahead, watching his chunky rear move from side to side as he climbed the stairs. It was still muscular. Still two-hands grabbable. I hated him.

In the anteroom at the top of the stairs, roving staff served canapés as sponsors poured through the door. Larking and laughing, they tore into food and snapped up champagne. Jude's new clients rah-rah-rahed as she talked to David Doran from Nutrinsic, flashing her gums at his every word. Photographers circled, noting down names. McManus stood with Pinafore Woman, now hysterically happy, an expressionless Horatio O'Neill and yet more flirty women, but his eye explored the room. Through the crowd, I saw Jim Harland. I lifted champagne from a passing tray and ducked behind Liam.

'There's a journalist who knows who I am.' I drank deeply.

'For God's sake, will you slow down with that stuff? I'm sure you don't need to hide, Tommie. Which one is it?'

'There's more than one?'

Liam looked round. 'About four.'

McManus's sharp eye found me. He stepped away from Pinafore Woman but she moved with him.

'I can't stay here,' I said.

'He'll follow you wherever you go.'

Someone touched my arm. It was Chris, with a glass of champagne. He dropped a canapé into his mouth and chuckled.

'My friend! Met all sorts today, loads of new contacts, thanks for that.' He leaned in. 'See your woman, your boss? See that riding gear?' He fanned himself like the canapé was on fire. 'Here, anyway, just wanted to say, one more week and yous'll have to go. Need the place for Dorota. Pay two months, I keep your deposit, that's you done.' He chuckled. 'Here you go, mate.' He handed a business card to Liam, who looked baffled. 'Take it easy.' He strolled away, lifting canapés as he went.

Heads turned to the door and Pinafore Woman rushed across as Kevin staggered in, vey vey emotional.

'Who put me to bed?' he cried. Splashes of mud reached up to his knees. 'You?' He pointed at Pinafore Woman. 'In a *chalet*?'

'Mr Loane—'

He stumbled forward, pointing at Jude. 'Why you talking to *him*?' Glasses tumbled and platters slid as he lurched into a table. 'What's with the britches?'

'Kevin.' Jude writhed. 'Have you—'

'You're all bazzards,' Kevin slurred. ''Cept you, McManus.'

'Mr Loane . . .' Pinafore Woman held up her hands.

Stan the doorman moved in. 'Come on, you.'

Jude crept forward. 'Kevin, you know . . .'

Kevin swung round with his fist. Wily Stan ducked and Jude got it in the gums. She collapsed, hands to her face as screams and shouts rose, cameras clicked and bodies launched at a bewildered Kevin and scurried to Jude.

McManus looked at the door and back to me. Head down, I

bypassed blood and chaos and followed him outside where he grabbed my hand and ran. He'd spent his youth charging round fields and I'd spent mine reading a thesaurus in my room. Wine, gin and champagne sloshed. I would either vomit or die. Behind us, Liam slapped along, laughing.

I heard someone call my name. It was Harland. I overtook McManus.

We almost slid down the stairs and bolted through the emptying reception, past the Morrisseys draped over grey and orange settees, all three unconscious, or close to it. Hao's shirt was ruined. The envelope slid from my hand and I tried to break free, but McManus's grip was firm. Liam picked it up but fell behind. Harland appeared on the stairs, followed by more people. We ran along the windowed corridor, into the frosty car park, past the front of the hotel and down the side of the old house.

McManus stopped and doubled over, letting go of my hand. His breath charged into the air. Every heartbeat rattled my teeth as night rolled over my skin. I felt in my pocket for cigarettes.

'Thanks,' I gasped. 'I only have a few questions.'

Feet crunched along the pebbles and McManus pressed me into the darkness by the wall.

Liam wandered by. 'Rory?'

'For God's sake,' McManus muttered.

'Don't worry,' Liam grinned, joining us. 'We lost them.'

'Liam, why don't you see if you can get us some hot whiskeys,' McManus said.

Liam's grin faltered as he looked from McManus to me. 'Alright,' he said, backing away uncertainly.

'So,' I said. 'How would it change things for you if you won the Wyman Prize?'

McManus removed his jacket. 'It's your skin, to begin with,' he said. He draped it round my shoulders. It smelt of tobacco and an old house.

'Do you ever worry your passion will run out?' I asked, lighting up.

He moved closer. 'Take your sunglasses off. Let me see.'

I took them off and his small eyes inspected mine. 'Your bruise.' His skin was smoky, soft like worn fabric.

'Isn't poetry just self-indulgent wankery?'

'Your sense of humour.' There were short white whiskers on his pitted chin. 'Your breath.'

This was my opportunity. Liam deserved this. So did she.

'I'm not like her,' I said and kissed him. He moved back, fingers to his lips as though I'd bitten him. He kissed me forcefully, his bristles scraping my mouth. It began as revenge and then I was lost, quickly, as he moved his hands under the jacket, below my top, into my jeans, no more Liam, no more Blob, Georgie, Gloria, no one, nothing, just hands, mouths, mindless in the dark.

'I got the drinks.' Liam's voice was low, edgy.

McManus broke away with a surprised grunt and I followed him before I realised I couldn't, not here. McManus took the steaming drinks without a word and passed one to me. I drank quickly, scorching my throat, buttoning my jeans.

'Come with me,' McManus said.

'Where?' Liam said.

'Not you.' McManus took a step towards the front of the building. He waited for me. I should have felt triumphant, clever, avenged. But all I felt was the dirty birth of guilt. I took McManus's hand.

Liam gave me the manuscript.

'She's not right, you know,' he said to McManus.

We left him in the dark. More than ever, I needed to be lost.

On the warm floor, on whiskey, above me white nasal hair and St Jude swinging back and forth on his medallion, I can never do this again, I am coming to an end, I'm not here, I'm not anywhere, the world ends here at his lesbian hands.

Let's get into bed
I'm OK here
I see what it is now
Don't write a poem about me
It's your bones

Windows and doors smash in, crashing so loud I'm crushed but only I can hear it. I scramble away, pull on my clothes, leave him on the floor under blankets. Grab the envelope, get out. I close the door quietly and the beautiful landing is silent, deserted, watching me. I pass into the door-lined corridor and down to the room where they held the drinks reception. Tornadoes are coming, here they come.

I lost her. I should never have brought her. I was in a hurry, I made her do what I wanted, so I could do what Jude wanted and Jude was worthless. I was worthless.

Into the cupboard. No one will come here, at least for a few hours. I kneel on the floor, pull out the manuscript, order the pages, concentrate, it won't take long.

I broke Blob.

And when they're in order, read them.

Where will I go?

Read. Faster.

Liam. Don't think, it will kill me.

Born in Belfast of working-class stock, sex at fourteen, Glasgow with a sailor, pregnant, goes home, thrown out, miscarries, on the game, more sex, goes to college, on the game, sex, sex, sex, writes poetry, joins a poetry group, off the game, Troubles begin.

No us.

I read on.

Naked people, people you know, sex, sex, sex, evil matriarch, silent lover takes to his bed, pregnant, silent lover gets better, war, pregnant again, silent lover tops himself, attempted bathroom terminations, tenacious parasite, never-ending mute duty, *In Utero*, Troubles end.

And that's all.

Nothing about us. Just that she blamed me for her lover's, my father's death.

But nothing new.

I leaned on some kind of unit. I needed a shower, a drink, food. I pushed the manuscript with my foot. I settled for a cigarette.

More noise and I covered my ears with my hands. But this was different, not a phantom. It went on and on. It was the fire alarm.

I crushed the cigarette on the floor but it was too late. I gathered up the manuscript and joined the exodus.

26.

The gardens shone with heavy frost. Directed by shouting staff, I drifted into the car park with bewildered, bovine crowds. Alarms blared and people asked questions that couldn't be answered. Chris was there, the nose, Pinafore Woman, Liam, the bob with the glasses and Rory McManus, vulnerable and confused in their nightclothes and blankets. One person stood with a blanket covering head, shoulders and torso. A fully dressed person. And she stood with Jim Harland.

Harland didn't smile as I lifted the blanket and entered Georgie's dark Dettol world.

'Where the hell were you?' Her breath warmed me. 'You disappeared.' In the safety of her blanket, her breathing was almost normal.

'Where the hell were you?' I whispered. '*You* disappeared.'

She lowered her voice. 'You abandoned me. That journalist rescued me.'

'He wasn't rescuing you, he was seizing the moment.'

'He got me a room, which was more than you did. Here's your jacket. You should wash that.'

I wriggled into the jacket, swapping the envelope from hand to hand. 'What do you mean, a room?'

'A room with a TV and room service, you perv. I watched eight hours of *Friends*.'

'How awful.'

'I enjoyed it.'

'You owe him now.'

'I didn't agree to anything,' she said. 'He understands that. He

221

looked for you. He said you ran away from him.'

'I thought he wanted . . . Look, I got it.' I held up the envelope. 'I read it.'

'Oh my God.' She brought the Dettol between us. 'And?'

'We're not in it.'

She froze. 'What?'

'It's about her life, not ours. She mentions that we're born but she doesn't mention us by name. She doesn't really say that much about us.'

'Oh, thank Christ.' I felt her shoulders loosen. 'Oh, thank Christ. Oh my God. I don't have to tell Darren. Oh, thank God.'

I rubbed my neck. 'I have a confession to make.'

'What?' Her voice was guarded.

'That journalist?' I whispered.

'What?'

'I sort of promised him a story.'

'For God's sake, Tommie, why?'

'I need money.'

'What for?'

'We're behind with the rent.'

'I told you moving in with that fat idiot was a stupid idea.'

'And my car died.'

'What are you going to tell him?' she said.

'I don't know.'

She pleaded. 'You won't mention me, will you?'

'No, I won't, but the thing is, if I start this, Gloria might respond.'

'Tommie . . .'

'I can't see her just taking it.'

'You can't do this to me, Tommie. We're safe now.'

'I don't know where else I can get money.'

She bobbed. 'Don't. Please. Please.'

'Ladies?' Harland's voice came from beyond the blanket.

'Yes?' Georgie said.

'It looks like it was a false alarm,' he said.

'Jim?' Georgie asked.

'*Jim?*' I hissed. 'Are you *friends?*'

'We talked. He was very supportive.'

'He'll use it all against you.'

'Stop being so paranoid.' She turned her head. 'Jim, could you give me a lift home? And Tommie?'

I had nowhere else to go. I had nothing left to make decisions with.

'And could we stop at a shop on the way?' she said.

'Oh yes,' Harland said. 'Final excerpt today. Let's see what she says this time.'

We huddled Georgie into Harland's large Renault like the victim of a kidnap. I slid in beside her. There was a ghost in the mirror, with make-up so smudged, it disguised a black eye. I watched the herds move back inside, Harland among them, going to check out.

Harland's shabby car stank worse than mine, not just with smoke and dirt but with sweaty man-dust. Under the blanket, Georgie sniffed her Dettol and we waited for him without speaking.

On the way back to the city, we pulled into a garage. A fan of cold yellow was spreading across the sky and gulls wheeled. Harland asked if we wanted anything. My head thudded with dehydration and my mouth was so dry my throat hurt, but I shook my head. He came out with the newspaper held high, tapping it.

'Look at this,' he said, getting in. He angled the paper towards us.

Georgie pushed back her blanket. She was flushed pink and her hair was electrified.

On the front cover, a banner ran under the masthead detailing the contents: spring's must-haves, holiday hideaways, restaurant deal, final excerpt from the Gloria memoir, next week exclusive preview of the extraordinary Hugh Phillips' diaries, and a thumbnail photograph of Gloria and Phillips together.

'Rumour is,' Harland said, flicking the paper. 'He's gay. She must be the fag hag. She pulls some moves.'

I gave in. I *was* like her. We even chose the same kinds of men.

Harland turned the pages until he found the excerpt. She was naked. Naked on the chaise longue. The picture was taken side-on so only the curve of her monumental bazongas could be glimpsed. Beyond that, Rubenesque legs extended into little trotter feet. She smiled coquettishly. She had new teeth. Below was a photograph of the pale blue front cover of *In Utero* which, according to the caption, was now one of Amazon's fastest-selling volumes of poetry.

Harland scanned the excerpt. 'Blah, motherhood, drudgery, art – Oh look.' He flashed his teeth at us. 'She admits motherhood was difficult. And that's verbatim. Blah blah. McManus teaches poetry class, recommends her work, awards, blah, he leaves for post in England, she wonders if she will ever see him again, blah blah.' He crunched the paper into his lap. 'Substantiation for your story. What more do you want?'

Frozen brambles had forced their way through the fence at the side of the garage. A curled leaf dead under frost and a feather in the mud.

I tuned in to hear Harland's voice. '. . . plenty of material.'

'Drop Tommie off first,' Georgie said. 'It's on the way.'

We pulled up in front of the house. Frost coated my doorless Fiat inside and out, and behind my car was Darren's BMW. Georgie rearranged the blanket so she could see out, then opened the car door. Darren opened his own door, slowed by apprehension. She moved in under his chin and he kissed her head, drying his tears on her hotel blanket.

'Aw,' Harland said. 'That'll be the hubby then? And after one night away.'

I opened my door. 'Thanks for the lift.'

'Did you think you were invisible last night?' He poked his tongue into his molars.

I pulled the door closed.

'I saw you and McManus. Other people did. Everyone knows the ladies love McManus, but I'm the only one who knows who upi are, *Tommie* Shaw.'

'What are you saying?'

'I'll be supportive.' He unwrapped a pack of gum and waved it at me.

I shook my head. 'What are you going to do?'

'Nothing for the moment,' he said, chewing horsily. 'I'd rather do it with you than without you.'

'I just need some time.'

'You're stalling. Give me your story and I won't need hers.' He nodded in Georgie's direction.

I looked at her, in Darren's arms. 'How chivalrous,' I said.

'And your motive is pure? How much is it you want?'

I stared at my knees and told him what I owed.

'You might as well do it for nothing. You really don't like her, do you? So when can we talk?'

'I just need to get my thoughts together. One more day.'

He ducked to look at the house. 'I'll drop by tomorrow.'

'I'll be at work.'

'Where do you work?'

'I get home after five.'

'That'll do nicely.' He drummed the steering wheel and showed me his teeth.

I climbed out and stood beside Georgie and Darren. We watched Harland pull away.

'I don't know what you did, Tommie,' Darren said, holding Georgie tight. 'But she's back and she's happy.' He swung as he cuddled her. 'I was thinking we could get a new suite?' He spoke into the top of her head. 'A new one this time.'

She mumbled something into his chest and looked at me. Fear made her eyes wide. I didn't invite them in, pointing out how tired we all were.

A skim of frost coated the plastic sheet and crept across the carpet tiles in the kitchen. I switched on the electric fire and turned on the lamps, even though it was getting light. I climbed the stairs slowly and pushed open Blob's door. He hadn't been home. I knew that already.

In the kitchen, I drank water with painkillers, flicked on the water heater for a bath and set about making tea and toast. The plates, crumbs and mugs from yesterday were still by the sink. If Blob didn't come back, Chris might give his stereo and records to Dorota as a house-warming present. And she would probably dump them.

I switched on the TV and changed from channel to channel.

He'd come back for his things. He just couldn't put up with me any more, the friend who scared him, tortured him and pitied him enough to swing him a role in a tawdry TV ad. His confidence was thin to begin with, and I'd provided the proof he was as talentless as he suspected. We would look for new places to live. I would go back to reading and he would find new friends. He was good at that.

I made the bath ferociously hot and eased myself in with more tea on the side. The avocado walls dripped condensation and I moved my fingers through fine droplets in the air. Water trickled from my arms, echoing lightly. My chilblains zinged and pulsed but I kept them under water. The bath cooled and I added more hot. It wasn't enough. I pressed my nails into my arm until I punctured the skin.

It was unfair to hurt Liam professionally so I hurt him the same way he hurt me. But I didn't see it at the time. I was drunk and selfish and reckless. I'd destroyed his relationship with McManus. I'd damaged his career after all. What if McManus left the Fellowes

Agency? It would be my fault. However thoughtless Liam had been, he didn't deserve that. And I could so easily have loved him again. And maybe he me.

I rose and walked water across the bathroom floor, looking for Blob's razor. On the windowsill. This way. Sideways, down. Water vapour sucked through my lips.

Dressed in clean clothes, wrapped in blankets and towel soaking up blood, I stared at the TV.

I was rubbish.

What if Gloria found out? How could rubbish take on Gloria? Humiliating her, stealing her trophy, her ticket? How presumptuous, how foolish. That was what Gloria called me – a little fool. I'd put Georgie at risk. Me. Georgie looked at me with fear. Me. We could pre-empt Gloria, tell all before she got a chance, but there was no way Georgie would agree. Gloria was everywhere, she knew everyone. I was a fool. She was right.

I was rubbish.

The frost stayed in the yard all day and I sat in the light and let tornadoes shake me loose. The sun moved round hazily and gave up trying, and with the dark came the dread. I turned up the TV, drink frozen in my hand. I wouldn't sleep. I'd lost the knack. I wouldn't sleep again.

I was the night of the living dead. Bits were falling off, I couldn't keep them on. There they go. Judgement gone. Needed that. Perspective, hold onto it, it's mine. Gone. Sense of humour. Sticky in the gutter.

A knock on the door like a question but I couldn't answer. Knocking, knocking. Nothing, I was smoke and shadow. I had no language.

This is the kind of place I like. Cold, dry, dull and empty. Black granite rocks, a mercury horizon and below, fine grey sand, damp on my legs. Leaning back, I watch sea hush over shale. One seagull. Another. Huge and ocean-going. I hear the beat of wings on wind. A feather. No, a snowflake. More of them, slow and heavy.

I push my fingers into the sand and feel the grains, sharp but painless. Some stick, some fall. I press my palms in, and my heels. The sand resists, playing with me.

It's not that I wanted to die that day. I just wanted not to live.

In that case, you succeeded.

Mo? I'm sinking into the sand.

You can't be alive and dead at the same time, sweetheart.

Where are you?

It was an accident.

I'm dissolving.

I am the grains.

The bliss of no thought.

A woman made of sticks on a patchwork vomit settee. Frantic Poles on the phone, learning English fast.

Come up through sand
    Come on
    Up
    Thomasina?
    Mo?
    'Come on, up.'
    Mercury that's white-blue aids sleep
    'Thomasina, wake up now.'
    I miss Mo
    Where is this?

27.

It was kind of Dorota to lend me some clothes. I'd never met her before. Her eyes, eyebrows and lips were drawn on and yet she had beautiful features that didn't need make-up. She kept her yellow-blonde hair in a high ponytail and, having learned her English in a Belfast taxi depot, her accent was a wonder. Only seven weeks until her baby came and she was looking forward to her mother's visit as much as the baby's arrival.

I sat on a bench outside the hospital in the loose jeans and baggy blue coat she left, smoking my last cigarette before I called a taxi. They didn't quite believe me when I said it was an accident. Did I feel despair? Only at the end when, with wasted fear, I thought depression was back to swallow me. And maybe a little bit, now that I appeared to be wasting everyone's time. A nurse reprimanded me quietly for taking such drastic steps to solve insomnia.

I didn't mention the voice, worried it might spark off a new area of investigation. It sounded like Mo and yet it wasn't her. The consultant psychiatrist was a strapping lispy Swiss man and I agreed to further treatment even though I was sure I wasn't depressed. I'd been admiring his glutes through his sensible trousers and I didn't normally fancy anyone when I was depressed. But I didn't tell him that.

Outside, the light was bleach white and glinted off passing cars. Sunglasses would've been useful but I'd lost mine somewhere. I watched an aeroplane pass overhead, sun streaming along its windows.

'I know.' It was Blob's voice. He stood at the end of the bench, watching the plane. 'I wish you were on it too.'

The bench rocked as he dropped onto it. He pulled his coat round his bulk. 'Chris said you might be coming home today.'

'Not home for much longer.'

'It's a shithole, let's face it.' Blob crossed his legs at the ankles and shoved his hands into his pockets. 'You know how we said we wouldn't talk about things?'

'Yes.'

'Well, let's not.'

'I'm sorry, Blob. I thought it would—'

'Aht!' He held up porky fingers.

'You *are* talented.'

'Stop it!'

'It's just that you're really big and you look like Morrissey and the role you're waiting for hasn't been written yet. Maybe you should write it.'

'Have you seen my handwriting?'

'I really thought I was helping, Blob.'

He tapped his brogues together. 'I'll say just one thing and I'm never going to mention this again. It's not you, it's me. Then Chris phoned to tell me what happened and I realised, it's not me, it's you. You don't have a clue what you're doing. I need someone like you to help me lower my standards.'

'That's six or seven things.'

'You're a nightmare.'

'You're an abomination,' I said warmly.

'I got you something,' he said. 'Your sister has been ringing ten times an hour and I can't take it any more.' He twisted round to open a white plastic bag and pulled out a box covered with pictures of glamorous people showing their teeth.

'What is it?'

'It's a phone, you brainless bint. All set up and ready to go. Eleanor lent me some money till my cheque comes through. May left me some money but I haven't got it yet. I paid Chris. Get the phone out.'

I stretched out my arm to take it, cuts stinging. I had woken with a scratched gullet from a stomach pump and an overdramatic bandage on my arm. It wasn't that bad.

'Thanks.' I opened the box and took out a mobile phone. I had a phone. A small black mobile phone. I had officially joined the ranks of the living. I turned it over in my hand like a dead wasp. 'Thanks very much, Blob.'

'Babe.' He acted out great concern. 'Are you feeling alright?'

'I'm fine.' I focused on him sharply. 'Why?'

'Well, unfortunately, I have some very good news.'

I'd spent a few days sleeping and answering questions. Thoughts of Blob, Harland, Georgie and Liam nagged and plagued but I was too tired and fuzzy to focus. I had lain around, growing back the bits I lost on the night of the living dead.

'Eleanor saw it yesterday.' He took the *Northern News* out of the plastic bag. 'Look at this, you bitch. You're famous.'

There was a photograph of me in the arms of Rory McManus, standing at the side of the hotel. At least I was wearing the sunglasses. At least he didn't have his hand down my pants. I was lucky really. The headline read:

POET STILL A'MUSE'D'

There was no journalist associated with the accompanying paragraph, but it had to be Harland. He must have run out of patience when I wasn't there on Monday night. McManus pictured with mystery woman, the latest in a long line of lovelies charmed by the charismatic poet. No mention of my name. I might get away with it.

'That's just the beginning,' Blob said. 'Look at this.'

He pulled out another newspaper. There was a picture of me with McManus and his hand was quite obviously down my pants. He obscured me for the most part but my face was visible, attached to his, and I had no sunglasses. The headline read:

UPRORIA! RANDY MCMANUS BEDS GLORIA'S DAUGHTER

It was the *Daily Mail*.

I leaned back weakly.

We'd reached a point of relative safety and I'd landed us right back in it. There was no comment from Gloria – yet – but she must know. Georgie and I had spoken on the hospital phone each day but she hadn't mentioned it. Either she hadn't seen it or she was protecting me. She had seemed angry, aggressive and borderline hysterical on the phone; in other words, completely normal. I was certain she didn't know.

Gloria would take this very personally and she had plenty of ammunition to fire back. This was a fight I couldn't win. All I could do was try to limit the damage.

I got Georgie's number from Blob's phone and dialled.

She answered timidly, not recognising the number. 'Hello?'

'It's me. This is my new phone.'

'Oh my God, are you alright? I phoned the ward but they said you were gone—'

'I'm fine, I'm going home.'

'Well, that fat idiot friend of yours—'

'Listen, Georgie.'

'He knows I can't—'

'*Listen*, Georgie. Have you seen the paper?'

'No.' She took a hesitant, scratchy breath. 'Why?'

'Is the Dettol handy?'

I told her about McManus and the picture and held the phone away from my ear as she honked and counted. She wasn't getting any better at controlling it.

'Listen, Georgie.'

'How could you—' Honk. '—do this to me?' Squeak.

'I'm going to talk to her.'

'You—' Honk. '—what?'

'I'm going to talk to her.'

She counted breaths. 'Do you think it will—' Honk. '—do any good?'

'It's all we have.'

I listened to her count. 'This just won't end,' she squeaked.

'I'll call you and let you know what's happening.'

'Oh—' Honk. '—God.'

'Bye, Georgie.'

Honk.

She hung up.

I needed to get moving, I needed to find Gloria. I stood up fast and sat down faster, head spinning.

'You're pathetic,' Blob said. 'Come on, we'll get some lunch. The ambience is good at your brother's. I'm on a diet and there's nothing I can eat.'

'You don't think anyone will recognise me?' I asked.

'No one will know you without your spectacticles, babe. Or without some man's hand up your twinkle.'

'Let's go home first. I need to get changed.' Into a hotel blanket that covers me from head to toe.

I phoned work from the taxi but it rang out. I assumed they were busy after the Festival furore. Getting punched in the face was probably very good for business. Patricia was right – Jude always had something up her sleeve.

Outside the house, my car sat on bricks. Someone had taken the wheels and both doors were missing. It was scrap now. We had shared seven hateful years and it was time to say goodbye. I patted it on the roof and it gave me a shock.

The trench leading into the house had been filled. Inside, the wall had been bricked up and there was a door-shaped hole, draped with the remains of the plastic sheet. In the yard, the rubble had been taken away and the ground cemented over. Ducts and pipes rose up like sinister weeds. Blob dropped onto the settee. It had new throws and cushions.

'The brothers Grimm left those for you,' he said, waving at the sink. A bunch of flowers had been jammed into a pint glass and beside it was my copy of Bob Dylan's *Bringing It All Back Home*.

'Will they be back today?' I asked.

'They're coming to put down carpet tomorrow.'

My prince had come. My princes. I would have to thank them. And apologise.

In my room, I changed into comforting black and pulled Diane Sands' address book out of my drawer. I fingered through until I found the number for the Fellowes Agency. I would have to ask for another favour. I entered his number in my new phone and stopped. I owed him a real conversation, at least.

It was a short bus ride to Orbital's and I phoned work on the way. It still rang out. I sent Jude a vaguely apologetic text promising to be back tomorrow. She didn't reply. I assumed she was test driving a horse and needed both hands for reins and Pimm's.

The bus stopped on the opposite side of the road and a scattered queue waited outside. I wanted to ask Orbital how Mo was. I didn't realise how much I missed her and her reasoned point of view until I had heard her voice – or her sort-of voice.

'Looks like we'll have to wait,' I said as we crossed the road.

'There she is!' someone shouted.

I looked behind. Who?

Blob screamed, clutching my arm. 'Oh my God, I dreamed of this!'

Four men and women launched themselves from the front of the café calling my name, asking for a moment of my time. Blob laughed wildly as cameras clicked. Happy as Christmas, he grabbed my hand and we ran, past the boutiques and charity shops, into the residential street, past the parked cars and furious dog, Blob screaming along in front: 'I need a sports bra!'

Journalists behind: 'Ms Shaw! Ms Shaw!'

Me in the middle, vomit or die.

The street curved gently and at the end was a T junction. A large

Renault slid up and stopped in front of us. I looked back. The journalists were getting close. I opened the door and flung myself in. Blob waved at the cameras.

'Get in!' I shrieked.

Screaming with delight, he clambered in and Harland took off before he closed the door. Dizzy and heaving, I held on to the dashboard. A 200m sprint is not ideal when you just get out of hospital, no matter what you were in for.

Shakily, I took out a cigarette. 'Thanks, Mr Harland.'

'Jim.'

'I love that café!' Blob bounced in the back.

'This was exactly what I didn't want.' I wound down the window as Blob boomed superlatives in the back.

Harland looked at me. 'You didn't want someone to pick you up?'

'You gave me away.'

His eyebrows hammered anguish. 'I did not. I told you other people saw you.'

'You told them who I was.'

'I did not,' he protested. 'It was your sister.'

'Georgie?'

'Astra.'

I smoked silently, my heart cramming in beats. So she wasn't willing to live and let live. The karmic wheel was Orb's thing, not hers. I should have known that. She saw an opportunity to hurt Gloria and she took it. I wasn't her target, I was her weapon. I just happened to be expendable.

'She phoned to ask me why I didn't leak your identity,' Harland said. 'I told her I was going to work with you. She said I was small-time and she'd go elsewhere.'

I watched him drive. With his worn jacket, washed-out hair, abused nose and stinking car, he *was* small-time. He'd never get anywhere by being so deep-down decent. He looked at me straight, no coercion, no ham.

'I've been holding onto this story for you and I've been supportive and now I'm begging. Please, please, Tommie Shaw. Will you give me an exclusive?'

Pedestrians, cars and buses moved along the road. We were invisible to them. That was how I liked it.

'I want to do that again,' Blob bounced.

'Yes,' I said.

'You will?' Harland said.

'Yes. But I need time.'

He shook his head wearily. 'You're stalling again.'

'I'm going to talk to Gloria but I have to find her first. I'll tell you everything about our meeting. That's an exclusive, isn't it?'

'You'd give me that?' He looked suspicious.

'Yes,' I said. 'But in the meantime.' I looked back at Blob. 'I know another story you might find interesting.'

Harland dropped us in the city centre and we went for a breakfast pizza to celebrate Blob's imminent infamy. I left him to the fried eggs and pepperoni and hurried away to look for the Fellowes Agency.

Gloria's book was in the window of Waterstone's, the cover showing her naked, heavily Photoshopped, with flowers over the frightening bits. She was probably doing a book tour or giving interviews or whatever else authors did. She could be asked about the photograph and she had the opportunity and motive to maul us.

Diane Sands' address book put the Fellowes Agency in a tall Georgian terrace near the City Hall. An intercom displayed the names of several businesses. I'd walked past the building countless times but never knew who was in there. I pressed the buzzer for the Fellowes Agency and said I had a delivery for Liam McMullan.

Inside, the hallway was dim and draughty, and smelt of paper and scorched coffee. Their office was at the top and I felt my pulse in my ears as I climbed the stairs. He could ask me to leave. He should. I'd brought it on myself.

At the top, a small white sign gave the name of the agency. I knocked lightly on the door and tiptoed into a cramped reception where a window overlooked the City Hall. Sandwiched between a photocopier and a desk piled high with papers, an older woman looked at me over her glasses.

'Delivery for Liam McMullan,' I said.

'Yes?' She looked around for my package.

'I'm it.'

She lifted her phone and tapped in two numbers with a pencil.

'Liam? A woman is delivering herself to you.' She tapped her pencil on the desk, listening. 'No, she's fully dressed,' she said. She looked me over. 'Yes, quite.' She hung up and turned to me. 'He'll be with you shortly. Have a seat.'

I sat in one of two stiff wooden chairs. On a table beside me were trade magazines still in their wrappers. Buses rattled by outside.

Behind the woman, a door opened and Liam stepped out. Seeing me, he simply said, 'Come through.' There were no kisses.

I followed him into a long narrow hallway with three blank doors. He opened one and led me into a small office. It too had a window with a view but every wall was stacked with books, manuscripts and documents, every surface scattered with envelopes, files, mugs and clutter. I stayed by the door. He stood by the untidy desk, hands in pockets.

'Sorry about the mess,' he said.

'Me too,' I said. 'I really am.'

His voice was hesitant. 'Are you alright?'

'I'm fine. Is everything OK between you and Rory?'

'God, yeah. We've been comparing notes.'

'Really?' I said with horror.

'Just kidding. It's fine. It's all work to him. It's not to me but I have to look after the big star, don't I?'

I moved forward. 'Liam, it was a mistake. I was drunk and I . . .'

'I know why you did it, Tommie.'

'You do?'

'I tried to warn him,' he said. 'But you, your . . . episodes . . . they just make it more interesting to him.'

He thought my sleeping with McManus was psycho. Well, maybe it was. 'I'm having . . . treatment now, Liam.'

'That's great.'

'Yes. It is.'

We were quiet. We spoke at the same time.

'So—'

'Could—'

'You go first,' he said.

'No, you.'

He swung from side to side. 'I was just wondering if you still wanted to go for a walk?'

'A walk?'

'You don't have to. It's just an idea. I'll understand if you . . .' He drifted into silence.

Don't do it, he'll mess you around, he'll leave you in pieces. Don't don't don't. 'A walk would be nice,' I said.

And there it was, that smile. The one I wanted to eat.

'Liam?' I moved closer.

'Yes?'

'Could I ask another favour?'

He sucked in a breath and held it, closing his eyes. 'I'm always going to have to jump through hoops, aren't I? What is it?'

'Do you know how I can get in touch with Gloria?'

'Is this about the picture?'

'Yes.'

He chewed his cheek. 'The quickest route would be through Rory. Just call him.'

'Call him?'

'I could do it for you but I think he'd like to hear from you again.'

'You don't think . . .?'

'Don't worry. I think you've given him everything he needs.'

Liam glanced at the phone on his desk. 'Do you want to call from here?'

Calling the man I'd slept with out of revenge, in front of the man I used to sleep with and wanted to get revenge on, was excruciatingly weird. And what if breathy simpering girl came back? I couldn't control her. This was getting messy again.

'Use my chair,' Liam said. 'It will be easier.'

I sidestepped along the desk, squeezing past documents. Liam watched as I sat in his worn chair.

'Star-seven-three on speed dial.' He leaned over. 'Here, let me.' He lifted the phone, close enough for me to feel how warm he was, to pick up his woody smell. I could see inside his shirt. His neck, the beads. I looked away.

He handed me the phone and waited as it rang. I rubbed my neck.

'I'll get us a cup of tea, will I?' He turned for the door.

I'd never known him to be sensitive before. Maybe he had changed. Or maybe he caught all my looks but just ignored them. Or maybe he was thirsty.

I got through to the same Midlands university.

'Could I speak to Rory McManus please?'

It was the woman from Yorkshire again. 'Sorry, who?'

'Rory McManus.'

I spelt his name and she burst into realisation:

'Oh, I'm sorry, it's just your accent, it's so strong! Where is it from?'

'Northern Ireland.'

'Indianapolis?'

'*Irlande du Nord.*' Wait a minute, where was breathy simpering girl?

'Norway?' the woman asked.

'Ireland.' This was me speaking. Wow. And I meant it.

'Iceland?'

'Ire. Land.'

'Sorry?'

'Botswana.'

'Oh, that's fantastic,' she said. 'I always wanted to go there, after those books came out. I'll just put you through. One moment.'

I understood. Breathy simpering girl had locked herself in the wardrobe. She didn't like sex, she didn't like the mess. Perhaps I should have sex with everyone I was going to phone. Or if that was impractical, maybe it was enough to be liked by the one or two people I liked back. Breathy simpering girl kicked the wardrobe door, foiled at last.

The extension rang for a long time before he answered. His hello was quick, as though he was in the middle of something.

'Rory? It's Tommie Shaw.'

'Well, hello!' His voice softened. 'How lovely to hear from you.'

I covered my eyes with my hand. I couldn't bear to look at the phone. 'Nice to talk to you too.'

'It was wonderful to meet you, Tommie. I mean that. I want to thank you.'

'You do?'

'Her imperfection is a fascinating area. It was being with you that revealed it to me. Thank you.'

'I don't mean to put a spanner in this, but I'm not really all that perfect.'

'You are a lens, Tommie. A lens. You were exactly what I needed. My God, it's exciting. Your differences gave me an entirely new perspective. I've started work already.'

'Er, that's great, Rory.' I lifted a pen and doodled my grave at the edge of Liam's notepad. 'Rory, I wonder, would you mind giving me Gloria's number?'

'Yes, of course, Tommie. She understands what it is to be a muse.'

I jotted down the number as Liam returned with two mugs of tea. He sat in the wooden chair on the other side of the desk.

'Thanks for your help,' I told Rory.

'No,' he said. 'Thank *you*.'

'And Rory?'

'Yes?'

'You won't tell her I'm going to call, will you? I'd like it to be a surprise.'

'Of course not. Goodbye,' he whispered. 'And thank you, Tommie.'

I hung up, rubbing my creaking neck.

'Get the number?' Liam said.

I nodded.

'I told you there was nothing to worry about.' He crossed his legs. He was wearing those disappointing cords. 'So where would you like to go for a walk?' He put his hand between his knees and swung his leg.

'The beach.'

'Isn't it a bit cold for the beach?'

'I like cold beaches. No one else goes.'

'When would you like to go?'

'Ring me,' I said. 'I have a phone now.'

'Welcome to the modern world. What's your number?'

'Er, I don't know. Hold on.' I hunted in my bag for my phone and pressed some random buttons. 'I don't know how to find the number.'

He leaned over. 'I used to have one of those. Look, I'll show you.' He took the phone and pressed a series of buttons I would never remember. If he didn't move away, I would climb inside his shirt and sniff him to death.

'See?' he said, turning the phone to me. 'Easy.'

The hairs on my arms rose under his breath.

'Don't look at me like that unless you mean it,' he said.

'I mean it,' I said.

We toppled files, spilt the tea and squashed a biro on his desk. I found his tattoo.

28.

I pivoted on the side of the bed and stared at the phone, heart pumping like a fox before hounds. She would hear it in my voice. Goose bumps ran down my right side. If I waited long enough, I wouldn't do it. I pressed call.

It rang three times before she answered. I forgot she didn't answer with hello.

'Gloria,' she said, emphasising the first syllable the way Handel did.

Now I remembered why mangled posh accents bothered me so much.

'Gloria,' I said. 'It's Thomasina.'

She hung up.

I sprang to my feet and kicked a handbag across the room. She was the only person who could do that to me. I thudded downstairs.

'She fucking hung up!' I flung myself on the settee.

Blob was settling the needle on the stereo. 'Just you let it out, nutjob.'

The Velvet Underground's 'Sunday Morning' sparkled round the room. Blob settled onto the other settee.

'I'll phone her,' he said. 'You're rubbish on the phone. I can be anyone you want.'

'I'm not sure that will work.'

'Of course it will. I'll say I want to set up an interview and then ta-daah, you appear,' Blob boomed in snappy RP, '*Daily Telegraph* perhaps?'

'What if she's already spoken to someone from there? That will be the problem with most publications.'

'I could make one up?'

'She'd know.'

Blob wriggled his fingers. 'Oh, I've an idea. I could be . . .' He assumed a hesitant and retiring Manhattan tenor. 'Bob Allen from the *New Yorker*.'

'That's your real name.'

He resumed his normal boom. 'Babe, she never knew I existed, not even when I sat in the same room. If it does sound familiar, she'll think it's because I'm well-known somewhere.' He shrugged and became Bob Allen again. 'The *New Yorker*. From New York. If you can make it there, you can make it anywhere.'

An hour later, Blob dropped the needle onto the middle of Miles Davis's *Kind of Blue*. The charity shop sticker was still on the cover. 50p. She was worth it.

He stood in the kitchen, lit a cigarette, pressed his glasses with his thumb and hung his head. He called her number.

'Uh, hullo, is that Ms Shaw? Hello, my name is Bob Allen, I'm with the *New Yorker* . . . No, I got your number from a friend of mine . . . Who? Well, his name escapes me for the moment—'

He marched across the kitchen, hand out in desperate supplication. Who did I know that she would know, but not too well so she wouldn't call them to check out Bob Allen? I whispered the name of the photographer who Photoshopped her into nubility and stood by, chewing my hair.

'Amanda Hamil . . . *ton*, Amanda Hamilton, yup, that's the one,' Blob said. 'I met her at an exhibition in New York a few weeks ago . . . Yes, talented, very talented . . . I'm so bad with names, I'm sorry . . . Thank you, thank you . . . Well, right now I'm in Belfast, England . . . Oh, I'm sorry, I'm not strong on geography . . . I'm doing an article on cultural renaissance. Well, obviously, you're a part of that, yes, completely . . . so, if you are in the city, I'd really like to meet up . . . That would be perfect. Very accommodating, really, you're very kind . . . That's a good time for me also. I look forward to it very much. Goodbye, Ms Shaw, goodbye.'

He hung up, straightened, stretched his arms wide and bowed.

I chewed my hair. 'I don't know, Blob.'

He shrugged. 'I'm a genius.'

We looked round. A phone was ringing. Mine. On the settee. I picked it up. It was the number I had dialled for Gloria. I swallowed and pressed the green button.

'That was pathetic,' she said. 'If you're that desperate, meet me tomorrow at six. The Merchant Hotel.' She hung up.

I slept for three hours and read a book on the history of indoor plumbing. Blob stayed awake as long as he could and rattled the kitchen with seismic snoring. I didn't know whether he was babysitting or keeping me company but I appreciated the gesture.

29.

I dragged myself through the bright streets to work. Blob's phone had buzzed us awake at 9 AM. It was an offer of more voiceover work and he pulled me to my feet in a jubilant dance. I would have given anything for more sleep – now that I'd figured out how to do it – but it was too late. I had to go back to the magazine.

Buddleja was sprouting at the front of the building and a thong was slung up against the wall. A bee droned by on cool air. The front door was open but reception was empty. In the office, Patricia, Bill and Seamus sat on desks like castaways. The radio played low but the computers were turned off.

'Oh Tommie,' Patricia said, her twinkling eyes red-rimmed.

'What's happening?' I asked. 'Where's Lisa?'

'The receivers were in,' Bill said sourly. His tie hung loose. 'We're out.'

'We thought you knew,' Seamus said.

I shook my head. 'I was sick.'

'Lovesick, you mean,' Bill said. 'We saw the paper. You dirty mare.'

'But what about Devine Energy's money?' I said, ignoring him. 'Wasn't it enough?'

'I think there was some kind of disagreement between Kevin Loane and Jude,' Seamus said.

'It wouldn't have been enough anyway,' Patricia said. 'We owed too much to too many printers.'

I didn't have to write the article about the Festival. I wasn't an Arts Correspondent. I could go back to temping and never have to write anything more than Post-it notes again. I resisted the urge to jump and clap my hands.

'What will you do?' I asked.

'I've reconsidered,' Bill said. 'I'm going to try a life of crime.'

Patricia touched her spray-hard hair and made a wild guess. 'Find another job?'

Behind me the door opened and Aoife joined us, smiling. I had never seen Aoife smile at anyone other than clients. I sat down heavily.

Never again would I write about denture repair, skin tag removal, animal psychics or back, crack and sack. Never again would I sway before Jude's fetid feet or buckle below her gin-blotched eye. And we thought we had nothing to put on our CVs. Never again would I find such Dunkirk spirit. I would miss this place.

Patricia boiled the kettle and I switched on my computer for one last look at my email. The usual spam, a few from clients looking for editorial and one from Kevin Loane. I opened it.

To: Tommie Shaw
From: Kevin Loane
Subject: Devine Energy

Tom

Please accept my sincerest apologies. I believe I may have offended those of a more sensitive nature at the Festival. Alas, creative juices got the better of me. I'm sure you of all people understand.

Unfortunately, I've had to withdraw the feature from the magazine. The Festival organisers felt they didn't require any further publicity from us. They were quite insistent.

With hindsight, I should have let you present all the testimonials, going by the success you had with McManus. But we live and learn. Look out for Devine Energy in the *Northern News*. I just had a conversation with a journalist who was very interested in our unique ethos and ground-breaking support for creative people. God moves in very mysterious ways.

Regards
Kevin

❦

We spent the day sorting through desks and drawers, ignoring phones and emails, and foraging for things to pilfer. Before we left, I asked Patricia to do my make-up one last time. She wiped, swiped, brushed and smoothed, and gave me back my shit-together face. We put on our coats and Seamus turned off the lights. There was nothing I wanted to take.

We stood outside in the half-light, rush hour traffic filing past. A car stopped as Seamus locked up. It was Jude's 'classic' Alfa Romeo, crusty with rust and blue with fumes.

'Oi!' she crowed, getting out.

'Morning,' Bill said as she strode through us.

Her teeth looked odd. I couldn't put my finger on it but she could. She had temporary crowns at the front and every few seconds she had to press them into her gums. She shoved her key in the door, pushed through to reception and turned off the alarm. She stood in the dark, glinting.

'Do you know she could have saved this fucking magazine?' she hissed at me before questioning the others. 'Do you know who she is? She's *Gloria*'s fucking *daughter*.' She pointed a stiff finger at me. '*Gloria's fucking daughter!* You had so many fucking angles. And now look at us.'

She was right. I could have given her an exclusive; it might have helped.

'Now it's over,' Jude breathed. 'For all of us.'

Bill turned to me, then shook my hand.

Seamus did the same. Then Patricia, twinkling sadly. And Aoife, with a nod.

Jude slammed the door and I heard her scream. 'Who the fuck took my fucking light bulbs! Fuck, my teesh!'

'Bar?' Bill said.

'Bar,' we all agreed.

Brisk night air made my eyes water. I walked through bustling streets and dabbed carefully for fear I might ruin my shit-together face. I had left my colleagues in the snug, their wishes of good luck following me into the street. Seamus said he was opening an all-day dance café and Lisa was going to work for him. We were invited to the opening. He said he would text us the date and I held my phone tightly as I walked. I had all their numbers.

Propelled by adrenaline, quaking with fear, I smoked three cigarettes on the way. Sweat glued my fingers to my palms and the air couldn't dry them. Georgie and I had spent years in hiding. Any kind of pressure or pain sent us reeling, so we created quiet lives in which we avoided the lows and missed the highs. But that was being alive and dead at the same time. It was time to come out of hiding. It was time to face Gloria.

A wide flight of sandstone steps led to the door of the Merchant, an Italianate hotel where a discreet concierge greeted and directed clientele. Behind me, cars crawled along the narrow road still snagged by the rush-hour traffic. Parked to the right was the hotel's Bentley. Was Gloria staying here? I had no idea whether she lived in this country or elsewhere. I had given her so little thought in recent years. We shared nothing except genes. Not even regret. I hoped she had mellowed but from what I had seen and heard, I doubted it. I wished I had a medallion like McManus's.

I climbed the steps, taking gallows breaths. Quartz glinted in the sandstone. The concierge nodded as I slipped inside, through the high stately room filled with quiet diners and into the bar. She was alone by the window, in front of her a silver tea service and a newspaper. She wore a white top which draped low to show McManus's 'lost vale'. Nausea carried lightness to the ends of my fingers. She hadn't seen me. I could still run. My feet started to move but they carried me to her. She looked up, expression cool.

'My goodness,' she said, touching her neck. 'I forgot how very like me you are.'

I had her features but none of the colour or the drama. Her mass of curls was mostly white, her skin lightly tanned, and she had the solid build of Britannia. With her hard jawline and pale eyes, she was striking. And she knew it.

I sat on the leather chair opposite.

'Still all in black,' she said, tapping sweeteners into her tea. 'Still thin. How do you do it?' Her voice was thoroughly anglicised.

'Stress, Mother.'

Her jaw twitched. Everyone was to call her Gloria.

'Is that a black eye?' she said.

I touched my face. I had dabbed too much.

She stirred her tea. 'Still having your other little accidents?'

A waiter approached. 'Would you like to see the menu?'

'Just water,' I said. He withdrew and she leaned forward.

'Let me see your arms.'

'Gloria . . .'

She sat back like she'd scored a point. 'You haven't changed.'

'Gloria, I came to say I'm sorry.'

She puffed out a little laugh. 'I have to say I wasn't surprised.'

'It was a mistake.'

'You were a mistake. You both were.'

Every act was one of aggression. We used to crumble under this. But we weren't children any more and if Mo believed I could do this, I had to try.

'If you didn't want children, why didn't you prevent them?' I asked.

She sat up straight. 'I was stoned, darling.' She rattled the spoon

249

into the saucer. 'Off my head.' She brought the cup to her lips, watching me. 'But you're right. Some people are meant to be mothers, some people are meant to do other things. Mo was there, she took the brunt.'

'I'm beginning to understand how much.'

She showed her quality teeth. 'What? Did you think I was a little harsh?'

The waiter brought iced water and I drank. Even their tap water was tasteful.

'Did you know Pete and Mo were sleeping together when I was pregnant with you?' she said.

I never knew my father and yet I'd picked a man just like him. That must have hurt her, but Mo and Pete were still married. And they did live in an idealistic commune.

'Wasn't it that kind of place?' I asked.

The fabric of her skirt fell as she crossed her legs. They looked like they had been carved by Bernini.

'I don't expect you to understand, Thomasina.' She looked at her subtle matt nails. 'You and I share an outward resemblance but that's as far as it goes.'

'I do understand.'

'You couldn't possibly,' she snapped.

I looked at the ceiling. 'OK, I don't understand.'

'I was trapped after Pete died. I had nowhere else to go. I had one little bastard and another on the way. And what a pair you turned out to be. One stole and fought, the other never stopped crying. You were still whining when you were nine or ten. You never stopped, Thomasina.'

'I think that's an exaggeration.'

'What would you know? You weren't on the receiving end.'

'I fell out of a tree when I was nine. You would whine if you dislocated your shoulder.'

'And those pathetic teenage cries for help,' she said. 'At least Georgina had balls.'

'They weren't cries for help, they weren't anything—'

'I was investigated by the social services because of you.' She jabbed a finger on the table. 'I almost had to go to court. You're a destructive little attention-seeker and you haven't changed. You would take everything from me.'

I set my thumbnail against my lips. I should've known not to answer back. Things escalated and that's how noodles were thrown. She was always on the defensive but I would have to find a way.

'Look, I'm sorry,' I said. 'I don't want to argue.'

She gave me a wary look.

'Can I ask a question?' I said, striking a balance between reluctant interest and obvious sycophancy. 'Just a question, just something I'd like to know.'

Her chin moved forward in a way that reminded me of Georgie.

'Do you think Pete meant to die?'

She laughed. 'How do you expect me to answer something like that?'

'Mo and Orbital always said it was an accident. I just thought, well, if anyone will tell me the truth, you will.'

She touched her halo curls. 'Theirs is a rather simplistic view,' she said. 'Pete would get very low. He would lose perspective. When I told him I was pregnant, he wanted me to stop working. I couldn't stop writing because he was feeling low.'

'You mean, your poetry killed him?'

Her jaw twitched again. 'You should watch that sense of humour, Thomasina. It will get you into trouble.'

'It's the only thing that keeps me out of trouble, Gloria.'

'Not this time, evidently.' She sat back and sighed in mock contentment. 'Isn't this nice? We're having a chat. Who would have thought?'

It was our first, but only because I was smoothing the way for my last request.

'Is that when you were writing your "war poems"?' I asked.

She paused. 'Pete understood art, usually. Art has no boundaries, no fear. But when I brought freedom fighters back—'

I almost snorted the water. 'You did what?' That wasn't in her book.

She looked away. 'This is utterly pointless.'

'No, no, I'm interested. The farm was full of hippies and their children and you brought who, the IRA, the UDA, who? Were they armed?'

'Must you always pick fault with me?'

I needed to be careful. But I also needed to know.

'What were you trying to do, Gloria?'

'Record their struggle,' she said, as though it were obvious.

I looked round. The hotel was a beautiful, restful place. It had opened long after the Troubles were over. The farm might have been unrealistic and founded out of fear, but who wouldn't have enjoyed a cocoon from the conflict? She'd ripped theirs open and exposed them. But it was Pete's home and he had nowhere else to go—she trapped him before he trapped her.

'They only came back because of the drugs, you know.' She gave a little shrug. 'But that's Mo for you.'

'Mo was your friend.'

'Mo took in strays, that's all.' Her clipped tone was final.

Mo must have known I would pick up on it. Gloria's constant truth-twisting and fault-finding were too much; there was something desperate about them. I didn't understand it before. It was a cover for how inadequate she felt, and she shared those feelings with no one. But Mo knew. Pity translated into kindness for Mo, but I wasn't sure what to do with mine. It hung there, unapplied.

'So do you think it was an accident?' I asked quietly.

'He took anything he could get his hands on.' Her voice was cold. 'He died when I told him I was pregnant with you. That's all I know, Thomasina.'

I sipped my water and watched the smokers outside, shivering happily under parasols. Orbital said Gloria drove Pete round the bend, and she probably did when she brought terrorists home for the sake of her art. But she would never accept blame: everyone else was at fault and it was I who pushed him over the edge. Reproach was her way of coping, just like I had my sense of humour and Georgie had her bleach. The problem wasn't us, it was her. It always had been.

I finished the water but my mouth was still dry. 'I just have one more thing to ask.'

She shifted, running her tongue over her teeth.

'I saw your book in Waterstone's and I had a look through it and I wanted to thank you for not mentioning us. I know I made a huge mistake but I really am sorry, he is a very attractive man. I just wanted to ask if you would try not to mention us in the press. It's just, you know, with Georgie's . . . thing . . . and my . . . thing, we didn't want—'

'Oh, I promise you, Thomasina, I won't talk about you.' She pushed her teacup away.

I sank into the chair, letting relief flood through me. 'Thank you.' Maybe she had mellowed. 'Thank you.'

She lifted her newspaper. 'Why would I, when that would give away my next book?'

My heart stumbled, snatching my breath.

She stood up. 'Did you think I agreed to meet for old times' sake?' She smoothed her skirt. 'You offered me a chance for research. *In Utero* was the best thing I have ever written. There were fifteen years of hell behind it, culminating in one daughter's teenage pregnancy and the other's attempted suicide. My publisher thinks it's a hit. Mo painted an interesting picture but meeting you in the flesh was' – her eye explored me – 'disappointing. Such a pity Georgina couldn't be here but Mo said she has problems that way. Don't look so shocked, surely you know me by now. I have to go, I have an interview tonight. Goodbye, Thomasina.'

30.

I could hear my own breath in the cubicle. If anyone came in, they'd think I was getting it on. I turned in a pointless circle, oh fuck, oh fuck, oh fuck. I was a fool, a little fool. Of course she was writing about us. It was melodramatic and juicy and the worse she made us seem, the better she would look and feel. I took out my phone. Aoife, Bill, Blob, Georgie, Harland, Liam, Seamus, Patricia. Liam had programmed in three numbers.

'Tommie?' he said.

I panted down the phone. 'Liam.'

'What, are you running?' he said. 'Is this a dirty call? What are you doing?'

'I don't know, I don't know what I'm doing.'

'Do you want me to come and get you?'

'No, I don't know, oh shit.'

'What's wrong, what happened?'

I told him about Gloria.

'Go outside, have a cigarette,' he said. 'Try to calm down.'

I speed-walked through the hotel and stood under the parasols, passing phone and cigarette between shaking fingers.

'Are you there?' he said.

'Yes.'

'How quickly could you write the book about her?'

I chewed my hair, rubbed my neck and smoked, smoked, smoked.

'You still there?' he said.

'I think so.'

'What do you think?' he said.

'What about Georgie?'

'Gloria's going to write about her anyway. She'll just have to face up to it.'

'Joe isn't Darren's son,' I said.

Liam was quiet. 'Well, unless you want to go through the courts to stop Gloria. But Georgie's hardly going to be able to keep that from her husband. And isn't she agoraphobic? She'd never make it through the briefings.'

Damned if we do, damned if we don't.

'Write it, Tommie, seriously. Her book is about to get totally panned, by the way.'

'People will love it.'

'Well, there is going to be a movie but don't think about that. Just do it.'

I breathed deeply. 'I need to talk to Georgie.'

'Give me a call when you can. Don't worry. We'll work something out.'

I clicked off and pushed back my shoulders, pacing along the side of the hotel. People passed, chatting and laughing lightly. Georgie answered after a few rings, the time it took her to lock herself in the bathroom, probably.

'Did you talk to her?' She coughed as breaths snared in her chest.

'Yes.'

'And?'

'It's not good.'

I told her what Gloria was planning and what Liam had suggested. There was no panic, no hysterical honking. Nothing.

'Georgie?'

A shaky breath gave away tears.

'Is he home?' I asked.

'Downstairs.'

'Do you want me to come to the house? I can get a taxi.'

'No, I'll do it. I'll do it now.'

'Will you call me back?'

'Yes.'
She was gone.

She didn't call as I walked home and I hoped it was because they were talking, trying to find a way through. I couldn't imagine how he would react. He was devoted to her and Joe but the family was built on an affair that preceded it. He would be crushed.

The lights were on in the house but I could hear no music. I let myself in. Orbital sat opposite Blob, his long limbs like collapsed scaffolding. Blob looked up warily. Orbital approached and touched my arm.

'Tommie, Mum's dead.'

Georgie phoned at eight the next morning. I hadn't slept. Music played, neighbours knocked, Blob was missing, the TV droned on and no one noticed the universe had been turned inside out. Dead was a bludgeon of a word. I went temporarily deaf, I didn't know what Orb was saying. How could Mo be dead? I still felt her in my head.

Georgie's voice was low. 'It's me.'
I lit up. 'Well?'
'He's gone.'
I listened to air scraping through her chest.
'Where?' I asked.
'His mum's, I think.'
'What's going to happen?'
'I don't know.'
'What about Joe?'
'We'll tell him together.'
'I'm sorry, Georgie.'

'I shouldn't have let it go on. I suppose I shouldn't have done it to begin with.'

'Georgie, there's more bad news.'

Her chest caught and she coughed.

'Mo died yesterday morning.'

'Oh, Tommie. Oh, no. Are you OK?'

I rubbed my eyebrows. 'I'm fine.'

'Tommie . . .'

'I wish I'd visited more.'

'Oh, don't cry. She understood. She wanted us to have our own lives.'

'I'm just tired.'

'Me too.'

We listened to silence, neither wishing to let go.

Blob whacked in through the front door, bubbling with excitement. He held up the *Northern News* and sat down to flick through the pages.

'Tommie?' Georgie said.

'Mm?'

'I couldn't have done what you did. I couldn't have talked to her.'

'Yes, you could.'

I heard a lighter flick at the other end of the line.

'The old Georgie is still in there somewhere,' I said. 'Fucking fiddlers.'

'Wish I knew where,' she said softly.

Blob prodded the paper violently. There was a picture of him bearded up in his God costume, just like the Devine Energy logo, another of him with Kevin Loane in front of the Devine Energy building, and a huge headline:

GOD IS GAY!

'Call or get a taxi if you need me, Georgie.'

'I will. Take care.'

'You too. Bye.'

Blob sucked in a huge breath. 'God, she is so demanding. Now pay attention to me. Look, look, look.'

I sat on the settee and read the article. It was, as Harland promised, supportive: ground-breaking new ad campaign rubberstamps new more inclusive Northern Ireland, future-focused company, talented marketing man, new gay icon.

'I'm worried, Blob,' I said. 'What if this wasn't such a good idea? What about religious nuts or gay bashers? What if someone has a go at you? I shouldn't have started this.'

'Babe, this is what I always wanted.' His chins wobbled joyfully. 'It's outrageous. It will travel far and wide. Bring it on.'

'But what if—'

'Go to bed, Fatty.' He dismissed me with a flick of his fingers. 'Begone.'

'I won't sleep.' I bumped into the door and dragged myself upstairs.

I called Harland from my bed.

'I saw the article,' I said, pulling covers up to my chin.

'Good, isn't it?' he said. 'That should get them excited. We're getting calls already. I hope your friend's ready for this. You talked to Gloria?'

'Yes, but I'm going to have to ask you to wait again.' I curled onto my side.

'You're taking the piss, aren't you? Have you seen the *Mail* today?'

'No.'

'Pic of you and Gloria, talking.'

She must have primed a photographer. Nothing was beyond her. As Harland said, she was on a quest to fill the papers.

'Did she make any comment?' I asked.

'None. Plenty of editorial assumptions. Like she gave you the black eye.'

'Really?'

'*Did* she give you the black eye?'

It wasn't very grown-up, but she started it. 'Yes,' I said. 'But don't tell anyone. There's much more but you'll have to wait.'

'Is this about money? Don't fuck about, Tommie Shaw.'

'It's not that.' I pressed my face into the pillow. 'I'm writing a book about her. Or something.'

'You'll give us the serialisation?'

I woke myself up snoring.

'What the hell was that?' Harland said.

'Sorry, I have to go.'

I slept for three hours and woke to hear a voice. It wasn't Mo's. It was mine.

31.

We stood by Peter Benedict's family grave in the cemetery, just across the way from where we used to get pissed. My father's parents were buried there, then him, and now Mo. The sun was smothered by cloud, and tiny flecks of snow chased and swirled. Mo's sister Kathy stood next to Astra and her dusty academic husband. In front of them, Jack and Dan watched and scratched. Orb stood with Betty, next to Blob, me and Georgie, and behind us, Mo's friends, some of whom I recognised from the farm. Beyond them, crowds had come to say goodbye to Northern Ireland's first lady of vegetarianism and its first proponent of recreational drugs.

Georgie was on Diazepam, prescribed rather than recreational. She was calm but adrenaline kept her from zoning out. I was getting by on so little sleep, I had passed through the looking-glass. I was floating. There were faces in places they didn't belong and slamming doors on the stairs. Blob shocked me by saying I should see a doctor and quietly hid everything sharp and anything chemical, even cleaning products, of which there weren't many. I said it was unnecessary and accused him of collusion with Georgie. He said that was proof I was completely mental.

I didn't see Chris's limo pull up and I didn't see Gloria get out. She had, of course, tipped off a photographer, although another had arrived separately and was chatting to Harland. It was Astra's shriek that made me turn. Georgie's hand was slow but the slap was hard and echoed across the graves. Gloria swung round under its force and fell towards me, hands splayed, mouth open. Her thick shoulder caught me in the chest and I folded, limb by limb.

'Tommie?' Blob knelt beside me.

Ow.

They peered down at me.

Harland, this one's for you.

'Tommie?'

I'd hit my head on a gravestone.

'Somebody phone a . . .'

A headstone. A grave situation. I'm star-struck, ha ha . . .

Gone.

It was the best sleep I'd had in years.

32.

We sat behind a curtain and drank gin from Lilliputian glasses. Blob's ego was too big for economy and we had the best seats on the plane. I had to be careful I didn't nod off, mixing gin with antidepressants. I took them to stabilise my sleep patterns and for the relief they gave Georgie and Blob.

Blob was still taking calls as we boarded. Priggish protestors had waved measly placards outside Devine Energy for a time, but he had developed a respectable online following and had been interviewed by news teams from the US, Australia and across Europe. He wasn't famous for long but his voiceover career had taken off. He was known in the business as the poor man's James Earl Jones and he said he was 'printing twenties'.

The McManus episode had been the height of my fame – for now. Gloria was still finding ways to stay in the limelight but she didn't mention us. A few newspapers printed pictures of her 'attack' on me at Mo's funeral but she successfully sought retractions.

Mo left me her piano and Astra sent me a solicitor's letter. We found £1000 rolled up and stuffed behind the pedals. When I called Orbital, he said to keep the money and the piano. In the karmic wheel of life, I was meant to have them. I made enough on eBay to buy a new old car that smelt of peaches.

My phone beeped during take-off.

'Can you turn that off please?' A passing steward threatened me with a smile.

'Sorry.' I fiddled with the phone, opening the message before I turned it off. I'd been waiting for this. It was from Georgie. One word: *Positive.*

It was odd to have someone so bright and well-balanced in the family, but when Georgie and Darren sat down to explain things to Joe, he calmly told them he figured it out around the same time he realised there was no God and everything in life was a meaningless construct, but he hadn't wanted to upset them. They got him a new iPad and new carpet for his room.

Now she was pregnant, she would have to give up smoking. I had been thinking about giving up, but Blob said you couldn't go to Amsterdam and not smoke. Hanneke was meeting us at Schiphol and she had a full itinerary planned.

The plane rose quickly through the clouds. They weren't as thick as they seemed from the ground and above them, the brilliant blue was blinding. My breath caught in my throat. The heavens were glorious.

Tara West is an Irish author based in Belfast, Northern Ireland. Her first novel, *Fodder*, was published by Blackstaff Press to widespread critical acclaim and established her reputation as a fresh and original new writer. Her short stories are punchy and pithy, and give a flavour of real life in Northern Ireland. Tara appears regularly at literary and cultural festivals, and has received a number of Arts Council Northern Ireland Awards for her writing. She works in advertising and is a member of the Society of Authors.